Acknowledgments

This is my first book. The reality is that I probably have a ton of people in need of thanking, starting with the people who believed in me from the very beginning. So firstly, this is for my English teachers, for being the first to be excited about the stories I tell.

For Frankie, for being the writing partner I always needed, and for being the cover artist I couldn't live without (I tried...it was sad). For all the feels, the funsies, the 3000 mile cups of tea, the endless geekery, and the all-nighters. I can't thank you enough.

For Chaos, for reading. And reading. And reading.

For the Dead Pete Society, my writing support group.

For Mama Mindy.

For the real Wex and the real Berge.

For all of the followers I've somehow accumulated without having a book to give you until this very moment.

For you, brave reader, for taking a chance on me.

Chapter One

The poor son of a bitch was dying a horrible death, and yet Bergeron Nacht was at least ninety percent sure he didn't care. For some reason, though, he was bothered that he couldn't remember the guy's name. *What was it? West?* It shouldn't have been important, but his feet stopped anyway. "Oy! West, right?" As the words left his mouth, it was immediately clear halting was a mistake. West was built like a pit wrestler—easily twice his own mass—and without the momentum carrying him forward, Berge slowly bowed under the weight. He tried shifting the heavy man up higher onto his shoulders, but the dying bastard seemed determined to wilt into the snow. "West! Oy, West!" The next attempt to redistribute his weight buckled Berge's knee. He dropped—hard—with West on top of him, driving him into the powder.

The impact knocked all of the breath from

Berge's lungs. And the behemoth on his chest made it impossible to breathe. He managed to nudge a shoulder between them and lift enough to suck in a much-needed breath of air. It gave him enough space to pull his arms free. "Death's balls, guy, but you're fucking heavy," he growled, shoving at West's seeping shoulder. Red oozed from the man like a wrung out towel, dripping between Berge's fingers. He turned his face away, trying not to get any of it into his eyes. Zanje always warned him that the most vulnerable entries to the body were through the eyes and orifices. And any open wound, not that that ever happened. He tensed every muscle in his body, struggling against the man's much bulkier frame, writhing free with excruciating slowness. When he finally slid free, he clambered a short distance away and pushed himself to a seated position, panting to catch his breath. He buried his hands in the snow and lounged back, heedless of the cold.

West groaned with pain. Berge looked in his direction for no other reason other than that West was the only thing to look at in the desolate winter. Other than the blemish of blood and flesh, the landscape as far as the eye could see was pure, unbroken white. The snow around the bleeding man was black and red and growing redder by the moment. A ragged red and white path led back the way they'd come, blood in Berge's footsteps as he'd carried the man across. The cracks in West's skin were slowly draining him dry, a symptom of late-stage Red Death. West didn't have a day left before he was nothing more than a scarlet smear in the snow. Poor bastard.

Berge looked away again, considering his options. He patted his chest pocket, finding comfort in the musical ring of coin. By the gold's reckoning, West's father had already decided that Berge's duty was fulfilled. It didn't matter that he was still dying. The guy shouldn't have paid before his task was completed. Trust was an ill-advised virtue in this day and age. Berge shook his head and grinned. "The old man didn't follow protocol," he complained to his unconscious charge. "Shouldn't have died if he wanted his opinion to matter, right West?" He frowned and looked back at the dying man. "West isn't your name, is it?" He scrubbed a hand through loose, unruly curls over and over, thinking back. The dying father had said the guy's name over a hundred times, droning on and on about the dying guy's accomplishments. Apparently 'West' was a bit of an inventor. That wasn't something to brag about. There were those that would kill him for that, thinking he might mean to eradicate magic in retaliation for what had been done to science. "Resh? Rex? Fuck, I don't know," he relented. "I give up."

He had the gold. He didn't, however, have the product. That, he'd dropped on the floor. Zanje was going to be pissed. It put him in this gray area of morality where funds had been exchanged, services *hadn't* been rendered... but the man's father had fucking *died* while Berge was standing right there! Berge ran his hand through his hair again, thinking about it. "I'm not the good guy. I should have just left you there," he muttered. "Right? Anyone would. Your father paid me and-and-and *died*. You'll be dead soon, anyway, and I don't care. I don't. I don't fucking care. I don't know *you*. You don't know *me*. Would you carry me through knee deep snow? No. No, I wouldn't either, and I don't weigh half as much as your monstrous *head!* That's crazy. This, this is crazy. That's it. That's it! I'm done. I'm going." He stood and dusted the snow from his pants. "Bye, West!" He took one step, then stopped and turned back to the guy. "Er, whatever your name is."

A small, sleek fuzzy creature leapt up onto the man's back and settled back on its haunches. It blinked foggy, unseeing eyes at him, tiny whiskers twitching as it tasted the air. Berge glowered at her, wondering how long she'd been hiding, waiting for her moment. She loved hide and seek. "What are you doing, Ashes?" he asked tiredly. The smoke-colored weasel didn't respond, but settled in a bit more.

"We're leaving that guy. He's dead." She stared back at him, unblinking. Her long body was comfortably settled between West's shoulder blades, wedge shaped head fixated on Berge. She'd likely gravitated toward him because his body was warm, feverish from the disease that laid waste to his flesh. He could almost hear her thoughts: *a warm body is a body that isn't dead.* "Well, he's *as good as!* I know what you're doing," he accused the weasel, pointing at her. "You put your cute face on his lumpy, ugly body so that I forever have to associate that big lug with how adorable you are." He paused and pulled his face into an exaggerated frown. "It's working, too, god damn it."

He turned to look in the other direction. The way behind them might have been long and arduous, but the trek up the hill to Zanje's castle was going to be the hard part. His insides withered at the thought. West's massive frame already had his lungs and legs burning. Berge shook his head. "I can't do it, Ashes," he decided. He refused to look at her. She was just too cute. If he looked now, he was going to end up dragging that giant fucker up that hill. "Don't look at me like that," he warned without turning. "Not unless you're planning on helping me carry him up Bitch Mountain. I am *cashed —out.*"

He sighed and analyzed the incline of the

hill. He wasn't really analyzing it so much as delaying the inevitable. He wasn't one to quit at halfway, and he'd already hauled West this far. How obnoxious it would be to have carried a man this far to save him to then only leave him to die. He shook his head, confused by his own reticence. His clothes were permanently stained with the blood of the innumerable men and women he'd killed. Why did this one matter? "West!" he shouted, turning on the guy in a fury. "This is *your* god damn fault!"

All he saw was Ashes, his eyes drawn in to the tiny white point upon the darkly clothed hillock in a field of white. For a twitchy little weasel, she could be surprisingly stoic when she chose to be. Her foggy eyes remained locked with his, unblinking in her defiant face, her chin as high as it would go. Whether it was because of the weasel or because of something else—something confusing, something he would not analyze today—the hem hawing was over. He made his way slowly back to the fallen man. He knelt, gripped West's arms and shoulders, and hauled his huge body up over his shoulders. It was an impossible weight for a man with such a slight frame, but an unfathomable potential for magical prowess came with certain advantages. When he was sure he had a hold of the guy, he stood on shaking knees, grinding his teeth from the effort.

"Can't die without your name," he explained to the unconscious bearded man. "'Cause trying to remember will drive me insane. Heh. That rhymes. You bring out the poetry in me, sir."

Ashes climbed his pants and his shirt and curled up in his front left pocket. His pocket inflated slightly as she took a deep breath. One, full throated groan later and Ashes was well on her way to a nap. "Sure, Ashes. I'll carry you, too." Berge sighed and started the long, slow incline. That led to a steeper incline. Step after shaking step, he approached the hill upon which Zanje's castle stood. Its eleven towers rose high into the sky. "I don't suppose either of you are going to help me up this *fucking hill.*"

Maybe both of them would die on Zanje's mountain. But the possibility of Berge dying a hero was so unlikely it was laughable. He smiled, then laughed a little for himself. Berge wasn't about to die a hero. Which meant Berge wasn't about to die. Good enough for who it was for.

"Who's that?" Zanje demanded without turning. She was tinkering with something on her counter. It was always hard to tell what it was she did with her time, but that was mostly because Berge didn't care enough unless it affected him.

"I don't know," he wheezed, worn out from

the uphill battle.

She capped a tube, held it between two fingers, and inverted it back and forth several times. She returned it to a metal rack. "If the next words out of your mouth aren't why you brought him here, dripping blood and filth in *my* lab, I'll—"

He dropped the man on the floor roughly and threw his hands into the air. "You'll *what?*" he challenged in kind, panting. "Fire me? Kill me?"

From the cold concrete floor, the big man moaned in agony. She ignored the interloper and gave Berge a look from under her eyebrows. It was that look she sometimes got when she was feeling extra superior, as if he was a toddler who'd just thrown a tantrum. Like maybe if she spoke slowly enough, he'd see her point and simply agree. "Berge."

"It's a long story."

The corner of her mouth curved into a wicked smile. She wasn't budging. "I've got time."

"Well *he* doesn't!" Berge protested, indicating the now slowly waking patient upon the floor.

Zanje crossed her arms and said nothing.

Berge's mouth twisted with disgust. He'd hauled a man twice his size several miles and then up a mountain, all in an effort to get him to Zanje before he died of the fatal illness plaguing mankind. He still wasn't sure why, but it was a decision he had committed to, and now that he had reached his goal, Zanje was being a bitch—as usual. "Can we talk about this later?"

"No." Her face went back to neutral. Waiting.

He fumed, scrubbing at his face, raging on the inside but without an outlet. He needed her. She knew it, and therein lay the root of every problem he had. "I—well, you see..." He blew out a breath, grumpy, unsure of what to say. How was he supposed to give her an answer he didn't have himself? "There wasn't a doctor there. And the old man...the fucking *dog*...and I dropped—"

Her expression darkened. "You dropped *what?*"

"Wex." His raspy voice cut through their argument. It was low and gravelly, hovering on the precipice at the edge of an open grave, but like the vampires they were, they zeroed in on the source, attracted to the advent of a death. They both looked at the stranger. While they were busy arguing, he'd rolled over onto his back. He used an arm to shield his face against Zanje's blue witchlights' steady glow from above. He took several deep breaths. The air rattled on its way in and gurgled on its way out.

"My name. Is Wex." He flailed the other hand weakly. "You were. Wondering. Heh."

Berge grinned, celebrating inside—finally, his name!—and turned back to Zanje. "There you go. His name is Wex. *Now* will you help him?"

"Why?"

And back to that. He didn't have an answer for her. And Zanje, being Zanje, didn't do a single thing if she didn't have a reason to. Whether or not Wex lived didn't affect her one way or another. In fact, letting him die lay more in her interests. Saving him meant exhausting her resources. Letting him die meant nothing at all. And the money had already been collected. Berge didn't have a bribe for her, either, except —"I'll give you my cut."

Her eyes snapped up to his and took on a predatory gleam. She smirked. "You've got yourself a deal, Berge."

His heart skipped a beat. "Good! Get your little typey bottles." He fanned his fingers dismissively.

"No time," she rejected with a single shake of her head. "The new batch of reagents isn't ready yet. Go get me the Null."

His good mood evaporated. "Zanje, the Null can't handle another one. He'll need at least a few more weeks to recover."

Zanje glared at him briefly. "It's your

decision. Either the Null dies or he does." She ignored him after that, busying herself preparing her supplies, selecting tubes, needles... He turned his back on her and exited the lab.

The lab's brighter witchlight winked out of view as he disappeared down the dimly lit hallway. He stalked across the dusty stone to the door at the end of the hall. It opened with a torturous shriek into impenetrable darkness. Before he'd set a toe upon the stair, the reactions reached his ears. One of the Primes, weeping quietly, hoping not to be chosen. The Weak was beginning to hyperventilate. As for the Rare... "I hear you, you rat bastard," came his voice. No matter what happened, the defiant Rare maintained his pride. He didn't ever raise his voice, only quietly acknowledged Berge's presence in the basement. Berge might have admired the guy if he didn't hate him so much. The Rare had been an artist before he'd been a bleeder, yet he acted as if such an impractical application of his time was the highest calling.

There was a bang beside him as he made his procession. "Please!" A body flailed against the bars of the nearest cage. Inside the cage was a dirty old man just past the prime of his life. His greasy gray hair hung in knotted curtains around his face. Berge had forgotten about him, actually, and had to look at the cage designation to remember. He was a Major, one of the types that was fortunately fairly easy to find. He was new to the holding cells, and had only recently been bled for the first time. "Let me out of here! Mercy, sir. Mercy!"

On a typical day, Berge might have toyed with him a little, but time was critical. Instead, he charged right past every cell until he reached the one at the end. The tall, thin, bearded man within it was sitting curled up upon himself in the corner, shivering with his face pressed to his knees. "Hey!" Berge shouted to the man, rapping the bars. "Wake up in there."

"C-c-cold," he protested. "I c-can't. Can't."

Berge's lips twisted. The scene unfolding in the lab upstairs was bound to be a messy one. Late stage Red Death was no joke. Wex was probably going to die whether the Null was wasted or not. The Null, however, would die regardless, and then Berge would only have more work to do. There was going to be a lot of clean up. "I don't have time to argue with you, old man." He was of an age with Berge himself, though he looked to be much older now. He unlocked the cage and sparked a witch lantern. It settled just above his head and hovered there, moving with him.

The man in the corner squinted against the pale blue light. "B-berge." He sounded surprised. It made no sense.

"Yep."

His eyes widened, eyelids twitching against the blinding light. "You can't...I'll die."

"Yep."

The basement erupted into cries of indignation. A dozen voices screamed obscenities at him. Some begged him to show compassion. Some pleaded for him to show mercy. Some merely condemned him for his crimes against humanity. He laughed quietly and grabbed the Null by the arm. The man whined, lips quivering both from fear and cold, but he resisted little. He was already too weak from blood loss to fight. He only sobbed quietly, knowing his time was up.

They jeered all the way back to the foot of the stairs.

But the only man who didn't condemn him was the only person's eyes that Berge met. The brown eyes of the Rare gleamed darkly from deep within his cage. He sat serenely as always, reclined against the back wall of his cell. He met Berge stare for stare, like a wolf among dogs. "His name is Tragen," the Rare said softly. It sounded like a challenge, coming from him. It was his habit, to shove the names at Berge when he borrowed one of them, in case that one never came back. It was his way of trying to get under Berge's skin, to provoke his conscience and humanize his victims.

"It doesn't matter," Berge dismissed before guiding the frail man up the stairs. "None of it does," he added for himself. *We all deserve to die. And none more especially than me.* He didn't have a conscience. He didn't have a soul. He'd given up those things long ago, back when he met *her*.

By the time he made it back to Zanje's playground—she called it a laboratory—Wex's eyes were rolling toward the back of his head and drool seeped out of the corner of his mouth. "We might have already lost him," Zanje muttered unhappily. "Hurry up."

Berge nudged the Null forward. There was a chair on one edge of the room with buckles and straps. The Null knew the procedure well enough to get into the chair and allow himself to be secured. There was a time, not long ago, when that particular Null would fight Berge every step of the way to the chair. He'd even thrown punches and tried to bite him, then. But Berge was backed by Zanje's power, and Zanje herself was in the room, and by now the Null knew enough about her to know she was worse than Berge. He knew well enough not to invoke Berge's wrath, but he damn sure didn't want to provoke Zanje if it was going to be his last day on this earth. Berge didn't blame him.

After the Null was buckled into his chair,

Berge wrapped a different strap loosely around his bicep and tied a knot. He inserted a short pole into the loop, then twisted until it closed tightly around the muscle, halting circulation until the veins of his forearm swelled. Zanje switched him places, easing onto a stool bedside, cradling a clean glass globe about the size of a child's skull. She felt along one vein with her index finger and held out her other hand in Berge's direction. Berge scrambled across the lab and found the needles she had prepared, each attached to a hollow rubber tube. He carefully placed one into her awaiting palm. Without taking her eyes from her work, Zanje brought the apparatus close to her face. There was a thick, waxen coating like a dagger sheath on the needle to keep it sterile. She bit it gingerly between her teeth, then affixed the other end of the tube to a port at the base of the globe before proffering an empty palm again. Berge cursed inside his head, eyes darting about for the brown glass bottle with the alcohol. Zanje snapped her fingers. "Well, where'd you put it?" he demanded.

She spat the tube out and let it dangle, but she let him know she wasn't happy about having to drop it. "Right back where it goes, Berge. It's been in the same place for fourteen years."

"Has it really been fourteen years?" he

mused aloud as he shot across the lab toward the glass cabinet. "Always glass with you. How about a proper wood cabinet?"

"Wood is porous. It holds pestilence if anything is spilled on it. It'll soak up and hold Red Death until the end of time. Wood's about as dirty as it gets. Steel would be fine, except it rusts over time and is heavy besides."

"Not like anyone is going to lick your cabinet," he muttered. He fumbled with the latch; it was old and didn't work properly, and his fingers had always been clumsy.

Behind him, Zanje sighed with exasperation. "Take your time. He only dies if you're too slow."

He shook his head angrily and swiped the brown bottle from the most inconvenient location she could have possibly chosen—the bottom shelf. He snatched what he hoped was a clean rag off a peg above one of the counters. This he soaked with the alcohol before handing it to her open hand. She didn't waste any more time chiding him for his slowness, but returned to the Null's bare arm and the task at hand. She dabbed at the area with the bulging vein. Then, in one quick succession of steps, she swiped the dangling tube, bit down on the wax, tugged the needle free of it, and inserted it into the Null's vein.

"I thought you told me not to put things in

my mouth in the lab," he commented.

"That's because you're an idiot. I cleaned this. Get the clip."

He undid the clip on the tube, following the path of the blood with his eyes. The dark red flowed into the tubing, marching its way along until it spurted fitfully into the round, glass jar. At that, Berge swore. "That was the fucking problem, right there. I told you glass was a terrible idea. I told you a thousand times."

"You know I hate a man who exaggerates. 'A thousand times,'" she scoffed.

"Yeah. A thousand times. Steel is good. Steel is *excellent,* in fact. When you drop it, it doesn't fucking *break*." He stabbed a finger against it, causing it to wobble dangerously and earning him a healthy glare from Zanje, which he ignored. "*This* bottle is about as fragile as blown glass."

"Because it is blown glass."

Berge rolled his eyes. "Well."

"I get them shipped in from Anthia. Each one is worth your meals for a week. If you keep breaking them, it's going to come out of your pay. You have a tendency to forget, but I run a sophisticated business and I need quality materials. As to the glass, I need to be able to see into the bottle," she explained. "Blood clots." She watched the jar fill, glancing between the blood and the bleeder. "He's going into shock."

Berge's eyes jumped to Wex. It was the wrong instinct. Wex was the same as he was before—unconscious, but still alive, for now. His head was resting on his chest.

It was the Null who was losing it. His hands trembled violently and his eyes were darting back and forth, searching the veil for something that probably wasn't there. Just then his fingers curled into tight fists, his jaw clenched so tightly that it creaked and grated like nails on chalk, and every muscle in his body tensed up. Berge leaned over the man's face and smacked him lightly. "Don't die. You can't die yet. You're not done."

"It's tetany," Zanje observed.

"The fuck does that even mean?" He was dimly aware that she'd said it before, but not recently. "You and your science words."

"Lockjaw," she snapped back. "He's having a reaction to blood loss. It doesn't really matter. He wasn't going to live through this." Her eyes were all for the jar. It was about three quarters full, perhaps about the same amount as a glass of beer.

The Null pissed himself. Berge noticed the darkening splotch on his pants before the stench of it filled the air. "I knew this was coming," Berge grumbled, stepping away from the chair.

"Mm-hm," Zanje confirmed, completely unconcerned.

A pit settled in Berge's stomach. The Null's breath came in shallow, rapid pants. He was laboring, his body making the last ditch effort to try to survive. Berge sighed, disappointed.

"I don't recommend forming any lasting emotional attachment to the bleeders," Zanje cautioned.

She didn't care one way or another about his emotional attachments. He knew that firsthand. She needed him in prime working condition. Her only concern was that his grief might negatively affect his performance. "It's not an emotional attachment. It's a professional one. Do you know how hard it is to find a Null?"

"Seven percent," she answered readily.

"It was a rhetorical question," Berge grumped. He did waste a moment wondering why she'd agreed to save Wex. She didn't really need the money, and it wasn't like Zanje to do anything out of kindness.

The Null slumped over quietly. He sucked in a few ineffectual breaths, twitched a finger a few times, and then went still. "I was kind of hoping to sleep in tomorrow," Berge complained. It was mostly for himself. Whining was a therapeutic means by which he coped with injustice.

"Could have let him die," Zanje reminded

him, unperturbed. She reclipped the tube and yanked the needle from the dead Null. With her free hand, she dipped into her pocket, rummaged briefly, and extracted a lump of wax. It wasn't sterile, but neither was the needle. Once the needle was guarded again, she dropped it and let it dangle. The glass bottle she tipped upside down and hung from a wooden hook on the wall.

"Alcohol." She scooted her stool toward Wex's side, the Null already forgotten.

Berge retrieved the glass bottle of alcohol and the rag, uncorked the bottle and doused the rag, then handed it to her. "You're going to need more rags," she informed him as she began washing Wex's arm.

"You only had the one, on that peg." He went toward the peg, even though it was empty.

"They're in the drawer where they've always been."

He shook his head and began opening drawers, one after another. He found pins and needles, scissors and knives, little bottles that held who-knew-what. He swore and rummaged through them fruitlessly. It wasn't until he remembered that one of the cupboards had a drawer inside it that he found the rags. "Honestly. Who's idea was it to put a drawer inside a cabinet?" he complained to himself. He grabbed a handful and shut drawer and cabinet.

She threw the rag to the floor and demanded another one, then washed Wex's arm again. It took three rags until she was satisfied that he was clean enough. It was disorienting to see him so filthless. To Berge, Wex might as well have always been coated in blood.

Zanje made a swipe and recaptured the dangling needle, dropped the wax back into her pocket, and held the needle out behind her toward Berge. "Sterilize this," she commanded without turning. He uncorked the bottle again and poured fresh alcohol over the needle in her hand. She waited for it to dry, holding the needle away from her body while she observed how Wex was doing. His breathing was slow and sporadic. He was soaked from head to toe in sweat and blood. Berge started to question his sanity for having brought him here. Wex was so far gone that not even Zanje's god could save him now. He almost opened his mouth to tell her to abort their course of action, but to do so would give her too much satisfaction and make him look like a fool. It was too late for all of that, and the Null was already dead.

Zanje didn't bother with the tourniquet; Berge could see Wex's veins from where he stood. With skill akin to that of a well-practiced surgeon, she smoothly pierced the vein, then wrapped and lightly tied a strip of gauze around his arm to hold the tube steady. Finally, she stepped back and unclipped the tube again. The jar began to empty. "No promises," she warned. "Your charity case is pretty much a corpse already."

Her tone put him on the defensive. "It's hardly charity."

"It's not like you."

He frowned. "I know."

"Why, then?" she wondered, amused.

He shrugged but didn't answer. He didn't have an answer. Nine hundred ninety-nine days out of a thousand, Berge would have let anyone die—or killed them, just because—especially if their money was already in his pocket, man, woman, or child. It didn't matter. He didn't know why *this one* had suddenly become so important. Was it before the old man had died, or after? Was it before the glass jar broke, or after? Was it before he'd dragged the brute halfway across the globe, or was it after? "To piss you off, mostly."

Berge watched the glass jar empty. Blood, as a subject, had always fascinated him. The thick, syrupy liquid clung to the sides of the jar, leaving a short-lived rosy smear behind as it went. Berge had always favored the vibrant color of blood. It was about as close as he ever came to appreciating art. He never tired of looking at it, whether it was in a jar or on his hands or spattered against the wall. Blood was the only thing in the world he truly considered beautiful. It was life and death in one, depending on whether it was coming or going. In less than an hour, the same amount of blood that killed one man could save another. Zanje was many foul things, but in this she was a genius. No one in the world knew the things she knew.

If anyone did, the two of them wouldn't have made near as much money as they did now.

As the last of the blood drained into the tube, Zanje clipped it close to Wex. "We're done here. The rest is up to him." She pulled the needle and pressed a wad of bandage against the wound. "Wrap this, and then get out of here." She jerked her chin toward the door. "We need another Null. Two, if you can manage."

"I'm not going anywhere until I've had some sleep," he denied. He stared at the glass globe between his hands, admiring the sheen of red that was left behind as it slowly pooled in the bottom. *Two?* There were never *two*.

"I don't want you here if he wakes up."

If, not *when*. Berge heard the unspoken words. Sixteen years with the devil taught him how to dance with her. What she really meant was that she didn't want Berge sitting around waiting for whether or not Wex would survive. Wex could be unconscious for a week or more, depending on if his body accepted foreign blood, and to what degree it reacted. The one and only Null was dead. It could take Berge months to find another one. They might receive four orders requiring Null in that time. That was four missed opportunities for a hefty payload. People these days were willing to pay just about any price to not die, and the Red Death affected more people than it didn't. "I still need sleep," he reiterated. He set the globe down carefully and grabbed the bandage from the countertop. He took over pressuring the bandage against Wex's skin.

Zanje caught his eyes over the man's arm. She searched his face, reading into his soul what he didn't wish for her to see. Finally, she nodded once. "Alright, Berge. Sleep." She smiled, a mockery of a grimace that didn't reach her eyes and was gone as soon as it appeared. "Take the Null to the pit. I'll clean up." She spun quickly and returned to whatever she'd been working on before Berge had dumped Wex onto the floor of the laboratory.

Berge wrapped a bandage around Wex's arm, sneaking glances toward her workspace. He needn't have bothered; even if he could see what she was working on, he wouldn't have had the slightest clue what it was. He tied the bandage into a small, snug knot and took one last look at his charge. It might be the last time anyone aside from Zanje would see Wex alive. His head still lolled over. Blood still seeped from the hairline fractures in his skin. In truth, other than the cleaner arm, he didn't look any better. Berge resisted the urge to say goodbye to the man whose life he had inexplicably saved. He didn't want anyone to believe he might have truly cared. Some utterances were holes blasted into defenses.

He still didn't know why he'd done it.

He scooped up the Null. He weighed almost nothing. "Sweet dreams, Zanj," he grumbled, answering her mockery of a smile with a mockery of affection.

She answered as she always did to any hints of fondness, and chose to ignore him. That was the first time he appreciated her indifference, though. With her back turned, she couldn't see the naked concern in his face as he took one last look at Wex and silently wished him a speedy recovery.

The castle's front door opened up onto a darkness so complete that it even ate the witchlights shining through the windows above. His first breath was too cold for his lungs. He coughed, but the sound was swallowed up by the abyss.

He made the long, slow, exhausted journey to the pit, legs quivering from fatigue. The setting of the sun had dropped the temperature considerably. The morning powder snow became the midday wet snow became the evening ice crust. Were he alone, he might have been able to step lightly atop the surface. Burdened as he was, he had to chip through the layer with his shins. He nearly tripped a dozen times. "Don't worry about it," he consoled the dead Null, patting his shoulder as he shuffled along. "I haul dead guys for a living."

The new moon cast the world entirely in shadow. Anyone else would have been lost, but Berge had made the trek to the pit countless times. Zanje's methods were invariably unkind. He'd ceased wondering about why she wasn't more conservative with her 'subjects' if they were so hard to come by. He didn't dare ask. Anyway, if anyone knew the bitch at all, they'd have just known she was rough on purpose because she despised people. Their mutual hatred for all of mankind was what had brought them together in the first place. It was unreasonable to question it now.

He stopped in the middle of the woods, confident that he stood just before the pit. He tilted his head to the side, sensing. There was the familiar stench of death, old and new. For all the time he spent around humans in varying stages of death and dying, Berge practically wore that stink like a perfume. And, too, there was the foreboding sense of void, a feeling like one more step meant certain death. It was accurate, too; the pit was a good sixty feet straight down into frozen earth. Unless you could fly, there was no getting out of it. And if you didn't die of exposure or starvation, Zanje would only set you on fire.

He heaved his charge forward, leaning the man on his knees. The Null's head tipped down. Gravity tugged him toward the pit. A gentle shove was all it took. The dead man toppled over and plunged into the pit. The sound of a body hitting other bodies was too loud in the heavy silence. To Berge, it was the sound of freedom. Finally, he could sleep.

Chapter Two

Wex drifted in and out of consciousness. The fleeting images his sore eyeballs managed to capture weren't very descriptive. He mostly saw ghostly blue light and heard nothing but a pulsing hum of energy and sweet music. He could have been dead and he wouldn't have known the difference. He didn't have the strength to worry about it, though. The second his mind attempted to make sense of the situation, it shut down. Hard. When he awoke, his entire body experienced such excruciating pain that he almost immediately passed out. When he slept, he did so dreamless. At any given moment, he was either dead to the world or wishing he was actually dead.

It was a strange time.

The music was pleasant, though. Never before had he ever heard such sweet orchestrations (although that only furthered his belief that he was probably dead). He didn't recognize most of the instruments, though he knew the difference between strings and reeds and flutes, and in this he heard all three. Music was a talent afforded only to the wealthy. It took a great deal of money to hire the talents of a group of musicians, too, so he'd only rarely heard an instrumental. When four out of five people died before they'd had a chance to wrinkle, the arts sank into the sad backdrop. It was now seen as a frivolous endeavor, and those who pursued it in any fashion were mocked.

Wex appreciated it when the music played.

When Wex finally awoke fully, there was no music. The ever-present hum was there, as was the blinding blue light. He turned on his side to keep it out of his sensitive eyes and immediately hissed in pain. His entire body was sore from his scalp to his fingertips to his toes. He moaned and squirmed, trying to find a position that was comfortable, but it was no use. If he had to guess, his skin was painted with acid and his organs had been scrubbed inside out with rock salt. His head had probably been stomped upon and his eyes had been repeatedly smashed with a hammer. "Oh, God, I think I'm dying," he complained.

"Do it or don't. Don't waste God's time with your indecision." Her voice was clear, though cold.

He hadn't been expecting a response, and nearly jumped out of his burning skin. One eye shuddered open, though it took every ounce of his effort to hold it open. There was a fine, sophisticated lady sitting nearby. If she hadn't been so rude, he might have truly believed he'd made it to heaven. There wasn't a good adjective to describe the aesthetic of such a woman. Pretty was too soft, beautiful was too artistic, and gorgeous was too pious. She was flawless and unattainable, the kind of woman born to be a soloist. There would never be a man that could be considered her equal counterpart. It was in the bored slack of her lips and the sardonic slash of her eyebrows. It was in the decisive way her legs were crossed at the knee and the elegant way her fingers laced over them. But mostly...mostly it was in the naked contempt in every firm and disapproving muscle in her face.

What could he possibly say to her? In his uncertainty, he faltered and merely stared in mute fascination.

"How do you feel?" she asked.

"Awful," he replied and immediately regretted it.

Her lips twisted into a sour frown and her eyes narrowed. "Be specific."

It was only two words, but those two words spoke volumes. He found himself falling all over himself to try to be specific *enough*. "My head's pounding and may explode—I can't be sure. The blood in my head's pulsing at the ears and behind my forehead. My eyes feel like they're too big...like they're swollen and bruised. It hurts to have them open. I feel as if I've been dipped in acid, and my skin's on fire and cold at the same time. I feel like I've been gutted, and I'm starving, but I also feel like if I try to eat anything that I might throw up, or it might kill me."

"Hm." Her eyes took on a distant quality, as if she saw something in his explanation he hadn't meant to put there.

"Where am I?" he wondered. "And where's my father, and Maxine?"

"My partner brought you to me because you were dying and I possess the skill and technology to save you. You're in my castle. It's a ways out from any other civilization. He and I live here alone."

He took in her words, fragments of memories clicking into place. He did remember his illness, but he remembered his father's more vividly. The Red Death turned even the strongest man into a weak, disgusting blood factory. Blood oozed from every orifice and broke through the skin. The eyes turned red at the sclera. His father had been coughing up blood. From start to finish, Red Death took about a year to murder. "So my father...and Maxine?"

She stared back impassively, completely unmoved.

He squeezed his eyes shut and opened them again, testing his faculties. "I'm sorry. You probably don't even know. You said your partner brought me here?" He wracked his brain, but he couldn't remember anyone. She offered a small smile in confirmation but no words. "Well. Thank you, for saving me. I really appreciate it. Is he here somewhere, so I can thank him, too?"

"No."

"Might he be back soon?"

"That's not your business."

He got the distinct impression that she didn't want him there, but it dredged up more questions than answers. A negative opinion of her began to form, but he bundled it up and threw it into a dark corner of his thoughts. It wasn't a fair opinion; after all, she'd saved his life. Somehow, miraculously, he'd survived the Red Death. "How did you...?" He couldn't even say it. It was too unbelievable to be voiced. *No one* survived the Red Death. Anyone with even a spark of power had already tried that.

Her face betrayed nothing except cool rejection. "Definitely not your business."

Disappointing. He sighed. "That's too bad. Again, though, I do appreciate it. You saved my life. For that, I am forever thankful. There's probably no way I can repay you, but if I can help you in any way, please don't hesitate to ask. If there's anything, anything at all—"

"That won't be necessary."

It sounded a whole lot like 'get out of my house,' but even if he'd wanted to, Wex couldn't. "When I'm not dying, I'm actually pretty strong—"

"I already have one of those."

"—And I have a knack for building things. I made a pen that doesn't need an inkwell, and lenses that block out the sun."

"I have everything I need." Completely unfazed.

"I even made a vehicle that moves across the snow in a fraction of the time it would take to walk." His throat closed up and broke on the last syllable. He snapped his mouth shut and prayed for the best. He suddenly realized what he was doing, but was powerless to stop it. His father must be dead. He didn't know what had become of Maxine, but feared the worst. He owed his life to these people, strange though they may be. There was nothing for him at his father's house. This woman had the power to stop an epidemic dead in its tracks. If he couldn't put his variety of skills to work for her, there was nowhere else to go. His life had to have some kind of meaning if it had been deemed worth saving.

"Hm." She stood, more of a graceful unfolding than the hasty, clunky move humans typically made. Her skirt clung to her knees, a constant reminder of female perfection. She seemed to dress in a way that was meant to infuriate all that looked upon her. While he was distracted, she'd retrieved a glass globe full of water. She turned it over and hung it by a loop on the bottom from a hook in the wall. It was only then that he noticed the rubber tube running out the bottom. Her fingers traced the length of the tube until she reached the end of it. She tugged something off like a cap, and then, at last, she turned back to him.

His eyes went immediately to the weapon in her hand. It was short but sharp, like a sewing needle. When she reached for his arm, he panicked and tried to back away. Every cell in his body hurt the moment he moved. "What are you doing?" he demanded nervously. His eyes never left the thing in her hand.

Her piercing ice blue glare rooted him to the spot. His muscles quivered to a stop, though his heart thundered on stubbornly. "Your body isn't ready to handle real food," she explained impatiently. "The needle goes in or you starve to death. Your choice. I have important work to do, so make up your mind."

His stomach roared to life at the word 'food,' but his mind and his pulse rebelled violently against the idea of being poked with that thing. He thought through every stillframe second of her needle stabbing into his body and had to squeeze his eyes shut to try to put it from his mind. The panic rose and rose in his blood until he was sure he might faint. He couldn't even speak, but did manage to shake his head gingerly and utter, "Uh-uh."

He worried she might try to stab him with it anyway, but she didn't. Instead, she tinkered around with the glass apparatus for a brief moment, then turned and left him there. It wasn't until she had been away for several minutes that he cracked his eyes open again. The hanging globe was still swaying gently from its hook, the tube coiled placidly around the glass. The woman herself was across the room at a counter, shrugging into a loose coat. Her back was to him.

Above him, the blue lights intensified, and with it, the hum of energy. A few moments later, a heartwrenching string instrument that wasn't quite a violin quavered in the atmosphere between them, joined intermittently by at least two others in perfect harmony. That the haunting blue lanterns and the melancholy soul of the arts belonged to such a woman was as confusing as it was fascinating, but he'd lost his chance to ask about it. Instead, he listened, and he watched, as his savior fiddled with the pieces and parts of a magic he'd never understand.

Eventually, he dozed off.

He dreamed of Maxine. It was the first time he'd had a dream since he'd been brought to this place. In his dream, he walked in circles upon circles, leaving trails of his own blood in his wake. He was lost and kept accidentally backtracking, despairing each time he saw his own tracks. He called for Maxine, but though his mouth opened and his lips moved, his voice was silent. He bled his heart and soul out into the snow, sacrificing his strength and his lifeblood in search of his beloved Maxine. He staggered like a drunkard through hostile terrain, but Maxine was nowhere to be found.

At some point in the dream, his blood had attracted victims of the Red Death, though in his dream it was far worse. Those that had succumbed to the bleeding disease had devolved into little more than monsters, drawn to his weakness and frothing at the mouth, pink foam dribbling off their lips. He stumbled and shuffled, intent on finding his dog while they gathered behind him and followed him around, waiting for an opportune time. He knew they were there, but dying in search of Maxine was better than living without her.

And then, he heard her whine. He crashed to his knees in the bloody snow, fully aware that the crowd of dead and dying men and women had been waiting for that very moment. Just ahead, Maxine limped into view. She was weak and injured, too, though it was because she'd been attacked by something. Her flesh hung in ragged strips from her ribs and her fur was wet and dark with blood. Nonetheless, her fearful eyes were as determined as his own. She limped heavily toward him, leaving a messy trail of pink and red in the snow. She collapsed only a few feet out of reach, crashing into her shoulder with half her face buried in the snow. Her eyes were apologetic, only sorry she couldn't make the last few feet.

Even in his dream, he was hysterical, crying so hard that he couldn't even breathe. He didn't care as the horde descended upon his body. He tried to break free from their inhumanly strong grip. He ignored their teeth and their nails digging into his skin. He fought against them as they tried to keep Maxine and him apart, shrieking voiceless obscenities at any and all within earshot. His entire body hurt.

Meanwhile, Maxine's eyes kept repeating what she didn't have the words to say. *Sorry, sorry, sorry.*

When he snapped awake in the same place, beneath the same blue light with its same strange hum, he curled up into a tight ball and tried to calm down. He kept telling himself that it wasn't real. Victims of the Red Death didn't behave like that. Maxine had to be alright. She just *had* to be.

His heart was just returning to its normal pace when the woman opened the door and stepped inside. She paused when she saw him awake, staring down her thin nose at him where he lay. "You can stay," she informed him. "I won't feed or pay you, though."

It was unexpected. And asinine. "How am I supposed to eat?"

She made a face and crossed her arms. "Let's get one thing straight, Wex..."

"How do you know my name?" he wondered aloud.

"You told us."

"Oh."

"I don't care whether you live or die. Berge is the same. Why he dragged your corpse up here eludes me. He's not known for his *soft heart*," she scoffed. "I'm allowing you to stay because your...vehicle...may prove useful to my needs. Make no mistake; I can clearly see you're desperate to stay, which tells me you have nowhere else to go. We are not friends. We are not allies. You work for me. The moment

I find you more trouble than you're worth, I bury you so far underground that not even the moles would find you."

He licked his lips. "And if I disagree?"

"I bury you. Same applies." She didn't miss a beat.

So he had no choice. Despite that, a bizarre wave of peace passed over him then. Perhaps she wasn't a kindhearted person, but neither could he believe her wholly evil. She *did* save his life. "It would be my honor to help you save lives," he replied honestly.

Her face took on a skeptical expression. Then she pressed her fingers to her forehead and shut her eyes briefly as if to recalibrate. "You can call me Zanje. The man who carried you here is Bergeron Nacht. There are more than a hundred rooms in this castle, but only the main tower is currently used. You're welcome to take any empty room. Beyond that, you're on your own. Don't expect anything from me."

He nodded in understanding. "Can I ask one small favor?"

She tossed her head impatiently. "Why not."

"I can't really move yet, and I need to go get my dog."

She blinked, then replied, "Absolutely not."

Her answer and the coldness of her tone took him aback. "She's all I have left, and she needs me. She probably hasn't eaten since I left. How long have I been out?"

Her eyes narrowed. "This isn't a zoo," she chastised. "We're not in the habit of housing smelly animals."

He bristled. "Maxine is *not* smelly. And she's no trouble at all, I promise."

"No."

He challenged her stare for stare, unsure of what else to say. As she said, he had nowhere else to go. He needed to stay in the castle with Zanje and Berge, and she keenly knew it. She wasn't in a position that required compromise. Even without Maxine, he'd need to stay. His father raised him to have some respect, and surely keeping him alive was one of the favors requiring recompense. He thought about his nightmare, and the apology in Maxine's eyes. She fought tooth and nail against death to return to him. He could do the same. So he struggled to reach a sitting position, simultaneously leaning forward, pushing with his hands, and trying to gain a little momentum. His teeth ground together as he tried to muscle through the hunger, and the pain.

"What are you doing?" Zanje wondered aloud. She didn't seem concerned so much as confused.

He blocked her out, bending his willpower toward trying to sit. Sweat broke out upon his brow. Cramps assailed his guts and the soles of his feet. He could feel the fibers of his muscles overstressing in his neck and shoulders, but he didn't care. *Maxine…I'm coming, baby dog.* He squeezed his eyes shut and focused on that sad, broken limp from his dream. And then he toppled over and crashed onto the floor face first. It broke his nose open and his teeth cut into his lip, the taste of blood and concrete filtering over his tongue. Upon opening his eyes, he saw the sharply pointed boot of the castle's mistress, tapping impatiently.

"That looked productive," she scolded.

"I'm getting my dog," he wheezed, ignoring the jab.

"If your dog ever sets foot in my castle, she's dead. My work is very sensitive to contamination and disruption."

He struggled to breathe, his cheek pressed to the cold floor. "Fine. We'll sleep outside, then."

"You're going to attempt to travel more than five miles in knee deep snow for a mutt?" She sounded tired.

"She did it for me." Not really, but she *would have.*

She sighed, exasperated. "You get to explain it to Berge," she muttered, "if you even survive." He watched as her feet shifted position and then left the room. The door shut behind her, leaving Wex alone to deal with his folly.

Wex took a deep breath. His ribs might have been broken in several places. Every breath stopped short with stabbing pains. *Alright, Wex,* he told himself. *What are we going to do?* He didn't have to think hard before the answer rooted in his mind and wouldn't let go.

Rebellion.

He gritted his teeth and placed his palms firmly against the floor. He pushed against the floor with all his might. Instantly, his eyesight dimmed, flashed over with blinding pain. His head swelled and pressed against the inside of his skull. His arms and legs trembled violently, weak from his brush with death and disuse. He sucked in a deep breath and threw the entire force of his will against the shackles his body created. A snarl and a roar tore from his throat, and slowly, slowly, his heavy body raised off the floor. He managed to get to his knees, leaning onto the bed that had previously held him during his ordeal. His hazel eyes locked onto the blood soaked sheet while he tried to capture his breath.

I almost died, he realized suddenly, patting his arms and looking for the weeping cracks that had once fractured his hide. There was nothing there but clean, unbroken skin. *I should have died here on this bed. That's my blood. That's how close I came.* He thought of his father, and how convinced the old man was that there was a God. There was a time when the old man was dying that he assured Wex everything would be fine. He told Wex that if he was dying, God meant for that to happen, too.

Suddenly Wex's face broke with a wide grin. He chuckled. It hurt to laugh, but he relished it anyway. "I robbed God," he said aloud. He tipped his face sideways and looked up toward the ceiling, laughing all the while. "Father wouldn't think it was so funny." But he kept on laughing. It seemed the right thing to do, since he'd survived God's plan to kill him.

Knowing he should have died gave him a burst of strength. He drew one knee up and placed his foot against the floor. He rocked forward, using his momentum and a strong push from his one foot to rise to his feet. His body still might as well have been a corpse, reanimated by a man's need to find his best friend.

His stride was wobbly and slow going. He had to lean against the wall and shuffle forward at the pace of ninety year-old man—if such a person existed...most died by sixty—but he moved forward. It gave him plenty of time to observe his surroundings. The castle was a well-lit place, brighter in places it was needed, such as the laboratory. Zanje's blue witchlights hovered in the eaves like brilliant stars. She must have been powerful indeed to be able to keep them burning throughout the entire building at all times. Most people could only maintain a handful of lights in close proximity to their bodies.

The castle was a mostly empty place. Besides the room he'd come from, the rest of it seemed pretty sparse. He made his way down the hallway and peeked into the open rooms on either side, but all the rooms were empty. There wasn't furniture nor carpet nor even paintings adorning the walls. It seemed a strange, lonely place, and it left him with more questions than answers about the two people whose lives he'd inadvertently joined.

He reached the end of the hallway. There were two locked doors—the supposed bedrooms of Zanje and Bergeron—and a toilet room. He stared into that last one for a few minutes while he rested, awestruck that they had such a thing. It shouldn't have surprised him, given that they lived in a castle. It was implied that they had at least a small fortune. They could afford things like running water and a sewage system, but Wex had never seen such a thing. Magic, the amazing force pervading their lives, had many miraculous uses. But much like curing Red Death, plumbing sewage was likewise not one of its virtues. He considered entering the toilet room to have a look around, but ultimately decided that it would cost too much effort. Of course, once he decided to resume his arduous journey to retrieve his dog, he realized something depressing.

The staircase leading up—and thus toward the exit—was not at this end of the hallway.

He leaned back against the end of the hallway and looked toward the other end like a pining lover. It seemed so far away. With a sigh, he began the long, slow, arduous task of traveling the hallway again.

Chapter Three

Nerys found her favorite alcove in the street cafe and slung her bag over the chair. It was tucked in close to the building, protected from the north wind. Little places like these were hard to find; most people didn't bother with any kind of business revolving around a social interaction, nor would they risk depending on their patrons' opinion of the current weather. Since the Red Death had become an epidemic, the human race had become reclusive, believing it was safer indoors. Truthfully, no one really understood how the disease spread.

Nerys didn't want to waste her life worrying about it. She'd rather spend her life doing things she loved than cowering in a dark room.

A waiter dropped off a coffee in a brightly colored mug. "Thank you," she murmured politely as he returned to his counter. She positioned the little mug in such a way that it wouldn't interfere with her work. Then, she settled into the chair, flipped open the bag, and pulled out her workbook. It flipped open to her saved page easily. She smiled at the sight of all of the little blossoms flattened and dried to the pages.

"Sorry, I forgot your sugar," the waiter apologized as he reappeared. "Oh, what's that?" he asked when he saw her book.

Her smile widened. "Flowers."

"How did you find flowers in the winter?" he inquired politely.

"I grow them indoors," she explained. "I have a greenhouse."

"Oh, that's nice." He set the sugar down and leaned over her shoulder. "So you must close the petals in between these pages? Is that how they dry?" She nodded. "What do you do with them then?"

Her fingers fluttered nervously over the pages. She considered hiding the flowers from view, but her pride won over. "I'm an artist," she admitted. "I arrange them on sheets of paper and coat them with glue. They make pretty pictures to hang on a wall."

"Oh." He nodded, trying to show he understood, but she heard it in his voice like she heard it in everyone's. None of them understood why a person would waste time on impractical pursuits. Anyone could catch the Red Death at any time, and the moment that happened they had less than a year left to live. Why bother with improving talents when it might all be over tomorrow?

She flashed him one last smile but didn't bother explaining further, accepting that it was no use. He smiled back and ducked away, leaving her to her work. She was grateful for his absence. She disliked handling the fragile blossoms in the presence of those who didn't fully appreciate them. Gingerly, she gather up a handful of violets and dropped them upon a blank white page. Humming to herself, she arranged them in a circle upside down. Then, she uncorked a small bottle of glue. She mixed it in a small dish with a little water, then used a fluffy brush to coat the flowers with a thin sheen of glue. She carefully flipped the flowers back over and stuck them to the page, then left them to dry while she sipped her coffee.

While she enjoyed her coffee, she watched the people walking by. There was a sad story written into their demeanors. Most walked with their chins tipped downward, watching their own feet as they moved about their business. Even those that traveled together didn't really talk to one another. She recognized the illustration of their logic; there wasn't much of a point in making lasting connections if one or both of you might be doomed to die soon. Her gaze settled upon a young couple. They walked side by side without touching, without talking. As they approached, passed, and walked away, her heart ached for them. *How sad*, she thought, *to be together but not understand true love*. It seemed so tragic.

Life was so dark and hopeless now, and no one ever seemed intent on making it a better place. Disease was terrifying, and fear of it sent people into hiding. Away from the invisible contagion. It seemed like everyone had switched into survival mode, as if they were in a stasis—no hobbies and no aspirations, just the bare minimum they needed to hunker down and make it through until the threat had passed. Except, it wasn't passing. And still, man remained isolated.

In the deepest place of her heart, Nerys harbored a desire to change the world for the better. She didn't have many talents. Her magic was dim and impractical. Her one passion was growing her flowers and arranging them in ways that were pleasing to the eye. It wasn't going to cure the Red Death or bring peace to families that had lost their loved ones, but it might bring a smile to someone's face. One more smile could go a long way toward lasting serenity. It was this idea that kept her going, though she was continuously trying to think of something more impactful.

A flicker of movement out of her peripheral

drew her attention. She glanced sidelong down the street as a small, white creature ambled up the cobblestone walkway. Her curiosity piqued, for she'd never seen such an animal in the city before. It was a cute little rodent with a long body that moved in a comical way as it trotted. She wished she knew how to sketch better so she could capture the moment. As it stood, she'd never see such a thing again.

Then, to her surprise, it stopped just outside the railing of the cafe patio on the other side of her table. Its little whiskered nose rose into the air, twitching back and forth. "Aren't you just the cutest thing," she cooed to it. Its face turned toward her, ears pivoting forward. It was then that she noticed the milky blue gray of sightless eyes. It struck her as odd that such a vulnerable critter was ambling down the streets of Naiora. She wondered if she should pick it up and take it home. It seemed like the kind of animal that might make a good pet. She was concerned about its ability to survive blind. It did seem quite thin to her eyes, though it might have been a trick of its shape.

A low-pitched, sad whistle announced a coming breeze, but she was too busy watching the strange creature to notice. Then a gust of wind hit so hard that the chairs around her scooted inches at a time. Her jacket snapped forward, hugging her body, but the wind blasted straight through the fabric. Her hair blew around her face. She tried to manage it so that she could see, but the snap of fleeing paper reminded her of all of her fragile flowers and her project with the violets. "No!" she wailed. She reached out to try to save them, but as soon as she did her hair flapped wildly into her eyes again. She shrieked in frustration and leaned over her work. From that vantage point, she could see down upon the book that had held all of her precious flowers. Most of them were gone, save for a single frangipani blossom that had caught in the spine. The sheet of violets was nowhere to be seen.

Tiny little claws hooked into her pant leg. The little rodent from the street scrambled up her pants, then climbed her jacket and snuggled up against the back of her neck. Her heart skipped a beat, partially from surprise and partially from fear. It was a friendly-looking creature, but if she knew one thing from growing flowers it was that sometimes, good looks could hide bad intentions.

The wind died down. She breathed a sigh of relief. Then, careful not to disturb the critter that seemed intent on burrowing into her neck, she shut her bound notebook. Naiora wasn't typically a tempestuous place. It hadn't *looked* like it was going to be a stormy day, but without any of her flowers, she wasn't going to be able to get any work done. Best to just call the day a wash and get back to her greenhouse to start a new batch of dried flowers. Sighing, she shut her book and began gathering her things. She was in the process of buttoning the closures of her bag when he spoke.

"Ashes honestly seems to like you." He spoke as if he was talking to himself, in a voice that was quiet and somewhat confused.

She was so startled by his sudden and stealthy appearance that she forgot to move slowly to accommodate the animal on her neck. Her head swiveled too fast in his direction—up and up, for he was very tall even for a man. The creature she presumed to be Ashes dug its claws into her neck. She yelped and reached for it instinctively, needing it to be off.

But he was faster. His hand shot out and gripped her by the wrist. She gasped involuntarily, fear briefly stopping her heartbeat. She stared, her mouth slightly open, trying to understand exactly what was happening. He smiled sweetly, though to her it looked more like a predator trying to charm its prey. It terrified her, but she couldn't move even if she'd wanted to. "If you hurt her," he warned, "I'll tear you apart." He sounded as if he meant it, too. He held her and looked toward the creature upon her neck. "Ashes, come on back." He made clicking sounds with his tongue. The rodent springboarded off of her neck, which made her hiss in pain, though she remained as still as she could. It jumped through the air and landed on the man's coat, then climbed up his shoulder and dropped into his pocket. The pocket bulged and moved a little before going still. The two of them made eye contact, and all of the warmth drained from his face.

She swallowed, for it was clear to her in that expression that he meant her harm. She tried to jerk her arm free and make a run for it, but his grip tightened, enough to make the bones in her wrist shift painfully. She cried out in pain, then shouted for help, looking up and down the street at passersby. Those that were close by ducked their heads and walked on past. Her cries grew more frantic as he hauled her up by the wrist and tugged her backwards into his body. Her chair tipped over backwards with a loud bang. One arm encircled her stomach and held fast while she kicked and clawed, flailing and struggling to be free. She yelled a wordless war cry as she put everything she had into breaking away. None of the general public showed any intentions of stepping in to help. She should have expected that, though it upset her more than she cared to admit. It was her against a man twice her size and at least four times her strength, but she wasn't about to give up. She threw back her head to try to catch him in the face with her skull, but he was too tall even for that. Her head thudded against solid sternum instead.

Behind her, he just laughed and held fast, amused by her ineffectual effort to escape. Above the pungence of too-close man, she inhaled the scent of damp, musty sugar with the hint of something acrid. It wasn't a fragrance she knew. His face pressed against the side of hers and he hugged her tightly, swaying with her entangled in his embrace like a lover might. "This is my favorite part," he whispered past her ear. "The *fear*. 'What is he going to do to me? Why is he doing this?'" He sighed wistfully. "The best part is that *I* know. Whatever it is that your"—he stroked her hair—"pretty little imagination can come up with, *I* know that what you're going to experience is... *so much worse*. Most would rather be dead. And eventually, you *will* die. They all do.*" He lowered his voice even further, his words just hot, audible breath in her ear that made her shudder. "This is the part where you cry." He kissed her cheek, his lips lingering.

He was *vile*. The vilest. And because of that, she didn't want to give him the satisfaction of her fear. It proved to be impossible. She watched another man—a big, strong man that probably could have beaten this guy blindfolded and with one hand—walk past. She almost shouted for help. But as he continued to watch over his shoulder as he kept on walking, she chose not to. The man who held her would have liked that too much. It was already obvious that she was on her own, and she was losing. No matter what she did, her attacker was in total control. The tears slid down her face, but she did manage not to sob or beg. It was something.

The mysterious sweet scent grew stronger as he pressed a wadded up damp rag over her nose and mouth. She panicked, unable to breathe but for the sharp chemical already pervading her nostrils, and in her blind hazy struggle, she sucked in as much air as she could. It tasted like a wine cellar and stuck like sugar to her tongue. Her mind fuzzed over and her limbs grew heavy.

"Shh…" he cooed in her ear. It was far away, though, and growing ever more distant. She was certain she was dying, and that he was easing her toward her grave. "Shh…"

The ginger went limp in his arms. She was heavier than he gave her credit for. He slung her over his shoulder and steadied her with one arm. With the other, he extracted his typing kit from the pocket that wasn't Ashes' nest. He set the card paper down on the table and weighted it down with her coffee mug—after finishing the coffee—in case the wind blew. The typing card was another of Zanje's creations. She'd tried explaining it to him, but as with most of the ideas she had, the terminology and the methods were lost on him. He didn't care enough about how it worked to pay attention to her long-winded explanations and try to understand. The fact of the matter was that her little creations worked. The *how* and the *why* were irrelevant.

He had no need for weapons, though he kept a tiny knife on his belt. The blade was only about as long as one finger and had only one purpose. He unsheathed it, held it firmly between his forefinger and his thumb. He pushed up her pant leg, bunching it around the knee so it didn't slide back down. He went to make the cut, but stopped short as his eyes fell upon her bare leg. His eyes drifted to half mast as he appreciated her pale, unadulterated skin. She looked so soft... as if no one had ever touched her in her life. Too innocent, almost childlike. His knife hand turned, and he brushed the other three fingers up and down that leg, imagining all the things he could do to her.

But unconscious women weren't his thing.

He turned his hand back around and made a small cut into the meat of her calf. The blood welled there. Using the tip of the blade, he collected a large droplet. He flicked the knife as one might a cigarette, and the droplet fell upon one of the three circles on Zanje's card. This he repeated for the other two circles. Then, he wiped the blade on his shirt and resheathed it. Zanje always chastised him for not cleaning his blade properly, but if she really had a problem with it, she could go get her own damned test rats. "'At least use the sleeping agent,'" he mimicked. "They're all going to die anyway. Why should I care if they get sick in the meantime? If Zanje wasn't so rough on them, maybe I'd be a little more concerned with keeping them alive longer. Well, Ashes? Am I right, or am I right?" He patted his pocket gently. Ashes hissed, irritated at having been woken up. He smiled to himself.

He turned his attention back to the card and tap-tapped gently. Whatever substance— reagents? Maybe?—Zanje had dried onto the cards, they reacted with blood. Depending on what all three of the circles looked like, he'd know which of Zanje's designated blood types the woman over his shoulder had—Major, Minor, Prime, Null, Rare, Weak, Baggage, or Junk. He couldn't tell them apart, nor explain what made them different from one another, but she could. He kept tapping, waiting for one of the droplets to separate, indicating a positive result. But nothing happened. "Hmm," he hummed to himself. "That can't be right. I never get that lucky." He whipped out another card—his last card—and his knife. He was even more careful than the first time, taking extra special care to use just enough blood, and that he didn't accidentally drag the substance on the card from one circle to the other. He cleaned his blade, put it back, and repeated the tap-tapping. Same result.

He grinned. "Null. Lucky me." He briefly considered hitting a dice table, but dismissed the idea immediately, remembering. He hadn't gambled since the night he'd won Ashes about ten years ago. He scowled and shook the cards off, spraying little droplets of blood everywhere, then stuffed the cards in a pants pocket. Zanje made him promise not to leave the cards lying around. He got the sense that she was worried someone else might figure out what she had done with them and steal her technology. She couldn't have been afraid someone might try to separate her from her laboratory; her Craft was peerless.

As he left the rundown coffee shop, he nodded amicably to the waiter. The man stared right back, glowering. It made him laugh how no one ever stepped up to try to save the lives he claimed. He was the Reaper, and for the most part the public treated him like exactly that, as if it were a common occurrence for a man to show up out of nowhere, drug an unsuspecting victim, and walk away with them slung over his shoulder in broad daylight. No one ever dared challenge him. When he was out and about, he was the king of the streets in every corner of the world. Even in places he'd never been before, his name was known. *Night King. Soul Reaper. Shadow Man. Blood Mage.* He had many names.

He swaggered down the streets of Naiora with his new captive over one shoulder like a sack of grain, taking in the sights of the city like a tourist. Naoira...it was a pretty name for a place that was such a literal shithole. The gutters smelled strongly of human waste. The paving stones were cracked, interrupted here and there by ankle-breaking potholes. Windows were boarded up, roofs caved in, doors hung askew on their hinges. Even the sky looked sad and bored. He made eye contact with all and sundry, tipping his chin and offering greetings. He drew looks. He drew whispers. In return, he smirked knowingly and just kept on. The reactions of the populace were the heartbeat of the world, and he had his fingers pressed tightly against the aorta. Civilization was dying, one ginger at a time.

A group of four men stepped out of an alley into his path, expressions resolute and grim.

They brandished knives much longer than the one he carried, and they looked as if they meant to gut him. He might have carried a larger knife, if he'd needed it. But sometimes, jewelry was more important than weaponry. He smiled. "Good morning, gentlemen."

"Hand her over, Shadow Man," one of the thugs said.

"No." He frowned. They knew who he was, which meant they should have known his reputation. That didn't explain why they were foolish enough to pick a fight. Sometimes they did, though, perhaps hoping to rid the world of him. He relaxed, tried his best to appear bored. His blood heated, roaring into an inferno within his veins. Perhaps they were a remnant of his sordid past. If they were thugs from the past here to collect on a debt, they might not know about the power he'd borrowed from Zanje. But then again, if they were, they should have known his real name. No one was ever allowed to borrow money with a pseud.

The four of them advanced one slow step at a time. Berge let them come. "Easy now, Reaper," the man he presumed to be the leader continued. "You've had your run of the streets for long enough, and we've had about enough of you." He strode forward confidently enough, but it was evident in the way his hands trembled and the quaver in his voice that the guy was terrified, and rightly so.

"Who's 'we'?"

"None of your—"

He was interrupted by someone else. "Where are you taking them, you bastard? What are you using them for?"

"Give us your witch," another snarled.

"Zanje?" he asked incredulously. "She's all yours. Come get her any time."

They exchanged looks, confused.

"You don't know her very well, do you?" he challenged.

"What does she want?"

He shrugged. "World peace. Maybe. To rule the world. Why don't you ask her yourselves?"

"She means to bring an end to us, doesn't she?"

He grinned. "We did that well enough on our own. Whether you believe it was the will of God, or the folly of man, or the triumph of science gone wrong...we're dying. It's just a matter of time, now. And look at us." He took a single step forward. The four of them stopped dead in their tracks. It was pathetic. "Here we are, squabbling over the ruins of once-great cities. Killing each other for fun, or maybe because we'd rather bleed to death from a wound than shit blood as we die. Fighting each other over sleeping gingers. Merciless. Friendless. Godless." He took another step.

They raised weapons with shaking hands. "So go on, now, gentlemen, and pretend you didn't see me. Life is meaningless. We're already all as good as dead. If you save her, you'll only buy her a few more years before death takes her instead. What do you say?"

They held fast in much the same way, trembling but resolute.

"Well," he purred. "I did give you the chance." Zanje's blue witchfire ignited at the feet of the leader like a pot on a cookfire, swallowing him up in tall, thin, licking flames. The man screamed and flailed. Berge relaxed back on the heels of his feet, even shoved his free hand into a pants pocket. His gaze locked onto the flickering blue flames. Fire was beautiful, almost as beautiful as blood. It had a limitless hunger he could appreciate. It cared not who it burned, nor how many it consumed. It just burned and burned, gobbling up everything in its path. If he had his way, he'd set the whole world on fire and watch it burn to ashes.

Unfortunately, most of the world was coated in snow more often than not, and it was soggy even when it wasn't. A pity.

The man's fellows succumbed to a brand of panic they'd never known. One made fearful noises, eyes wide and staring, like a deer that knew it'd been found out. His legs quaked, as if couldn't seem to remember how his feet worked. Instead, he pissed himself and fell to his knees. "Poof," Berge whispered to himself, and the man's head caught on fire. He clutched at his skull, hands and arms shaking as he shrieked and tipped over, curling into a ball.

One of the other two *had* remembered how his feet worked, and took off at a sprint down the street. Berge raised his hand and narrowed his eyes at the man's back. A blue ball of fire shot from just in front of his palm, gusting through the air between them, tail fluttering. It smacked into the fleeing man, burst like a bottle bomb, and swallowed him whole. He died instantly, dropping to the earth in a heap.

"And the fourth..." he murmured, looking about. The fourth was nowhere to be found, but in the short amount of time that had passed, there were a limited number of places he could have gone. Berge took his time as walked toward and past the smoldering corpses, pausing a moment to appreciate the beauty of fire. What he loved the most about the witchfire was the color—azure and with a hint of pale purple and white. Normal fire did the job, but witchfire did it with *style*. He reached the edge of the alleyway and peeked around the corner. There he was, cowering in the shadows like the frightened animal he was. "Where you going?" Berge cooed. "I was just warming up."

"Please," the man begged. "This wasn't even my idea. Please, just let me go!"

He shook his head once, almost regretfully. "Can't do it."

"Oh, *please!*" he whined.

He hesitated. Pretended to give it some thought while the fourth thug panicked and panted. He gave him time to fear, enjoying the power that came with total control. "Alright," he at last relented, laughing on the inside. The man's jaw dropped, and he stopped his heaving and blubbering. Berge could only imagine what might be going on inside his head. He wondered if the guy honestly believed he was free. Berge turned his back on the dumbfounded expression and began casually walking in the opposite direction.

"Oh, thank you, sir. Thank you, thank you, tha—" Flames shot up between the two of them, engulfing the mouth of the alley.

"My pleasure," Berge said for himself, shifting the load on his shoulder. He repositioned his hand, sliding his fingers up between her thighs just because he could. Behind him, the fourth man began to scream as the fire crept close and closer. Without an escape, he would have to watch the fire as it stalked him and slowly ate him alive. Berge whistled a tune to himself as he began the long journey home. He hadn't expected to be finished so early. Nulls were a precious commodity. There weren't many of them and Zanje used them up too fast. This one probably only had a few months, if that.

Chapter Four

It took Wes two days to get to Lorent, though it should have only been a five hour walk. His body rebelled at every step. His muscles threatened to seize up. He was probably still half dead, a corpse waking up from the grave, fuelled by stubbornness and wanderlust. He slept when his body gave out, and when he awoke, he just kept going.

He still hadn't eaten anything. After refusing Zanje's injection—whatever that was—he hadn't had a chance to find anything. In all honesty, he rather regretted his defiant leap into the unknown. His body was barely holding together as it was, and if he wasn't sustaining it, he couldn't expect it to get him the six miles between Zanje's castle and Lorent.

That, and he only assumed Lorent lay to the west.

He wasn't much of a gambler, but even he had to admit that lumbering such a heavy vehicle without any fuel in the tank in a direction he basically chose at random wasn't the best calculation to get him home. It was madness at best, sheer lunacy at worst. And not that he'd tell anybody, but his conviction came solely from within. He firmly believed that if he was spared by the most gruesome death reserved for any man or woman at the last second, that fate could not mean for him to die of starvation or exposure. Whatever happened on his journey toward Maxine, he would survive it.

But if he didn't hurry, Maxine wouldn't. The last place she had been was inside their home. His father was probably dead and no one else would look there, which meant that she was locked up without food. And he still didn't know how long he'd been out. He'd asked, but in his panic he hadn't secured an answer and she hadn't provided one.

So when the squat crumbling brick buildings appeared on the horizon, he thought he was imagining things. For a spell, he was sure he was dreaming, or dead. It might have been a part of that horrible nightmare that initiated this journey in the first place. But as he shuffled even closer to the brown brick and saw people moving about between buildings, he nearly wept with relief.

No one greeted him. That just wasn't the

way things were done. He crawled along with one hand to the walls of the shops, ignoring the scowls of displeasure as he left fingerprints and smudges on the storefront glass. It probably did them a favor; wherever his hand smeared, it left enough of a view through the grime to finally see what was inside the building. He turned down the street toward his father's place and sighed with relief, for it finally settled into his bones that he'd made it at last.

He swallowed the knot in his throat as thoughts and concerns sparked to life in his mind. His imagination ran away from him, painting vivid images of what he might see. Maxine might still be right where he'd left her, patiently waiting with her nose pressed to the window. Or she might be tied up and starved to death—how long had he been gone?—she might have been killed, either by burglars or passing animals. Once the master of the house died, his home became fair game. Which reminded him of his father. Which reminded him that his father might still be in the house. His dead father. Probably rotting, stinking up the house. It had him worried that he'd be more anxious to leave than to pay his respects, and it made him feel like a bad son.

He scrubbed at his eyes and shook his head, trying to banish the images, but a fresh round replaced the old ones. The scenarios grew stranger and bolder, and oh! What he wouldn't have given to be able to run! His feet dragged forward like lead, one shuffling, limping step after another. His dim, blurry vision threatened to go black. His mind was heavily fogged and wanted to shut down. His body felt as if it were heavier on top than it was on the bottom, to the point where he wouldn't have been surprised if he merely tipped over and passed out a hundred yards from his house.

When he finally wrapped his fingers around the wooden handle, he released a deep breath and paused briefly to consider. He made peace with whatever was on the other side of the door. Or tried to. When it came time to pull on the door handle, he found it harder than he had ever imagined. He shut his eyes and took several more deep breaths, calming his nerves. His hands refused to obey his command. He simply wasn't going to pull the door. The fear of what was on the other side had him paralyzed.

But then he heard the high pitched whine from within, and his hands moved on their own. He yanked the door outward so hard that he stumbled against the front porch rail. Maxine launched from where she'd been bounding toward him and careened into his waist paws first. She springboarded off immediately, tail wagging so hard that the bone batted his shins hard enough to bruise. She hopped and bounced, her entire body flailing like a fish out of water. She kept whining, breathing so hard that she wheezed and groaned.

"Hey baby dog," he cooed. "Did you miss me?" He squatted down and held his arms out. She climbed up atop his shoulders and drowned his face in dog slobber. He spent a long time just holding her, grateful that a long journey was over, and that at least this part of it he'd survived. Half of the horrific images in his head were dispelled. Maxine was alive. Whatever happened next, at least *this* had gone right.

But it wasn't the only reason he'd returned home. With a heavy sigh, he stood, dreading the next part. Maxine kept wagging her tail and watching him from the ground, but she didn't leap anymore. She shuffled along beside him as he stepped into the house.

The first thing he noticed was that it didn't smell like corpse inside. For that, he was grateful. He didn't think he could take it if he had to witness his father rotting on the floor.

The next thing he noticed was the huge dark stain on the floor. It was obviously blood, and it had him panicked, thinking his father might have been brutally murdered. It was completely apart from everything else, though, merely a dark stain in the center of the floor. There was no body. There was no story, save for the shards of broken glass and the boot scuffs through it. So, likely not a wound. He bent down toward the floor and pressed his fingers to it. He was perplexed until he remember the clear glass globe in Zanje's lab. He fingered the shards, holding them up before his eyes, studying the curvature. Then he nodded to himself, accepting that this might have been one of those.

Which meant it had held blood. What he didn't quite understand was why.

He couldn't find his father at first. He searched, the den, his father's room, the kitchen. There was a sack of potatoes in the kitchen that was open and disheveled. It didn't make any sense until he looked at Maxine. "Maxine." Her head lowered and her tail wagged fitfully. "Were you eating potatoes?" She stopped panting, her muzzle closed, and she looked up at him without raising her head. After a moment, she headed toward the den, looking ashamed. "Hey!" She stopped. He shuffled his way over to her. "I'm not mad. I'm glad you had something to eat."

He still couldn't find his father anywhere. But, his father must have been present when Bergeron had arrived to save Wex from death, which meant the last time he would have known his father was alive was in his own room. The closer he got to his room, the more certain he was.

The bed was gone. In its place was a perfectly rectangular bed of black and silver ashes. Soot was dashed up and down the walls, but nothing else in the room had been touched. Oddly, the bed was the only thing in the room that had been burned. It was nothing short of miraculous, but Wex wasn't a fool. There was only one explanation for the state of the bed, and it was one involving witchfire.

It seemed he had another reason to thank Bergeron Nacht.

Chapter Five

Nerys and her captor spent three days traveling. Three days freezing on the road, ducking into abandoned ruins to sleep. There were always abandoned ruins; abandoned houses, abandoned farms, abandoned cities. Most of them weren't so much abandoned as they were extinct, especially the houses and farms. Once the families within them died out, that was it. There wasn't anyone left. The cities were much the same, though their downfalls had been longer. The population would taper off until the city could no longer sustain itself, then its inhabitants moved on to another city. There weren't many true major cities anymore, maybe one in a hundred miles or so with some smaller ones thrown in between.

They walked. Horses and other work animals required food and boarding, and most could not afford them. When the money ran out, horses were either sold or eaten. They might have still existed...somewhere. There was still a small pocket of the wealthy living in more pleasant climes, hundreds of miles to the south. Nerys had never seen it. This far north, it was rumored that the existence of a healthy, wealthy class of people was just a myth to make them feel better. Or to set them against one another. Nothing was certain anymore.

She'd have thought her captor handsome if he didn't frighten her so. His roguish black hair cut feathery slashes across his eyes, but they were eyes that held no mercy nor remorse. They were eyes that had seen death more times than life, deeply set in a craggy face that looked older than it probably was. Dark eyes of liquid malice that would sooner see her dead than walking free. She hated him, hated him all the way through his rotten core.

She had no idea where he was taking her, but it was north. Very north. Too north for the jacket she wore. The moment they left Naiora they ran into snow showers and she spent the rest of the journey trying not to freeze to death. He nudged her along, poking and prodding her rear end or simply running into her back hips first. That he hadn't outright raped her yet surprised her, but she lived every moment wondering when he would. The thought of his hands upon her made her sick, but he groped her constantly. He found excuses to grasp her in inappropriate places and he openly leered. She endured it during the day, but when he stopped them to rest, she couldn't avoid him. The temperature dropped precipitously when the sun went down, and for some reason his body blazed like a furnace. If she didn't lay close to him, she'd freeze to death. He knew it, too, and took full advantage. He slept soundly. She didn't sleep at all.

Before she'd been caught, she'd passed people every day who were aloof—or at worst indifferent—to suffering around themselves... but never had she met someone who actively harmed others. It was simply too terrible to comprehend. "Why are you doing this?" she asked.

"Because I enjoy it," he answered readily.

She swallowed bile. Her stomach hadn't settled since he'd picked her up. She lived in a constant state of indigestion, one kiss away from losing the contents of her stomach.

Anytime she chose to speak, he undressed her with his eyes until she shuddered and turned away. True to his word, he did seem to enjoy tormenting her. Their destination no longer mattered; she would be thrilled to see the back of him no matter unto what he delivered her. Until then, she endured; she kept her tears to herself and did her best not to react to his harassment.

Her only solace was watching the antics of Ashes, his pet weasel. She was a mischievous creature who played and slept in equal measure. She sometimes threw coins out of the man's pockets or spent half the day climbing up and down his clothes.

When they finally arrived at the base of a small mountain, she swallowed her courage and withered on the spot. Her eyes traveled up and up, awed by the way the castle's eleven towers disappeared beyond the clouds. Height was a mark of wealth; it cost a great deal of money to build into the heavens. The stone was an unrelenting deep gray color that looked black against the bright sky. There wasn't a bright splash of color or relief anywhere upon its severe edifice. It was the fortress of nightmares crowned with the spires of death. If she was to be taken into that place, she wouldn't go willingly. She could get lost in it easily and die trying to find her way out, and who even knew what kinds of creatures roamed the corridors at night? Her feet rooted to the snow, heels dug in, and she threw all of her weight in reverse against her captor.

The stranger rounded on her in exceptional fury, eyes burning like smoldering coals. His grip on her arm was iron, hard enough to leave a mark. She yelped and shut down, her legs going slack beneath her. Instantly, he was upon her, pinning her arms into the snow and crushing her there with his body. Her skin crawled, reviled. His answer was to sneer inches from her face. She turned her face away, sure he meant to steal kisses. Instead, he hovered over her face, head tilting back and forth, almost curious. He inhaled deeply and sighed, violating her with comments on how sweet she smelled.

She had to choose between escaping his attention and escaping the cold, and her traitorous body decided it was more against the subzero powder snow than her captor. She curled in upon herself, tugging her arms toward her sides and dragging his hands with her. He chuckled, amused, then helped her up and slung her over his shoulder. She tried to kick him in the face, but before she could connect with his hateful visage he only slid a hand between her legs to keep her still. "What's the matter?" he teased. "Scared?"

She couldn't admit to that. "No."

"Give it time. Let it really sink in."

By the time they reached the castle, she had replaced the old Nerys with one that was ready and anxious to do violence. Her eyes scanned her surroundings for anything that could serve as a weapon. She imagined gouging his eyes out, stabbing him in the heart, breaking every bone in his body, slitting his throat. The thought of him dying slowly brought her a modicum of comfort. Somewhere between the base of the mountain and the castle's front door, she calmed enough to allow herself to be carried. She let him believe she had surrendered, but in her mind she was only saving up her energy for the final push for freedom.

It was darker and quieter inside the castle than it was outside, though the hallways were well lit by witchlight designed to look like stars. That, she found peculiar; in such an oppressive place, with men as artless and lecherous as the man who held her like a sack of flour, *someone* was impassioned enough to grace the interior with a slice of beauty reminiscent of the night sky. It had to have been Crafted by the hand of another, for the brute toting her about didn't have an eye for grace.

He carted her down several hallways, each just as plain as the last. A layer of dust seemed to coat every surface and cobwebs sheltered every corner. She tried to memorize the layout, but there were too many hallways, and all of them looked the same to her. No personal touches, no deviations from the standard decor. Every door was plain, aged wood with iron detail and rings. Every stone pillar and support beam was so utterly plain that there was no telling them apart. If that wasn't enough, she realized too late that he was purposely retracing his steps to confuse her. He veered down the same hallways over and over. She lost all sense of cardinal direction and became helplessly lost. When at last he came to a stop in front of a door she hadn't seen before, she no longer remembered how they'd reached it. "I hate you," she finally said.

He patted her rear end and laughed. "Not half as much as you're about to." His voice was laced with venom.

The door creaked open onto a pit of despair. A cacophany of sorrow and horror rose to her innocent ears. There were at least a dozen voices of the damned in that hole, crying out for mercy, for freedom, for death, for release, for *something* long denied. She broke a little more each second, another hairline fracture in the foundation of Nerys Raphaen. She listened in mute horror, paralyzed, internalizing every word.

"Please, please, please, please, please, please!"

"Berge, you rogue bastard. Fight me like a man! Come on, let's go a round. Just let me out of this"—a crash sounded so loudly that Nerys startled back to life. Whoever had been speaking did so now through clenched teeth, enunciating and sharpening every syllable. "—*Fucking cage!*"

"Oh, God, save me!"

One voice wept quietly.

One less so.

Another screamed and screamed, a howl of pain and sorrow that only worsened with every passing second.

Nerys was too shocked to react.

The man who held her—Berge—chuckled softly to himself and released a contented sigh. A bright blue star of witchlight bloomed above him, illuminating the treacherous stairs to the world below. Finally, he set her upon her feet. "Your room is this way," he told her, gesturing downstairs with a courtly flourish. His thin frame blocked the doorway behind them. She briefly considered dashing past, ducking under that immovable arm. Then she caught a glimpse of the man's expression in the ghostly blue light and changed her mind. There was sparkling, violent amusement there. He *wanted* her to try to escape. He silently dared her to, the corners of his eyes turned upward like the smirk he wore.

"What is this place?" she whispered, horrified. She descended the staircase, but couldn't shake the feeling that she was lowering herself into the cradle of hell.

"You'll find out soon enough," he promised. The devil, following her down.

Her heart thudded, harder and harder, as he led her through what could only be described as a jail, or perhaps a dungeon. It was little more than a kennel for humans. The staircase let out at an intersection like a 'T.' Toward the left, the aisle disappeared into the blackness, unlit. God only knew what was beyond. A low, ominous echo originated there, like a warning. Her tormentor turned toward the right. There were two cells on either side of the aisle. Two of them were empty. Two held one man each. She could barely see them save for the thin blue glow around their silhouettes. It was impossible to determine whether or not they were even alive.

The jailer locked her alone in the cage in the furthest corner and left. The blue witchlight went with him, fading until it finally winked out, leaving her in absolute, suffocating darkness—with whomever was down here with her. It was dark, but it wasn't silent. At least a handful of voices wept, muttered, and wailed. The blackness closed in around her. She tried to make flame, but the air down here was too damp. She could barely make a spark, and it died as soon as she tried. She tried just to draw in a little heat, but to do so required pulling heat from the environment, and the dungeon was especially chilly. Her ears rang with the cacophony of noise in the enclosed space. Her breath came in frightened pants. It was maddening—she couldn't see anything, yet she heard too much. She was alone among terrified strangers, and the future was uncertain. She whimpered, at a loss for what else to do. "Can someone—" she swallowed, choking on the words. "A light, please?"

"It's best if you learn to go without," said a voice. It was calmer than the others. "But you're new, so I guess just this once." A small and fitful blue light sputtered into being. His fingers caged over it, barring across it. It illuminated his face as well. Dark eyes appearing black in the dim and otherworldly light. His mouth made a firm line that tended toward a frown. All she could see of him was his face, square and haggard. He might have once been a handsome man, but his scarred face had seen too much, and there was no joy in it now. "Better?"

"Much," she agreed. "It's too damp and cold for mine to work. My Craft is weak," she admitted. "But I've never needed it until now." With nothing else to do, she simply sat down. The floor was even chillier than the air.

"You still don't *need* it. No one *needs* it. What's your name?"

"Nerys. What's yours?"

"Simos."

"It's nice to meet you, Simos."

He snorted. "No it's not. Were you more fortunate, we'd never have met."

She had thought to be polite, but couldn't refute his logic. "What is this place?"

"Hell." His gaze dropped away from hers. He fidgeted with something on the floor, scratching at it out of boredom.

"No, I mean really."

"Hell," he repeated with the same conviction.

She frowned, sorry she'd asked. "Okay then."

"They bleed you," a woman's voice chimed in, hollow and haunted. She realized, then, that the rest had gone quiet, save for one woman weeping farther down the corridor. "They strap you to a chair and steal your blood."

"What?" Nerys squeaked, too appalled to say anything more eloquent.

"It's true," Simos confirmed. "Each cell in this godforsaken dungeon represents one of Zanje's blood designations."

"I don't even know what that means."

"Neither do we, other than that some seem to get bled more than others. I'm classified as Rare. Lissa, Kalyria, and Marc are the Primes. Primes get used the most, but by the looks of it are quite common. Tafford and Rowan are the Minors. Larric and Mirdoz are what's called Major. It's used about as often as the Prime. Fross is our only Weak, and Nellan, Seph, Megra, Illis, and Kopep are the seldom used type known as Baggage. The empty cell beside you is for Junk, but it hasn't been occupied in quite some time."

Her head swam with confusion, unable to keep all the names and types straight. "Okay."

"You're the Null, baby girl," a man from further down said.

"What's Null?" she asked.

Simos sighed. "It's ugly, but you've a right to know. Nulls are used a lot, as a sort of default when the folk upstairs aren't sure what they want." His voice had gone soft, grave almost. "And they're not very common, unfortunately. They bleed the Nulls more often than any other person."

Her stomach fell as her pulse quickened. She didn't like the sound of that. "What does that mean?" Her stomach tied itself up into a knot, dreading the answer.

"It means you're probably not going to be with us long."

"Oh." She hugged her knees and went quiet. Around her, the other voices had fallen silent as well, a soundless chant of human pity. The only noise was Simos, scratching at his cell floor. It began to sink in exactly what they were trying to tell her. Slowly but surely, she was going to die here. Her gaze slid sideways, looking for comfort from the only other prisoner she could see. He wasn't fidgeting... he was drawing, or something that looked like it. He had a sharp little stone in one hand and dug mercilessly at the relatively soft, damp stone of the floor. "What are you doing over there?"

"Writing."

Her ears sharpened, intrigued. "What are you writing? A poem?"

"No, they're names." He stopped and leaned back, then moved his fitful spark of witchlight over the floor like a wand. There were dozens of them. "The names of the dead. This one"—he pointed with the stone—"is Tragen. He was the last Null."

Chapter Six

Berge heard the mewling, whining, godawful sound of Zanje's music from the main entry hall. Zanje didn't know the meaning of quiet when it came to her music. She claimed that when the volume was too low, one could not 'fully appreciate the intricacies of the piece.' He rolled his eyes and considered talking to her later, but was too impatient. Cringing against the inevitably increasing noise, he climbed the stairs to the giant ballroom of the seventh floor. Her floor. The ballroom was the only room on that floor, and the view from the grand balcony made it Zanje's favorite haunt. He pushed open the heavy oak and iron double doors. The pressure differential sucked in air from the dozens of open windows, sheer red curtains whipping like banners. "Fucking hell, Zanj, are you trying to freeze to death?" He had to shout over her music, but the strings hit a crescendo and he barely heard himself. He strode over to the tall, arched windows all along the outer wall to close them.

"Leave it," she commanded with a graceful wave of her hand.

He ignored her and closed all of the shutters and the balcony door. The wind this high up rattled the shutters as he latched them shut. Belatedly, he remembered that his ability to ignore the cold was only a fraction of hers. The warmth that burned within them was a symptom of her mastery of natural energy. He chose not to comment on it, and instead went right to the important topic. "Got your Null."

"Shh," she shushed, holding up one finger and closing her eyes.

He scowled. Zanje was fussy about her music. He dropped onto the overstuffed armchair across from her, splayed out upon it as if it were a throne, legs thrown wide apart and one hand gripping each arm. He slouched and watched her intently, drinking in the sight of her while she drifted off the mortal plane, lost to the music. His eyes roved over her perfect legs, crossed and tucked under her, toes twitching in time with the percussion. She took a sip from her wine glass, then savored the drink over her tongue. She smiled and moaned softly with pleasure, then tipped her head back. For all intents and purposes, she basically forgot he was even there, which was just fine with him.

He slid his eyes down the elegant line of her neck and across naked collarbones, across the slope of her shoulder. His eyes stuck on the missing finger on her left hand. Unconscious of what he was doing, one of his hands curled around the bone that hung from a leather cord around his neck. The ability to use Craft was written into a person from birth and bound to the body. Without her token, he was powerless. He despised that. Despised *her*, just as viscerally as he wanted her.

The music played on in the background. He never could appreciate it to the same extent that she could. Music didn't make sense to him. The strings graced his eardrums with all the elegance of a high pitched squeal and made him want to claw his own brains out. The drums chafed at his ears with the same aggravation as a screaming child. Nonetheless, the music was important to Zanje's happiness, and she had so precious little of that. He didn't typically place Zanje's happiness high on his priorities list, but when she was happy *enough*…

The sound in the air stopped abruptly. Her eyes drifted open. "That was one of the songs you ruined with your inane chatter," she mourned. He narrowed his eyes and cocked his chin. "You forget that the song is recording at the same time it's playing. It picks up your voice, too."

He did forget. He always forgot because *he didn't fucking care.* "I got your Null," he repeated.

"I heard you the first time," she shot back, fluffing at her hair. "If you're looking for a reward, forget it. I'm not in the mood."

He frowned. "You're never in the mood."

"You're always in the mood, so we balance out."

"Your overwhelming gratitude is appreciated," he sniped.

"You get paid a portion of our proceeds. That's the reward you get for doing your job," she reminded him tiredly. They'd gone over it plenty of times. She hardly needed to repeat it, but she did it anyway, probably because she thought he forgot.

"A *small* portion," he grumbled.

"Mm, yes, and a larger one than you deserve."

He disagreed with her, but it was still more gold than he'd seen in a lifetime. He never forgot that particular detail. Still, it was obvious he wasn't getting sex from her today, so he stopped trying. "She's a feisty thing," he said instead, hoping to provoke her jealousy. It was, as ever, a wasted effort. Zanje was a cruel, heartless bitch who didn't possess petty human emotions. She ignored him. "You think you might let this one last more than a month?"

"I use what I need when I need it. If you want them to last longer, you should fill the cells with more of each."

"Gladly. Except your *godforsaken Nulls* are like myths on the wind. You're lucky I found this one so quickly."

"You're lucky," she corrected. "The only way it affects me is that we suffer a momentary lapse in business, but your well being depends on our income much more than mine does." She smiled a cruel smile.

He scowled again. He knew he shouldn't have settled for such a low cut of the pay, but at the time, *any* money seemed like a fortune. Ashes poked her nose out of his pocket. She tasted at the air. He touched her nose with the tip of one finger and made smooching noises.

Zanje scoffed. "Why you let that rat touch you eludes me."

"Weasel," he corrected. "And if it weren't for Ashes, I'd still be out there searching. She has an uncanny ability to sniff out Specials."

"You're imagining things. She's an animal, not a wizard."

"It's not hard to believe." He scratched under the weasel's chin. Her nose went straight up in the air. "After all, you're an animal, but you have special abilities."

She poured another glass. "We're not animals."

"That's exactly what we are," he contested. "Dirty, stinking animals." He leered at her.

She remained unfazed. "The only good thing about that filthy rat is that it finally convinced you to stop gambling."

His mood soured. He didn't like to remember that. "Yeah."

"Hm." She seemed pleased. Berge raised a brow at the empty wine bottle as she set it upon the floor next to the other one. The two of them made an exorbitant amount of money, but her wine habit—with the caliber of wine she drank—could bankrupt a king. Winemaking was another dwindling art, but like any business centered upon alcohol, stubbornly refused to die.

Perhaps a change of subject. "How's Wex?" he asked instead.

"Gone."

His gaze shot up, eyes wide. "Oh no." He'd been worried about that. Zanje had once explained to him why taking blood from one person and giving it directly to another was unwise. She usually had to do something to it in between to make it safe for transfusion. She'd tried to explain to him what she did, but he tuned it out. Something about antibodies and immune reactions. He understood the general concept. Fresh, unaltered blood could make a person sick unless it was the exact same type, and even then it wasn't a sure bet. They hadn't known Wex's type, so they'd gambled a little. Even if he had survived, recovery was going to be especially rough. "Damn, after all that."

She rolled her eyes. "Not dead, you idiot. *Gone*. He left."

Pure shock replaced disappointment. "How? Recovery should have taken a lot longer, right?"

She laughed bitterly. "Exactly. He's not recovered. Practically fell all over himself on his way out. Probably froze to death, honestly."

"How long ago did he leave?"

"I don't recall. A few days. I forgot about him as soon as he left."

"Why didn't you stop him?"

She gave him a bemused look. Of course she didn't stop him. Wex wasn't a Special, or he wouldn't have gotten sick. He had no use to Zanje, alive or dead. Berge could almost imagine that scene. She'd say, 'You shouldn't do that,' and he'd answer with, 'Well, I'm going to,' and then she'd just shrug and say, 'Your death sentence. Goodbye.' And because she *didn't* stop him, Wex was certainly a goner. Silently, he fumed. He hated putting forth any effort in the first place. To hear that it had been a wasted effort chafed.

Zanje retrieved a cigarette from the gold embossed case beside her. Berge's nose wrinkled away from it, but he watched her from the corner of one eye. He despised everything about cigarettes…except for the way they looked between her lips. She pressed the pad of one finger against the end. Smoke wisped up from where it touched. She looked over the cigarette from beneath her eyebrows and smoldered him with a look that robbed him of his breath.

He groaned from deep in his throat, *wanting* with every fiber of his being. She knew it, too, smirked around the cigarette and denied him regardless. "So tell me about this new Null." She tilted her chin back and a line of smoke trailed from where should have been his kiss.

He didn't want to tell her anymore. She had entirely soured his good mood. Of course, he couldn't let her know that. "She's prettier than you."

Zanje's expression told him that she knew better.

"She's younger, too. Probably about ten years younger than you. Red hair. Freckles across the nose." He waved his fingers before his own nose to show her where. Zanje wasn't taking the bait. "I found her about forty miles south. Something about that place—what's it called?—keeps the snow from falling most of the time. It's nice this time of year."

"Naiora?"

"Yeah, that's it."

She took a sip of her wine. He watched intently, and she caught him at it. "Naiora is at the bottom of a valley. The atmosphere there is too dry. If there's no water, there's no snow. And the mountains keep the cloud cover from drifting in." She flicked the cigarette over the back of her couch.

"How do you just know all of these things?" he wondered aloud, irritated.

She shrugged but said nothing. It brought her too much pleasure to make him feel unintelligent.

A body crashed against the door to the main hall. Berge was on his feet in an instant, heat in every blood vessel, ready to attack. Zanje languidly craned her neck over the back of the couch to see. Wex was wrapped around one side of the threshold, leaning into the room. His eyes drooped, and his beard had gotten a little out of hand. "Hey."

"So he lives after all," Zanje observed. She turned away from him and sipped her wine.

"Yeah, I'm here. Barely."

"That was a stupid thing to do," Berge admonished. "What were you thinking?"

"I had to go get my dog." He spoke as if it were the only option, like *not* getting his dog was unacceptable. Wex indicated the woman on the couch as he limped his way into the room. "*She* wasn't any help." He hobbled to the nearest chair and fell upon it. His head dumped into his palms. He rubbed both hands over his bare scalp and loosed a heavy sigh.

That bitch, Berge thought immediately. He was beginning to understand why he'd saved the guy. Subconsciously, he patted the pocket that held Ashes. "Did you find her?"

Wex smiled in the shadows of his hands. "Yeah. She's alright. A bit hungry, but that's typical."

"What's her name?"

"Maxine."

Berge nodded. It was a good name.

Zanje tilted her head backwards and spoke to Wex from beneath her chin. "Where is she?"

"Waiting at the door."

"Good. Did you bring that contraption you mentioned?"

He looked at her. "Yeah." He seemed confused.

She nodded, brought the cigarette to her lips and drew on it. "Then you're going out tomorrow."

It was Berge's turn to be confused. "What?"

She pointed with her cigarette hand. "He offered to work for us."

Berge looked between them. "Doing what?"

"Driving," Wex answered.

"Driving?"

"Driving," he confirmed with a short nod.

"Huh?"

"I made a vehicle that skids across the snow. Beats walking there."

"A vehicle?" Berge knew he sounded stupid, but he didn't care. Such a thing didn't exist.

Wex grinned and nodded again. "Yeah, that's what I said."

"What the hell is that?"

"Well, you get in it," Wex pantomimed, "and then you feed it some of your energy, and it goes."

"It goes." He sounded doubtful.

"Yep. It *goes*." His hand made a smooth motion.

"How far?"

"As far as you want it to."

"How fast?"

He shrugged. "I could get from here to Passdell in about three hours." He rubbed his hands together slowly as he spoke.

Berge snorted. "Bullshit." Passdell was about a hundred and fifty miles east. He made eye contact with Zanje, but to his surprise, she had gone still. To his horror, she was *listening*. Carefully. Travel and mobility were great challenges in the modern era. Only the wealthy could afford horses or even pack animals, for they took a great deal of feed and care. And although she could easily afford them, to her it was a risk not worth taking. Quorath was in the heart of the most blasted land in the world, and owning horses would only draw attention. And that, she did *not* want. He could almost see the numbers and maplines connecting in her brilliant mind. And as soon as he saw that, his brain did the same thing. With money. *Oh my God,* he thought, though he denied God's existence. "Prove it."

"I have a package for you to pick up in Becket," she informed him.

Berge's eyes widened. Becket was a hundred and eighty miles north, into the frozen wasteland. Zanje had never taken requests from anywhere that far, let alone anywhere that far north. "Zanj, that's suicide."

"He'll do it," she assured him. "He owes us his life." She flicked the cigarette again. Nonchalant and cold as ice.

"Well, I was hoping we'd get a little more out of his life than that." He sank back into his cushions. "It would be nice to let someone else do your dirty work for a change."

"But you love my dirty work," she retorted wickedly.

"I do. You're right. But we could get so much more done with two of me."

"Two Bergeron Nachts? I wouldn't wish that upon anyone."

"Not a problem," Wex interrupted.

Two sets of eyes settled upon him.

"I could go tonight, if you wanted."

"That's ridiculous," Berge said at the same time Zanje said, "Done." They made eye contact with one another. Zanje's lips curved in that malevolent, victorious way he loved so much. Zanje could bend a man into submission with nothing but the muscles of her face. His own face contorted with hatred. She played him too easily, and he let her, lapping at the fingers of privilege and poking his nose where he knew it wasn't wanted.

"Alright." Wex smiled for himself and got shakily to his feet.

She spoke over one shoulder without even looking at the man she was sending to his inevitable doom. "You're looking for a woman named Orelia. She runs an apothecary in Becket. When she gives you the item, keep it a temperature that's cold to the touch but warmer than the snow."

"What is it?"

"Best not ask that. Just keep it as cold as I said."

"Damn it, Wex, at least wait until your legs work," Berge insisted.

"Nope. Too damned stubborn. Besides, I don't need my legs."

Zanje's eyebrows spoke for her.

Berge watched the new recruit leave, respect growing with every wincing, tortured step.

When he was finally out of sight, Berge turned to his nasty accomplice. "Who's paying for this?" He mentally prepared a half dozen counters for the inevitable cut to his paycheck.

So it surprised him when she made a flippant gesture with her cigarette and shrugged out, "No one."

"What do you mean no one?"

"I sure as hell am not paying him. No one's making him stay. You're cheap. He's free. It's a good deal." She blew out smoke. "You like him, don't you? Don't get soft on me now, Berge."

"Wouldn't dream of it," he shot back.

"If his...contraption...is as good as he says it is, we can expand our reach to much further. I get requests all the time from places as distant as Copracache."

"Really?"

She nodded slowly. "I have them all saved up. We can fill them as fast as Wex moves."

"Not that I'm complaining, but do you have anything planned for all of this money you're not paying him?"

She was quiet for a long time before she answered. "Some things, Berge, I'm just never going to tell you."

"Wex!" The sun damned near blinded him, seared his retinas and shattered his brain. He shaded his eyes with a hand and searched for their added business mate. A dog barked and sprinted through the snow, tail wagging in a circle around the large rear end of a well-fed animal. Berge instantly forgot his stony demeanor and dropped to the snow on his knees. His voice took on the sing-song quality he usually reserved for Ashes. "Well, hello there!" His hands encircled the dog's square face, brushing the pads of his thumbs across the grizzled grey around her muzzle. Her chin was tipped upward, inviting a scratch. Berge could have sworn she was smiling.

"Dogs can recognize a guy that likes dogs," Wex said casually.

Berge clicked his tongue at her. "You're so pretty. Yes you are. Yes you are." He snuggled his face against the top of her head and kissed her. He breathed in the scent of clean animal fur and sighed. He'd always wanted a dog, but for most of his life he couldn't even afford to feed himself, and then there was Zanje. "Maxine," he murmured, remembering. Her tail wagged even harder. Berge's eyes rose to the man himself, though he had to squint against the bright sunlight. It was then that he saw Wex's vehicle. It had skids on either side and a traction belt to grip the slippery earth. "Oh wow…"

Wex smirked and patted the metal. "Yep, there you have it. The only one of its kind."

Berge stood and walked towards it, transfixed by the shining silver metal. It was like a mirror, reflecting brightly in the light. "What is that? Steel?"

"Aluminum. It's a lot lighter than steel. Let's you travel over the snow. I spent a lot of time studying how to smelt steel. If you temper it just right it's stronger than anything in existence. Although, did you know that hair, human hair, if you were to braid it into a rope, could lift this whole vehicle up with me and Maxine both in it? Tough stuff. Anyway. Steel, as everyone knows, is the preferred metal for metalworking if you want to make anything that lasts. The problem with steel is that it's really, really heavy, and since the machine I wanted needs to be able to travel over snow, which doesn't have a lot of mass and can bog down a vehicle, I didn't want that. I went with aluminum, which isn't really a metal people work with very often because it's not as durable. Actually," he added with a frown, "I don't think many people even remember how…"

Berge knocked on the hood of the vehicle. "Huh."

"Well, it's not fragile…it's just not steel. But. Aluminum, as it turns out, is easy to get your hands on. All you need to do is find bauxite. Lots and lots of it."

"The hell is that?"

"It's just a kind of ore that can be found in the earth. It's not very far underground. The land between Quorath and Lorent is rich with it. Took me about, oh, three days to find all that I needed. The bauxite itself is actually worked into clay in little bits, so you have to wash it all off. You actually have to scrub it and grind it all down to separate the bauxite from the clay. That took me longer than digging it up.

"But you're still not done," he continued. "Then you have to refine it, which involves mixing it with lime and soda and heating it up. Bauxite itself doesn't make aluminum. You still have to extract out the actual ore, the alumina, from the bauxite. It's a multistep process. So you get it really hot and mix it with these caustic elements—the lime and the soda—and they separate out in solution. When you filter it out, you get the alumina, and that's what you use to make the aluminum itself, which is what you need to work with to make this lovely beast behind you." He gestured toward his vehicle.

"When you free the alumina from the bauxite, you dry it into this lovely, shiny powder, and then—" He paused and regarded Berge with a grave expression. "How much do you know about circuitry?"

Berge had already tuned out. He was imagining how much easier it might have been to carry a man like Wex six miles in heavy snowfall with one of the contraptions Wex had made. "Not a damned thing," he admitted. His eyes roved over the back of the vehicle. It looked to be a kind of compartment. Berge was calculating how many bodies he could fit into it. By the looks of it, about three.

"Ah, well. Hm." He paused to think about how to explain it. Berge wished he wouldn't. "You know how the Craft works? How you manipulate energy with your body, and it translates as light or heat? You know, you can convert light to heat or heat to light, and all that?"

"Not...exactly," he admitted. He wasn't about to admit that he couldn't. Such an admission was dangerous. "I mean, of course I can do it, I just never really thought about how. I just do."

"Ah." Wex went quiet again for a second, composing thoughts. "Well, it's kind of like a river." He held both hands out as if he were about to clap but never did.

"Yeah."

"Water always flows downhill right? Well, circuitry is like that. There's a current, like with water, that goes from one defined endpoint to the other. It always goes from a higher point of elevation to a lower one. Downhill. So, with circuitry, the current is like the water, except that the current in this case is the energy, and the energy is what we use with the Craft to make light and heat. Do you know what I mean?"

"No."

"Ahh. Well. A circuit is just the energy that is used to make light and heat, and it goes from one point to another." He moved one hand toward the other to demonstrate, earnestly willing Berge to understand. "Do you understand?"

"Yeah, I get it." He didn't, but if he admitted that, there was no way that Wex was ever going to stop trying to explain it.

"Good! Okay, so if you take the alumina from before and you hit it with that energy, then it turns into molten aluminum, and that's when you can start to shape it! "

Berge's brain glazed over again, but he nodded at the times when it was appropriate to nod, every now and again interjecting with "Yeah?" and "Oh, really?" so that Wex could hasten toward the end of this godforsaken explanation.

After what felt like a lifetime, Wex finally concluded with how he'd added the skids—Berge narrowly missed another lecture on how he'd made *those*—and how he'd fashioned it to react to his own power so that it would move. It was clear that the man was proud of his invention, and Berge had to admit it was impressive, but he struggled to hold onto the reason he'd come out here in the first place. "Sounds a lot like science," he murmured without thinking. Wex went quiet. When Berge looked at him again, the other man appeared unhappy. "What?"

"This is the part where you tell me it's stupid and will get me killed, isn't it?"

Berge blinked and thought of Zanje's laboratory. He laughed. "No. I know how the world feels about science in general, but science puts gold in my pocket. I just don't know shit about it." He tapped his skull. "It never stays up there, with me."

"Oh." He relaxed, and it was only then Berge noticed he was tense at all, as if he'd been preparing for an argument.

That's when he remembered. "Hey, you don't have to do this, you know." Once he'd said it, though, he wasn't sure how to continue. It'd been too long since he'd tried to give anyone advice or caution them against something stupid.

"I know," Wex replied, as if he knew exactly what Berge meant.

He didn't. He didn't know the half of what went on in Zanje's laboratory. And if he did, he wouldn't be casually preparing for a journey almost two hundred miles into the great white north. "No, I mean it. You should go home. This isn't the kind of job most people can handle." He immediately regretted the implication of his words. Before Wex could open his mouth to counter it, Berge held up a hand and changed the subject. "Zanje told me you're working for free." He tried to convey with his expression what he didn't wish to say. *We kill people. We lock them up in little cages and bleed them for cash.*

"I never got to thank you for saving my life."

"It's not like—"

"I can see what you're doing here, Berge." He pointed with his great bearded chin toward the castle. "Your woman's got some kind of ability to reverse the Red Death. You brought me to her and she saved me with whatever that was. I get that you're hiding something about how it's done. You're probably trying to keep that quiet. Yeah. I get it. I won't say anything. But this is how it is. When you're handed a gift like this, you don't ask questions. You gave me my life back. By rights, that means I'm your guy. You don't owe me anything more than that. I can't ever repay you for what you've done, but I can try. Whatever it is that you do to save guys like me, I'm going to help you do it. You bring people back from the edge of death and give them back their lives. There can be no greater calling than that. Now, I'm not going to let what you did for me go to waste. My father taught me better than that. Maxine! Let's go, baby dog." He patted the seat of his snowcraft. The brown dog was overweight and seemed rather old, but she hopped up into that seat like a puppy without any trouble. Wex slid a pair of tinted, iridescent glasses over the bridge of his nose and grinned. "Thanks, Berge. You're a decent guy."

Berge didn't really know what to say to that —he definitely *wasn't* a decent guy. "Look, before you go..." He delved into his pockets and emptied it for everything that was in it. "Zanje changed her mind about payment, so here." He handed it over. "Don't ask *her* for your money, though. It will give her a chance to change her mind." Wex nodded. "You're probably going to die out there. Might as well do it with some food in you. It's not much, I know, but we'll get more. At least it should be enough to keep you fed."

"She really didn't have to. I'm just grateful to be alive." He accepted the money, though. A man needed to eat. "Thanks again. Don't worry about me, though. I'm a tough bastard. I'll be back by morning." He hauled himself up into the seat.

"Well don't wake me up then. I need my beauty rest." He smirked.

Wex rolled his eyes and shut the door to his vehicle. He gave another brief wave, then the contraption started purring, mechanical gears and gadgets waking up. Berge eyed the thing as the parts began to move, the skids tilting toward one direction and the tread spinning, propelling the thing forward. As the machine disappeared from view, Berge hailed Wex as the bravest man he'd ever met.

But why did he save him? He still didn't know.

Chapter Seven

She watched the newly fledged emotions play themselves out on the stage of Berge's face, confused, but amused. When she had met her co-conspirator, Bergeron Nacht was nothing but an unscrupulous, dirty button man. He was willing to do anything for any price so long as it brought him back to the dice tables that evening with a drink in hand. She found him drunk or hungover most of the time, but it had never stopped him from performing his duties with alacrity when she asked it of him. There was not a more despicable being in all the world, and this one belonged to her. Only to her. He knew and she knew that he had an obsession with her that only grew more pronounced with time.

He knew and she knew that it was *because* of how far she was willing to go to change the world.

She smiled to herself and finished off her last

glass of wine. Her thoughts drifted, buzzing pleasantly. Most often, her thoughts sailed into the future. It was a place where science triumphed over magic instead of the other way around, as it should always have been. She triggered one of her musical stones in the box on the mantle, choosing one at random. With another hand, she reached toward a table at the far wall of this ball room. Another stone sailed toward her, slowly, like a moon in orbit around its witch. She smiled lazily, reveling in her power. So many ignorant wretches believed that heat and light were the only forms of energy worth manipulating. Had they ever been as closely acquainted with the elegance of the universe—of the science they so despised and yet used unthinkingly—they might have known of the more sophisticated energies awaiting their command. Kinetic. Thermal. Nuclear. Potential. Sound. It was that last that pleased her most, for with it she could capture music within stones.

She sat up straight on her couch. Her head tilted over the back of it. She sighed with perfect contentment. She never understood how Berge always went crazy or wrathful when he'd drunk a little too much. Alcohol made her feel sleepy and relaxed, the only time she ever felt so. Any other time, she was a chaos within, filled with hatred, anger, and vengeance for the way the universe currently stood. Mankind had destroyed the looking glass into the intricacies of life, so completely that many technologies were lost. Had scientists not recorded their findings as they studied the mechanics of physics and biology, she'd not have advanced as far as she had. It fell upon her to rescue science, and she was working against a thieving mob of children playing with fire.

The music began, a tense yet tentative nocturne. The melody was bright and hopeful, though the foundation was more cautious and grounding. The effect was an almost playful story, rooted in sadness but trying to leave sorrow behind. It was too achingly sweet for her to hang onto her angst for the past. Her stress drained away, knots in her shoulders easing. The constriction in her lungs ebbed and allowed her to breathe more freely. When she shut her eyes, the music gripped her deep in the heart, almost alive, speaking straight to her soul, a voice for only her. The music was always the force behind her thought, for it injected civilization deep into her marrow and reshaped her. She longed for sophistication, was nostalgic for something she'd never been able to experience.

"Ah, Berge," she said aloud. He was her greatest asset. She prized him like a cherished pet, though she'd never let him know. His stormy wrath brought her sweet joy. He left messes everywhere he went, ripples in a pond, blood in the snow, little haphazard masterpieces he'd done in her name. Brutal and flawless.

No one else in the world had an eye for art like she did.

And Wex...she hadn't decided what she thought of him yet. He was certainly useful, but he seemed upon the surface to be too soft to suit her needs. If he jeopardized their operation, he would need to be dealt with. And, too, there was the matter of Berge's attitude towards him. What was that? And did it threaten her? Her thought was no. Berge loved her more than he hated her. As long as she kept Wex at a distance, as long as Berge's balance remained skewed in her favor, he was worth more than his risk.

She shut her eyes and let the music fill her up. The song coiled around her every finger, slithered through her veins like sugar. Slow breath after sigh waxed and waned, and for the length of the piece, she was merely a vessel of the divine. Her lips parted with awe.

When the last violin shivered and then went still, her eyes flew open. The colors to her seemed to be much more vibrant now. The red of the curtains like freshly spilled blood. The gold of the sun like a splash of godliness across the silver of the floor. She peered at her hands and saw the deep grooves of every line. She was alive. Deservedly so. And the fact that she was so very alive and livened ever further by the heart of a violin only gifted her with more righteousness.

She descended the seven flights of stairs with an open mind, observing the difference in the feel at each level. The closer she got to earth, the more average she felt. Upon the main floor she was common, a goddess forced to step upon the filthy earth where she did not belong. One level further into the cockles of the world itself, she was an intruder. It was the domain of sin, and it was here that she bled them, in the presence of the dead and dying. In the presence of the dirty souls that went to hell.

Did they know? Did they know how much their deaths benefited mankind? Did they know that in dying they were actually saving the godliness of man? Did they even suspect?

Her lab was silent and cool. Dry, as it should be. Clean and sterile. She took a deep breath, tasting a hint of the coppery fragrance she'd grown accustomed to. It was ingrained into the walls and the floor, a pungent reminder of her work. It brought her comfort, the spicy scent of blood and gore. It was the history of her progress written into the stone. Twenty-nine years since the last genius had made use of this lab, and she'd already accomplished more than he had in his lifetime, only because she was willing to do what needed to be done for advancement of the field. How many people had died at her hands?

Not enough. Not nearly enough.

Her fingers ghosted over her tools, shivering with excitement. They were tools Berge would never understand. Tools her father had handled too carefully and shown her how to use, but he held them with the gentle vigor of hands that weren't used to their purpose. They were tools to kill and maim and desecrate, to take a body apart and understand its inner workings. When they'd been created, they were intended to use upon the dead. It was controversial, yet acceptable, to disassemble cadavers to see how pieces and parts matched up, how blood vessels and bones connected, or how unfortunate mishaps deformed a person inside and out. Her father had been hesitant to use them. Procuring cadavers drew too much attention.

She used them. Differently. There was so much more to learn when one could see the systems as they still functioned. Less far back into the past, she'd used them to bleed her victims, trying to understand blood and bleeding and why some lived and some died. A lot of men and women had died then, before she knew about compatibility.

A book had helped with that. A book that should have been burned in the great purge, when all of the books of learning had been scorned and thrown into a great blue fire. Hundreds of years, maybe thousands, relegated to smoke and ash in a matter of days.

Her hand closed around the blade, but she didn't squeeze hard enough for it to pierce. The purge made her angry, for it was during that purge that her father had succumbed to their childish fears. Him and most of his books. But not all of his books. And the rest of the books were hers now. Sometimes she found new ones on her travels, and these she absorbed into her collection silently. And without fail, she killed the previous owner, so that it might never be known.

Witch, they called her. Murderess. Evil. She accepted it. Reveled in it. They feared her, wanted her dead. She loved that. Her father had once said, "If no one hates you, you're not doing it right." It could only mean she was magnificent at what she was doing. And in the meantime, her Reaper plucked them from the masses one by one, locked them up here so she could poke and prod and drain them with the science they so despised.

She set the cutting tool back down upon the

countertop and dragged a fingertip as she moved along the bench top. At the end of it was a cabinet. She kept it at a certain temperature, regulated with her own special magic. Inside the cabinet were cultures of the cells of her victims, turned over again and again. They evolved as humans evolved.

So, too, did the plague they hosted.

She opened the cabinet and looked inside it. How benign they looked this way. Just a thin veneer of human smeared across a dish. The virus that caused the gruesome anomaly known as the Red Death was invisible there. It was only when it was allowed to incubate in the bloodstream of a human that it manifested all of its more obvious qualities. 365 days exactly. She'd meticulously catalogued every single day. One precise, chiseled out year, each one exactly the same as the last. If that wasn't proof of a divine pestilence meant to eradicate man, there never would be one. It was too calculated. Too by-design. Manmade or godmade, it mattered not. It was a machine engineered for a single purpose. Slowly, mankind had evolved to resist it, and though she had made a lot of money off that strange trick of nature, she had only delayed the inevitable.

That cabinet...the death lurking within it... was to finish the job.

Chapter Eight

"Well, they seem nice," Wex said to his dog.

Her tail thumped on the seat next to him.

"I know, you didn't get to meet Zanje. That's probably for the best. I don't think she's going to be your favorite." He leaned over conspiratorially and lowered his voice. "I think she's one of those cat-people."

Maxine stopped panting for a second and stared out the side window.

"That Berge guy's alright, though. You know if it weren't for him, I probably would have died like Papa did. I wonder what Papa thinks about the way things turned out? He always said that whatever happened was just a part of God's plan. He didn't bat a lash when he got sick. Too proud, I think. I begged him to seek out a cure. I knew better, though. No one's found a cure. There is no cure. But you know what, Maxine? Berge and Zanje found a cure. Can you believe that? Huh? There's a cure now. You know what else?" He reached over and ran his hand over the spot between her ears. "I get to be a part of it now, too. Zanje asked me nicely if I wouldn't mind bringing the cure to people all over the world. You and I? We're saving lives now. Wonder what Papa thinks." Wex stared straight ahead into the wintery mess that obscured his journey. "Wonder if he'd be proud of me now, if he were still alive." He scratched Maxine's ears, trying to focus on keeping her smiling so as not to let his sadness overtake him.

"I was worried you wouldn't wait for me. I know how you feel about dinner time. I was sure I'd come home to find you'd skipped town with the first man to wave a bacon in your face." Her ears perked up at the word 'bacon'. Her mouth shut briefly, eyes wide, brows climbing up the peak of her forehead. Her tongue darted out past her nose. She stared at him intently, the small cab of his snowcraft growing rife with expectations.

Wex couldn't help but laugh. "I know you know the word 'bacon,' Maxine. I don't have any with me, though." She started sniffing in his direction, leaning toward him. "Would I lie to you? Go ahead, then, check." He waited while she satisfied her curiosity, searching for the bacon that wasn't there. "When we get back to the castle, I'll see what I can do." She didn't understand those words, and continued to stare.

Eventually she gave up and went back to watching the land move beyond the glass. She smiled, tongue lolling. Her brown eyes were bright and joyous as she looked out the windows and the windshield. It never mattered to her that the landscape was always the same —fields and trees, either covered in snow or being peppered with snow at any given time. She always enjoyed a ride in the snowcraft. "You know, I love you so much it's ridiculous. No matter how dark and dismal my life gets, to you all it comes down to is 'scratch my ears, give me bacon, and let's go for a ride.' What I wouldn't give to look at life through your eyes, just once."

Wex kept glancing between his dog and the path ahead, petting her ears constantly lest she forget how important she was for even a second. There were no roads heading deep into the north that he could use if he wanted to get to Becket as fast as possible, so he guided the craft through the clearest part of the landscape. Most of it was a spattering of treeless fields, but there was the occasional sparse forest.

Wex would have guessed that there were more trees to the north, not less. It didn't bode well for his journey. Where there were no trees, there was no wind break. When the gusts of wind picked up, they blasted thick billows of powder snow across his vision. Aluminum made for fantastic construction to keep the vehicle light enough to travel without getting bogged down in the snow, but if he drove it too fast, it also made for fantastic construction if he wished to learn how to fly. Sometimes, the wind squalled so hard that he could feel the craft lifting off the snow on one side. Maxine remained unperturbed, just as excited as the second they'd set out.

The further north they drove, the worse the storm got, surpassing Wex's expectations for what a dangerous storm ought to be. It was the kind of weather that kept a man indoors. He probably should have pulled over and waited it out, but the work was urgent and important, so he persevered.

His hands gripped the steering wheel fiercely, knuckles going as white as the snow outside, as the driver side of the snowcraft was blown off the ground, putting the vehicle at an angle. He shut the engine down immediately and came to a complete stop. The craft teetered for a moment, tipped a little more as the wind blasted just a little harder, then dropped back down upon its skid when the gusting relaxed. After he calmed his panic, he started the engine back up and continued north. "Whatever happens next, Maxine, I'm glad we met." She stopped panting and stared at him again. He could feel it but he didn't turn to look at her, instead concentrating on the path ahead. He didn't want to admit that Berge had been right about the stormy nature of the terrain to the north, but he had been right. "Why did I agree to this, baby dog? Yeah, it makes perfect sense to drive a hundred and fifty miles into the heart of winter, doesn't it? This is stupid. You know, if I could I'd turn around and go back."

He thought about how he'd woken up in Zanje's care, more than half dead and aching from head to toe. But his skin had stopped bleeding and his heart felt stronger. And though he still had a little trouble walking because his bones felt like they were still putting themselves back together, he was alive, and so was his dog. He hadn't done enough in his lifetime to deserve being alive.

His heart constricted, thoughts of his own illness reminding him inevitably of his father's. "Wonder if Papa put in a good word with the big guy," he mumbled with a brief sideways glance at Maxine. She was still staring at him, though her eyelids drooped in that way she had about her when she was too relaxed and about to pass out sitting up. One side of her upper lip was caught between her teeth, puffed out above one white canine. When she noticed him looking at her, she perked up as if waking from a half sleep, the droop in her eyes vanishing back to her too-awake doggy stare.

It gave him some perspective. She always looked at him as if he were the most wonderful human in the entire world. Under that animal scrutiny, he was forced to envision what he might look like through her eyes, had to consider why he was driving through a blizzard in the first place, and the reasoning *she* might come up with instead of his own. So it unfurled slowly in his heart, and it kept him warm as the winter shrieked outside. "You're right," he nodded, believing it with every fiber of his being. "We *are* saving lives. I *have* to make it through this storm. Failure is unacceptable."

Maxine's tail thump-thumped against the seat. Her gaze returned to watching the scenery flash by. If she'd had a voice, he could imagine what she might have said: *Damn right we are.*

A few hours after midnight, the storm took a turn for the worst. He had to slow the craft to a crawl, and even then he fretted. The vehicle was going to tip over for certain. Maxine would get hurt. He didn't care about himself, not really. In his mind, he had already died once. Every second of every day from that point onward was just a bonus.

But Maxine either didn't notice or didn't care. Eventually, he had to stop worrying, too, just because she had. His worrying was just a waste of his concentration, and at that point he just fixated on pushing the craft a little at a time, mile after agonizing mile. He drove slowly enough to avoid the constant gales, and he hunkered down and didn't move at all when the wind picked up and attempted to overturn him. It was slow, slow going, exhausting in mind, body, and spirit.

For the last few hours of the journey he drove in silence. The swirling snow was hypnotizing, bright twirls of light in the pale blue of the witchlight beam that illuminated the way ahead. His eyes couldn't keep up with the tracks they cut through the black howling abyss beyond. His already sore eyeballs threatened to close. He couldn't afford to sleep, not now. If he fell asleep, his energy would sleep with him. There would be no light, not heat, no forward progression.

If he fell asleep now, he might never wake again.

Worse yet, he wasn't even sure he was still heading in the right direction. The only indication that he was still traveling north was that the storm yet worsened. There was the sound of crystal shattering, and then ice chunks crashed into the side of his vehicle. At long last, even Maxine fretted. She jumped away from the source of the sound and into his lap, whimpering and trying to become a part of his body. He wrapped one arm around her while her eyes darted nervously from the passenger side door. Her head tipped back, and she made an attempt to kiss him that missed. "I know, baby dog." He gritted his teeth and ended up squeezing her a little too hard, but she didn't seem to mind. Outside, ice rattled against the windshield and against the body of the vehicle. He worried about the integrity of the windshield, wondering if it was soon to shatter. He didn't have a backup plan for that.

He took a deep breath, but he had to accept that whether or not he lived or died was completely out of his control. *Look out for me, old man.* The thought made him smile a rueful smile, for he realized that he'd finally jumped on board with his father's faith quite by accident. *Looks like I'm more like you than I thought, Papa.*

The snow began to relent as the colors peeked up over the horizon. Whether by divine intervention, sheer luck, or better skill than he believed of himself, the first poke of manmade structures sprouted over the next ridge just after sunrise. He bent over and kissed the top of Maxine's head. It woke her from her nap, but her tail thumped once in forgiveness. He parked the vehicle about a quarter mile from the edge of the city, obscured in the trees. The snowcraft drew too much attention, and he harbored a fear that someone might steal it.

Maxine trotted along beside him, tail

wagging happily as he sought out Zanje's contact in Becket. It took no more than an hour before a man could point him in the right direction. "Orelia? Yeah, you can find her in that alley around the corner there." He pointed and swooped his hand around to indicate the corner.

"Thank you, sir."

"Not a problem."

Orelia's was a tiny apothecary shop in a frigid, narrow alley. The sign hung out in front of the shop, filling the entire space between one wall of the alley and the other. Voices reached his ears before he'd quite made it to the doorway. There were bare hinges where a door used to be, but no actual door. He knocked at the frame. Maxine politely waited outside the doorway for permission to enter. They had been a number of places before that dogs were not allowed. She knew better. "Can I come in?" he asked peeking into the shop.

There were two women in heavy coats and woolen stockings there talking, but they both stopped midsentence at his interruption.

"Sorry," he muttered.

They reanimated as soon as the word left his mouth. The one behind the counter waved him in furiously. "No no no, child, come in. Come in!"

The one nearest him was much younger and

smiled. "It's a shop, honey bear. You don't need to ask."

He gave her his best smile and stepped across the threshold. Maxine waited outside, wagging her tail. "Oh." He glanced between the two ladies. "Can Maxine come in, too?"

Both ladies melted into pretty smiles. The elder of the two waved to his dog as well. "Of course she can. Come on in, Maxine."

Maxine's head tipped down, and she shuffled into the shop, tail wagging. She went right up to the younger lady and butted her hand. "I'm Tandy," the lady said to him before squatting to hug Maxine.

"Wex."

"Orelia. How can we help you, young man?" She leaned across the counter on her elbows.

He jabbed a thumb over his shoulder to point back the way he came. "I'm from down south around Lorent. I'm on business. Zanje sent me...?" Orelia's smile fled. "She said you had a package to send back to her. I came to pick it up."

Orelia rubbed her hands together. "Zanje. Yes. How do you know her?"

"She saved my life, actually. I'm just trying to help her out. It's the least I can do."

The lady behind the counter went still and looked surprised. "She saved you?"

"Yep."

"Really?" She sounded doubtful.

"I'm alive." He spread his arms wide and grinned, unsure where the conversation was going. It was awkward. He didn't typically have conversations with strangers that lasted more than a few minutes. He kept the grin stuck to his face, though Orelia kept staring incredulously and Tandy remained silent.

"Zanje saved you," Orelia drawled. "For free?"

"As far as I know. I didn't give her anything."

"This the same Zanje?" Orelia leaned over the counter to look down at Tandy. "You don't know any other Zanjes do you, girl?"

"No, ma'am."

"Hm." She pursed her lips together and combed her fingers through dark grey hair. "Hm. Well. That sure is odd." She thought about it, then looked at Wex again. The way she looked at him reminded Wex of Zanje herself. "She sleeping with you?"

His grin slipped. "No? Does that matter?"

"Maybe, maybe not," she huffed. "Just wondering why she puts herself out there to save you when it's going to cost me my shop to save Nyra. What makes you special?"

He didn't have an answer for that, but it struck him deep in the confidence. "I...I'm sorry," he offered.

"There's nothing to be done about it now, boy. That's just the way of things, I suppose. The rich get off for free and the poor suffer, year after miserable year. Your Zanje is the only one in the entire world who knows how to bring folk back from the Blood Plague, and she's not above yanking a person's entire life out from under them just to leave them with barely enough to understand how awful the shambles of their lives have got. Do you know what I'm saying? Wex?" Her eyes had sharpened to black little glittery lights in the winter light from the windows.

"No, I'm not sure what you mean."

Orelia shook her head and bit her lip. "Don't listen to me, boy. I'm a bitter old woman and my grandchild is dying. It's not your fault. You wanted a package. I'll be right back." She threw up one finger to tell him to wait, then pushed aside a curtain and disappeared into the back.

"Sorry," Tandy muttered from atop Maxine's head. She gave the dog one last kiss and stood. Maxine shuffled forward and shoved her muzzle beneath the girl's hand. Tandy smiled and petted her again.

"Quite alright. I don't confess to know Zanje all that well. She's been…alright…with me. She *did* save my life, so she can't be all that bad."

"That's wonderful. It's just that, up here,

we're a close community. We care about one another. We took collections for Nyra—she's just a little girl!—but Zanje's price changes like the wind direction. The more a person has, the more she takes. She raised the price, and when we sent back word that she'd already given us a price and that we had it, she called us all liars and basically told us that if we didn't meet the new price, then Nyra..." She frowned. "Her name is known throughout the world—having a cure for the incurable will do that—and it's never spoken with fondness."

"Noted." It troubled him, though. "Maybe I can talk to her about it when I get back."

"If you would, that would be nice. Orelia's shop has been in her family for six generations. If she gives it up, she won't have any source of income. But if she doesn't give it up, Nyra dies."

"I see."

"She's all she has left."

Orelia returned, a small glass bottle in one hand. "Here you go," she told him grimly. "The blood of a child. Feed it to your witch and make a deal with her devil, and give me my grandchild back." Her eyes wanted him dead.

"I'll see what I can do," he promised with a reassuring smile, trying to put the old woman at ease.

"You do that." She didn't smile at all.

He held his breath all the way back to the snowcraft, then let it out in a deep sigh. "Well, she was nice," he said to Maxine. The dog kissed his hand. "You probably think I meant Tandy. She *was* nice. That other lady, though…" Maxine kept licking, slow drag of tongue over rough skin. "You know what. You're right. She's just upset that her granddaughter's dying. I get it. I'd probably be the same way if it were you." That made him feel better. "We'll do our best to save her. So I guess that means we better get back to Quorath." He picked up a handful of snow, using it as a guide, then set the temperature of Orelia's vial to just a tad warmer than the snow, as Zanje had advised.

"Okay." He opened the door to the vehicle. "Let's go, Maxine!" She jumped before he'd finished his sentence. Settling herself on the passenger seat, thrilled at the onset of yet another amazing adventure with the human Wex.

That was when Wex realized driving back to Quorath entailed a reprisal of the storm, starting with the worst of it first. He sighed.

Chapter Nine

Zanje strode through the streets of Quorath, a black woolen overcoat buttoned tight around her chest and a cigarette hanging between her lips. The cobblestone roads were chock full of filthy, stinking, dying people. They edged past one another, on their way to or from one insignificant place or another. She avoided eye contact, unwilling to share any kind of connection with the general populace. Instead, she lifted the collar of her coat up to her ears and tried to shut them out. This was the one foray she made into civilization, once each day, for she couldn't expect to have a successful business if she never interacted with potential clientele. It was also, consequently, her least favorite part of every day.

It grew increasingly challenging, as time wore on, to pass through Quorath unnoticed. The survivors of the Red Death had big mouths, it seemed. Rumor spread of the black castle's healing witch, the only one in the world who could save them, if one could afford it. If she so much as stepped a toe upon the stone of Quorath, she was assailed by the bleeding, pathetic masses of the sick and dying, begging for aid. They grabbed at the hem of her skirt and kissed at her sharp heeled boots, begging for her to give them for free what she charged a kingdom for. Hypocrites, all. Only a few years ago, they whispered about the unnatural things that occurred in the cursed castle. They would have killed her if they'd had the courage. If she could make it through Quorath unimpeded, she ignored them. Occasionally, though, an example needed to be made. If they were fortunate, they'd only end up with a fresh wound.

The less fortunate...well. At least they suffered less. It would never be said that Zanje was undeserving of a little fucking gratitude.

She ducked under the sign of the tavern in the center of town—The Dead Kettle. It wasn't that she'd chosen such a filthy establishment for its easy-to-locate placement. It was the only place in all of stinking Quorath that was willing to order a bottle of wine she was willing to pay for. The owner's smile slid away the moment she entered. They weren't friends. "Zanje."

"Rord." She rummaged in her purse for her payment. "The wine, first."

"Yes." He snapped his fingers to get the attention of a lad in the corner. "Jack. There's a case of wine in the back. Go get it. Don't drop it! *Don't* drop it!" He turned back toward her, face schooled carefully neutral. "The man in the corner over there has been waiting for you for two days."

"I was caught up with my work," she explained. "The one over there with the beard?" She glanced his way. He was staring at her, eyes gone dead inside. A desperate man. He looked to be desperate enough. She resisted the urge to smile.

"That's the one."

"Good. I'll get to him after I get to the wine."

The boy reappeared, struggling with a heavy wooden crate of wine. He made as if to pass it over. She shook her head. "No, you carry it."

Rord's mouth fell open. "Zanje, can't you see we're understaffed? He's the only help I—"

She froze him with a glare. "I pay you thrice what that wine is worth, and you know it well. I appreciate your procurement of it, but my generosity only extends so far. He'll carry it, or you'll keep it and eat the cost."

Rord swallowed his protest, his grey brows furrowing with suppressed fury. "Well," he spluttered. "Well."

She smiled sweetly. "Boy, my castle is a mile east of here. You may leave the crate on the step."

The boy looked between them. At Rord, glowering in her direction, hoping—futilely—that his rage would change her mind, and at her, immovable and unconcerned. What must a young mind think of such a thing? It didn't take him long to come to the correct conclusion, however. He blushed and dipped his head, apologized to Rord with a sideways glance. "Right away," he mumbled. He set the crate down on the bar to retrieve his coat, then made forthwith for her residence, wine in hand.

"He seems like a good boy," she praised Rord. "Thank him for me when he returns."

Rord nodded, keeping his critical level of irritation to himself.

She turned toward the bearded man with the need, putting Rord from her sight and from her mind. She stood at the edge of his table. "You needed something." She crossed her arms and waited.

"Are you Zanje?" he asked.

"What do you think?"

He thumbed at his lips and glanced about from side to side as if afraid someone might overhear. "It's my wife. She's dying. Can you help?"

"Can you pay?"

He nodded slowly.

"Prove it."

He lowered his voice and leaned closer. "My father was the master of the Untamed. They're—"

"I know who the Untamed are," she interruped. The Untamed were one of the money lenders that wanted Berge dead, but the only ones who might have succeeded. They were nipping at his heels the night he'd skipped town in Raddolf. Which meant that this man was Haddig's son. "That makes you Dair, the Cur."

He nodded again. If he was pleased at all that she'd recognized him, he didn't show it. "Can you help?"

Her mind clicked together a handful of fragments. Of Haddig and his brutal methods of collecting on the debts he was owed. On how Haddig was the only man in the world Berge would rather run from than fight. "What happened to Haddig?"

Dair scowled. "He couldn't pay a debt."

Zanje practically purred with satisfaction. If Dair was even more ruthless than Haddig, it might serve her well to have him on her side. "I see."

He leaned forward even closer and hissed at her through clenched teeth. "Are you going to help me or not?"

She met him glare for steely glare, unflinching, glutting on the desperation and the pain. The Red Death did not discriminate, and affected the rich and poor, good and evil alike. And yet, it was Zanje that decided who lived and who died. That reflection stared back at her through red-rimmed eyes. The face of atrocity, begging for her blessing. She let the moment stretch, feasting on the need, the despair, the urgency. Finally, she tilted her face toward the door. "Come. Let's talk."

His breath of relief filled the space between with the sour rot of humanity. Her nostrils curled away from it. Were the man begging for his own life, she might have denied the request on that failing alone.

She hadn't expected for Berge to be waiting for her on the seventh floor. She really hadn't expected for Wex to be there, too. "Oh, good, you're both here." She turned to Berge and smiled sweetly. "Dair, the Cur of the Untamed, is downstairs."

Berge's eyes hardened right away. Zanje loved that. Despicable people always brought out the worst in her Night King. "I see you remember him," she drawled.

"Who's Dair?" Wex wondered aloud.

Berge held her eyes and spoke over his shoulder to the man at the window. "Dair is the son of a money grubber in Raddolf. It's my hometown."

"Oh."

"He almost ripped my throat out once with his bare hands." He crossed his arms and met Zanje's eyes. "So turn him away."

"He's got a lot of money."

"Yeah I bet he does. Is Raddolf even still there, or haven't they succeeded in destroying it yet?"

"I take it you aren't friends," Wex observed.

"We aren't friends," he confirmed.

"Holding a grudge is an ugly trait," Zanje reminded him.

"Then it's a miracle you're still as pretty as you are," he shot back. "Tell him to go fuck himself with a broken bottle."

"I told him we'd help," she told him with a sly grin. She leaned against a wall and crossed her arms, enjoying every moment of his volatile reaction. "I thought you'd be glad to relieve him of some of his wealth."

"I'd rather relieve him of whoever he's hoping doesn't die."

"Hm. Well, that's unfortunate, as it's not your call to make. I already told him we'd help."

"Then I guess you're working alone in this one. I'm not interested."

"That's not the arrangement you made. Accepting assignments is one of my responsibilities."

"Then I'll sit this one out."

"Fine. I'll do this on my own." She made as if to leave.

He swore. "No." He glanced sideways at Wex, then back at her. "No, don't try to do this on your own. It just ends up making more work for me in the long run."

"Of course. Where would I be without your manly assistance?" she pouted.

Fury returned to his face. "Don't start in with that."

Wex had remained silent for most of the exchange, but he spoke up now. "If someone is dying, we should help. Right?"

She grinned wolfishly, never taking her eyes from Berge. "Right."

He scowled and turned to Wex. "This guy is as shit as it gets. He'd steal your firstborn and sell it to slave traders to collect on a debt. This isn't the guy you want to help."

His eyes darted between them as he thought about it. "Well, it's not really for us to judge the worth of a human life, now, is it?" He looked back to Zanje.

"No, it really isn't." She preened under the moral dilemma. Berge wouldn't dare to disclose the truth of their moral fiber in front of a man who was a stranger to their operation. He couldn't risk their business being exposed for what it was. Couldn't risk Zanje's protocols being stolen. Couldn't risk the loss of a valued assistant. Berge's mouth was forced shut, and Zanje couldn't be more pleased.

"So let's help the guy," Wex opined.

"Yes, let's," Zanje agreed. She and Berge locked into a battle of stares. Those, she won every time. She had a knack for resisting the urge to blink, and more practice subduing people with her eyes than he had.

Berge swore. And swore, and swore some more.

His behavior seemed to cause the new hire some distress. "Come on, Berge. Can you really turn your back on a dying human being?"

Berge really did turn then, slinging one arm over the back of the couch and leaning over it. "Yes. Yes, I can. You don't know Haddig, and you don't know Dair." He flung his arms up then. "But you know what? Fine. Fine! Lead the way, heroes. Let's go save a life!" He practically leapt off the couch and stalked to the door beside Zanje.

She caught Wex's concerned expression from across the room and tried to offer a reassuring smile, laughing on the inside. As Berge passed her, swearing under his breath, she tilted toward him and said, "Grab the Null. He didn't bring a vial for me to type."

He swore even louder as he traveled the hallway, his words echoing up into the tall ceiling and empty corridor. "'Grab the fucking

Null, Berge,' she says. 'Whatever it takes to save the wicked,' *he* says. *No problem!* 'While you're at it, Berge, I'd like a glass of fancy wine and a feather fucking pillow!'"

Zanje blinked, then leaned into the hallway. "That reminds me. There should be a case of wine at the front door. Bring it here on your way back."

He punched the wall at the top of the stairs before starting down. "Death's—fucking—*balls*, woman, but you're a pain in the ass!" He took the stairs, shaking an injured hand and wearing an expression so pristinely irate that Zanje wished she had a painting of it.

She smiled and turned back to Wex. "Feeling better?"

"Much," he replied. "I, uh, left that vial from Becket on the counter of your...laboratory."

"Good."

He shifted on his feet and took a breath, obviously searching for the words to say. His mouth shut and opened again twice more.

"Something on your mind?" she asked.

"Yeah, um...When I was in Becket, your contact...Orelia?"

She blinked and lifted her chin.

"She's having to sell her shop to pay the price for your assistance."

"How unfortunate."

"It's her only source of income and it's been

in her family for generations. My father used to own a greenhouse that was in our family for generations. I mean we're talking from like the beginning of time. A *long* time ago. And it was a big greenhouse. He had something like eight to ten guys working for him at any given time. And back when he used to do that we used to have like, potatoes, and beans, and corn and you name it. Whatever it was, my old man grew it. He loved that greenhouse. Used to make decent amount of money selling the vegetables, too.

"He owned and operated that place until it burned down almost ten years ago. We were doing alright, but we didn't have enough to build a new one, unfortunately. Times were pretty hard after that, so I mean...I know where she's coming from on this one. Believe me. I almost got around to building a new one for him, but glass isn't cheap."

It was the first time she'd heard him say more than a few sentences. She watched as he rambled, fascinated, trying to follow the meandering paths of his mind. And then, when it seemed he'd talked about everything he meant to cover, he recalibrated, centering back on the one point he was trying to make. His eyes refocused upon hers as he said, "She said you raised the price after you'd already given one."

She waited.

"Did you?"

"Of course not," she lied.

"Oh. Well...I promised her I'd ask if it was at all possible for the price to be lowered."

"What do you think of that?"

"Well...Is it possible?"

"What do you think would happen if I gave away my services for free?" she countered instead.

He met her gaze levelly. "Maybe the world would be a brighter place."

"Maybe. But maybe not."

He seemed confused. "How could it not?"

"You seem like a smart man. I'll let you think about it for a while. See if you come to the same conclusion I have."

His face contorted as he considered her words. "Okay. I'll do that."

"When we're done in the lab, you and I are going to Raddolf."

"Just the two of us?"

"Yes, just the two of us. Dair and Berge will stay here."

"Is that...wise?"

Probably not, she thought. But it would be hilarious. "That vehicle of yours. How did you do that?"

"Oh. Well. I read about it."

"How? All of the textbooks were burned."

"Yes, the textbooks were burned. But there are still stories. There're fairy tales. Um, let's see…poems. Songs, even. They aren't as forthcoming with the details as textbooks were, but if you pay close attention, you can find things out that way. As for this one, it's a story my mother read to me. She loved all the old fairy tales. Like, the really old ones. *Old* old. Some stories were written down back then, but it was easier to just keep retelling them and my mother *loved* the old stories. She used to tell them to me all the time. At bedtime, as we walked to town, when we would cook together. I mean, she *loved* stories. If she'd have lived, I think she would have been a good writer.

"Anyway, I digress. We had a big book that had all of the old fairy tales. And there was this story about a smith. He was a really good smith, trained with the master smith of the town he lived in. But when his apprenticeship was over and he went off on his own, he started experimenting with new metals, and that was how he found aluminum. The story itself goes into great detail about how he discovered it. It was a series of accidents, from how he tripped on a rock and came face to face with bauxite and took a rock home because he thought it looked interesting to the time he accidentally crushed it when his roof caved in to how he spilled his lye on the pieces…all the way to the end of the process. The only thing that was different about the way the smith did it in the story and the way that I do it is that he had a means of generating an electrical current. Back then, they had that kind of thing. I just use Craft…"

She listened to him. Every word of it. She didn't see herself ever having a need to smelt aluminum, but the thought process was sound. Wex was a clever man. She was so intrigued by the things he had to say that she quite forgot she had work to do until Berge reminded her.

"I got your fucking Null, you vile cunt!" Berge shouted up the stairs.

She chuckled, reveling in Berge's palpable displeasure. "Duty calls."

Chapter Ten

She heard the muffled cursing as the man they called Berge neared. The dungeon took a collective breath and went silent, for the approaching voice could mean only one thing —someone was about to be selected. Someone was about to bleed and, from what she'd heard, someone might be about to die.

She shrank back into her cell.

The door banged open. "Oh, Berge, no one fucking cares what you think about the situation. Don't you know?" His feet banged their way down the steps as he continued his tirade. "Only *I* get to choose who lives and who dies. The rest of you must dance to my *shit whinging music* and shut your traps 'til the song's over. And if you don't fucking like it, too fucking bad! Because I'm Zanje fucking Vangelic and I fucking run this fucking business. You don't get a fucking dime unless I say so and let's not forget, you're fucking *broke* as *shit* without me. Get the fucking Null, Berge. Smi-ley smi-ley *smile*. I'm going to wipe that smile off her cunt-kissing face. I'll show her—"

"Having a rough day, Nacht?" The challenge issued from Mirdoz, one of the Majors. Nerys held her breath, terrified of how Berge might react to provocation.

The dungeon lit up with witchfire, wild tendrils of it sparking through the air. It illuminated Berge's face. The pits of his eye sockets and the shadows from beneath his hair combined with the pure hatred in his expression made him appear menacing, almost demonic. He bared his teeth in a rictus snarl and charged at Mirdoz's cell. Faster than a viper, Berge's arm snaked through the bars and wrapped around Mirdoz's neck. Nerys wasn't even nearby, but she gasped in fear and shrank back even further. Mirdoz's breath wheezed in and out as he struggled to breathe. "You've been itching to fight me, Major," he declared, his soft voice threatening in the dank dungeon. Not a soul spoke a word, save the tormentor himself. "Perhaps today you'll get your wish." Berge's face pressed up to the bars, projecting malice into a space that was already torturous enough. The man Mirdoz shared his cell with, Larric, whimpered from deeper within. Larric was a cowardly, frail man. Mirdoz often argued with Berge when he brought them food. From what Nerys had learned of her fellow prisoners, only Mirdoz was willing to stand up to him.

Until Simos proved otherwise. "Nacht."

Berge's sharp glare pierced the veil of darkness, locking onto the bars of Simos' cell and the man within. "Is that you, Rare?"

"No, it's me, Simos," the man corrected. Nerys watched him carefully. She liked Simos, so far. Simos sat with his back to the wall, one leg down and one steepled, one elbow resting upon his knee. "Come over here. Let's talk."

Berge shook and shoved Mirdoz, and Nerys heard the man collide with the wall of his cell with a grunt. He sucked in a much needed breath of air and gasped, trying to catch his breath. Berge forgot about him as soon as he'd let go. He made his way slowly down the corridor, step after slow and careful step. Most of the time, when Berge came down to the dungeon, there was a chorus of pleas for mercy and weeping, punctuated by Mirdoz's insults. This time, however, the prisoners were hushed, every one. Berge radiated banked menace in want of an outlet. He came to a stop before Simos' cell.

Nerys held her breath, watching the exchange. Simos seemed perfectly at ease in the deep blue witchlight shadows of his cell. He smiled a slow and lazy smile, one corner of his mouth turned up and teasing. "Do you want to talk about it?" His face tilted.

Berge's wrath tempered around Simos. His anger went from hot and formless to sharp and focused, and all upon Simos himself. He calmed immediately, and Nerys saw again the mocking criminal from before. "I'll tell you all about it on the way to the pit," he sneered. "When do you want to go?"

"I'm free now," he shrugged carelessly. "But if you're too busy, I don't have any plans for the rest of the week." He grinned, white teeth flashing in the low light. Simos was brave. Or stupid. Or maybe he just didn't care. Nerys couldn't imagine speaking to Berge that way. He could do so much worse to her.

His words reminded Berge why he'd come to the dungeon in the first place. "Sorry, Rare. I've got a date today."

"Sticking it in your harpy after work?"

"Not today," he sneered. "Today I get to poke the pretty new Null. Want to watch?"

Nerys could have sworn her heart stopped. Startled, she looked to Simos, but even Simos' smile had gone lopsided. His brow furrowed with something akin to sympathy. She couldn't have expected to make it out of her predicament without being chosen at least once, but with Berge in such a state, she couldn't help but worry that she might not survive even once. Her pulse raced, faster and faster, and when Berge leered over his shoulder at her, her vision blurred, threatening a blackout.

"Nerys!" Simos snapped. She blinked, struggling to stay awake. "Strength, Nerys. You're going to be alright."

"Maybe," Berge shrugged.

Something fell into her lap. It shocked her to awareness, for she feared perhaps it was a rat. Rats were awful, ugly creatures that were believed to carry Red Death. She yelped and nearly jumped out of her skin before her eyes fell upon the creature responsible. It was Ashes, Berge's weasel. The little creature's nose twitched, whiskers glowing blue with witchlight. "Ashes," she breathed, relieved. The weasel leaned forward and placed tiny paws on Nerys chest, nose traveling up and down as if unsure what she had found.

The ensuing silence was thick with tension. She felt the eyes of Simos and Berge upon her, but she focused on the little weasel and its adorable twitchy nose, and ever so slightly relaxed. It brought her back from the edge of a panic attack.

Then the keys in Berge's pocket jingled, and Nerys was jolted back to her reality. Her eyes snapped up to meet his—cold, merciless, and unforgiving—and Ashes hopped away. The weasel climbed up Berge's person and hopped into a pocket on his shirt. Meanwhile, the man himself regarded her with nothing short of hatred. The bars were moved out of the way, and nothing remained between them but dank, damp air. She swallowed, suddenly frightened.

He gripped her by the elbow and hauled her up. He practically dragged her up the stairs. The level one floor up from the dungeon seemed already infinitely brighter and happier than the level below. Blue witchlight illuminated every nook and cranny. Berge shoved her through a door so hard that her feet betrayed her. She went sprawling, catching her momentum with the frail hands of an artist. The concrete bruised and broke her skin. She rocked back on her knees and heels immediately, surveying the damage with grim sorrow. "I'm going to die here, aren't I?" she asked, resigned.

"Odds are good," Berge confirmed. "What did you do to Ashes?"

"I don't know. Nothing. I'm not sure what you mean."

"She likes you. Why?"

"I don't know. Does she not like people?"

"She's never had an opinion on people."

"Oh."

"She can't see."

"I know."

"She frightens easily, because she can't see. And she can only smell people like you. And she's old, so her hearing seems to be going, too. So if anyone touches her or gets close, she gets scared easily. That's why I don't get why she seems to like you."

"She's...cute," Nerys dared. She turned to watch him.

He stared her down for a moment. Then, in a rush, his breath left him. He sauntered over to one of the three beds in the room and lay upon it, one hand draped dramatically over his brow.

Nerys adjusted her position on the floor. His inaction confused her. She had thought that once he'd gotten her out of her cell, something terrible was bound to happen, given his mood. She knew bleeding was involved. She presumed he might do something more dastardly. Instead, he threw himself back onto a bed and sighed heavily. He looked almost...bored. She was content to remain uninjured, but her curiosity demanded satisfaction. "What are we doing?" she whispered.

Berge pointed angrily with one hand toward the levels above. "Pissing her off. Making her wait. Whatever it takes. Maybe if we wait long enough, the Cur upstairs will suffer for it."

Nerys was confused, but sensed an opportunity to increase her chances for survival. She didn't want to befriend the evil bastard that held her captive, but if she could find a chink in his armor, perhaps she could find a way to escape. "Who is she?" she wondered meekly.

"Zanje!" he all but shouted, losing his temper. He failed to elaborate any further, as if just her name should have been explanation enough.

She thought about pursuing the topic, warring with the decision of which information to probe for. Zanje seemed like a more important subject, yet Ashes seemed to bring out Berge's softer side. Too, if Berge's beloved pet seemed to take a liking to Nerys herself, perhaps it would do more toward ensuring her safety. "How long have you had Ashes?"

He peered at her from the corner of his eye, suspicious. She tried to appear harmless and merely curious, insofar as she could. His visible eye narrowed, trying to figure her out. Then he shifted his sights toward the ceiling and the witchlights above. He twirled one hand in the air and made them dance, swaying back and forth as if they were trapped in a disturbed pond. She watched the lights, too. It kept her from scrutinizing the man. It kept her safer. When he spoke, his voice was tinged with regret. "Ten years. I won her. In a bet."

"Oh. I see."

"No," he snapped. "No, you really don't." He took a deep breath and released it in a sigh. "It was a dog fighting tournament. There was this dog. Real mean dog. Big, too. Muscles all over." He motioned with his hands. "They called him Rapscallion. He killed every dog you put him in a pit with. I knew if I bet on him, it'd be a sure thing. I stole a great deal of money to place that bet. I robbed every residence in Raddolf, even the Untamed themselves. Then I took a chance on a sad, tired old dog named Dapper with no chance. To this day I don't know why. I just got a good look at him, and I saw something in his eyes. Like he was thinking. Like he'd had enough, and he wasn't going to tolerate any bullshit today.

"Sometimes things like that just happen to me. I make odd choices completely out of character. I stood to win a great deal of money. And when the fight happened, that's exactly what happened. Dapper won the whole god damned thing. He went in pissed off, like an old man woke up from a nap, just...*raging*, and he just shredded every dog there, even Rapscallion. I won. I fucking won." He paused. "And I don't *ever* win."

"Wait, so did you win money or Ashes?"

"Don't get ahead of me," he growled. "No, not Ashes. But I won *so much gold*." His voice took on a dreamlike quality. Nerys returned her attention to the man himself. His eyes had drifted closed, but he didn't look happy. "It was enough to pay back every debt I had and never have to work or gamble again. It was a dream come true."

"And Ashes?"

He glared at her. "You going to let me finish the fucking story or do you want to tell it?"

Her cheeks heated. "I'm sorry."

"I went to collect my pot, but Haddig got there first. I owed him a debt, and I think he knew I stole from him. He seized all of the money I won and was waiting for me. Him and his whole pack of Untamed. I wasn't going anywhere without my money, so I fought them for it. They beat my ass into the ground, robbed me of every penny I had left. Then Haddig dropped a cage by my face. Said that if I'd have gambled with my own money, all it would be worth was one blind and worthless weasel, so that's what he left me. By the time I could walk again, I thought about throwing the cage in the river.

"But it was Ashes. I shouted at the weasel in the cage, but that was before I noticed the cigar burns in her fur and how her mouth was hanging open. There was dried blood on her muzzle. She's blind. She can't see. I could only imagine how scared she must have been. Couldn't even try to defend herself. Fucking animals." The witchlights froze, Berge's hand suspended in the air. Nerys was certain he hadn't meant the weasel or the dogs, but the men who jumped him. "I spent my life risking it all for the big payoff. I finally won, and then about died for it. I watched my dreams go up in smoke. And all that was left—"

"—Was Ashes," she finished for him. It moved her, his story. She thought about the twitchy little weasel nose, and wondered if the weasel had always been blind. Then she noticed he was staring at her, as if seeing her for the first time.

His eyes narrowed, and he stood. "It doesn't matter. None of it does."

"What do you mean?"

He rubbed a hand over his face and then indicated their surroundings. "Nothing. Not you. Not me. Not Ashes. Not Zanje. Not Wex. The reality is…we're all dying. We just don't know when. At least you have that much."

"What do you mean?"

"At least you know your time is soon. There's comfort to be had in that."

Chapter Eleven

He stared down at Nerys's troubled face, trying to hate her. He hated everyone. That was his default state of comfort—hatred. He hated Zanje. He hated humanity. He hated every stinking human soul, none more than his own. Humanity was corrupt; it couldn't be salvaged. That was what had brought him to appreciate Zanje's company, and her perceptions more foul than his own. The Null was watching Zanje, her face twisted with concern. But, he noted with irritation, she kept darting glances at him, and in her hazel eyes he caught flashes of sympathy. *I don't want your pity*, he thought.

He didn't know what he wanted, though. He just kept living, another animal in the insignificance of the passage of time. He was here for this moment. He could die at any other. Then he would rot, if he wasn't rotting enough as it was. She caught his eye and then she smiled shakily, trying to be strong. He grimaced, wondering where her strength came from.

He'd never been a pleasant person. He never wanted to be a pleasant person. He'd never entertained the thought that he might have been, might currently be, or might aspire to be a good person. He was perfectly content with the sourness of his soul and the blemish it left on the history of mankind. That was the legacy of Bergeron Nacht. That was the story of the King of Night, the Shadow Man, the bottom of the barrel that plagued society. He was known, and not fondly. Zanje, too, was remembered, both for her miraculous work of science and for her rotten attitude. Together, the two of them made quite a pair.

And it was in that epiphany that he found the reason the Null disarmed him. He didn't want her, and he didn't know what that meant. He held the soft, yielding skin of her arm in his hand, and he wasn't thinking of defiling it. He wasn't taking pleasure in tightening the straps around her wrists and arms. He wasn't imagining her naked or crying.

Was it because of the Null?

Was it because of Ashes?

Was it because of something else?

"Berge."

He snapped up to meet her gaze. It was fearful, and nervous. And he didn't understand for a moment why she seemed to be reaching out to him for comfort. He opened his mouth to tell her so, but what came out was, "Nerys." He mentally kicked himself after. *Never, ever refer to them by their names,* he chided himself. They weren't people here. He couldn't see them as people. Everyone who came here died. They were test subjects. Cash cows. Not people. Not humans, capable of love and affection, fear and rejection.

Nothing at all like himself.

"I...I won't..."

"Die?" he finished for her.

She bit her lip and nodded, and a bloom of sympathy tightened his chest. Here she was, his feisty little Null, friendless and doomed. She should have kicked and screamed. She should have fought, earned his hatred, and hated him back. Instead, she'd imagined a friend where there wasn't one and asked for reassurance. Were it anyone else, he might have answered, "Only one way to find out." Instead, he found her eyes and held her gaze, suspended for several seconds. "Not today." He double checked all the restraints, slid a finger between the cold leather and skin too soft to be restrained to make sure they weren't too tight. "Don't watch the needle go in," he suggested in a low voice. "And whatever you do, don't give Zanje a reason to remember you."

She swallowed.

He took his own advice and left her bedside. Her breath quickened the moment he stepped away. He had to stop himself from going back, from even looking. Zanje sensed weakness in all around her, and that included him, too. If he showed any concern at all for the well-being of her Null, Zanje would see to it that Nerys died swifter than all the others that had come before her. So instead he busied himself with retrieving all the things Zanje needed for her work—the bottle of alcohol, the wax for the needle, a fresh glass globe. For a moment, he forgot about Nerys. Seeing the glass reminded him... "Seriously, Zanje, the glass has got to go."

Zanje was over at one of her counters, shrugging into an overcoat she only wore when she was working. She explained to him once that the coat was to keep her workspace clean. Berge suspected that she enjoyed the spatters of blood that wouldn't wash out. She was twisted that way. "The glass stays. Stop being such an oaf and you won't break them."

"I'm not a graceful creature."

"No one knows that better than I do," she sighed.

"I should go lock the door," Berge suggested, concerned for Wex's reaction if he came upon them now.

"No need," Zanje stopped him. "You don't

have to worry about him stumbling in. He hates this room." She came over to Nerys and settled upon her stool, needle in hand. "And, he's afraid of needles."

"Good," Berge said. "I'd be more concerned if he liked them."

Nerys chuckled, too. Zanje stopped what she was doing and glared at her sharply.

Berge held his breath. *Don't speak, you fool. Don't speak.* To her credit, Nerys dropped her gaze away from the woman on the stool. He exhaled shakily. *Good.* He could sort out his own existential crisis later.

Berge stood over Zanje's shoulder, avoiding eye contact with Nerys. Zanje dabbed at the inside of her elbow with the alcohol. Nerys's breathing quickened again. She was more nervous than most as they lay at Zanje's mercy, but there was nothing to be done for her now. She'd have to overcome her own fears without his help. As Zanje neared her with the needle, Nerys tried to lean away. Zanje didn't even flinch. "I never can figure out why they think wiggling will make this any better," she drawled, bemused.

It was enough. Nerys stopped writhing, though she did moan with fear and squeeze her eyes shut. *Better that way,* Berge thought. The needle went in. Nerys popped open one eye, then looked down at it. "Oh." Berge fought against a smile. Nerys had survived the poke. It wasn't awful. One needle poke wasn't all that bad. It was the repeated ones that caused the issues. She smiled and breathed a sigh of relief.

"Yes, that's it," Zanje derided. "Smile. The first one is the easiest."

Nerys blanched, and it wasn't only from the blood loss. Zanje patted her shoulder condescendingly and smiled. Zanje's smile was the most terrifying expression to ever grace a woman's face. After that, Zanje merely watched the glass globe fill. When it was done, she waved him over to stop the procedure. He caught Nerys's eye and smiled. She stared, wide-eyed, but distracted enough. He pulled the needle and put pressure on a hunk of gauze. "That wasn't so bad now, was it?" he whispered. She shook her head only just. He wrapped her arm, then unstrapped her from the bed. "I'm going to take her back."

"Take your time. I'm leaving you here anyway."

He blinked and looked at her turned back. She was squeezing the blood from the tube into the receptacle, intent on her work. "Leaving me here? Where are you going?"

"To Dair's, obviously. There's no one there that can be trusted to perform the transfusion. Wex will take me. But his contraption only seats two people. You'll have to care for his mutt, too."

Inside, he seethed. Then he swore when he realized what else she'd left out. "You're going to leave me here with Dair?"

"Yes. Although he's paid, now, so if you want to kill him, you may."

It was tempting. "Un-fucking-believable," he muttered. He helped Nerys off the bed. He steadied her against his body and glared daggers at Zanje's back. "Why don't I go?" he demanded.

"Obviously, because if you went, Wex's dog would starve to death. I don't mind, but he might."

Sound logic, though he hated to admit it. When Zanje was right, she was right. "Well, Dair doesn't have to stay here," he countered.

"Berge..." Nerys interrupted.

He ignored her as he waited for Zanje's answer. She chuckled and delayed her answer. "No, he doesn't. But I told him he could."

Just to fuck with him. He swore again.

"Berge..." Nerys tried again.

"I don't need this shit," he snarled at her back. "I'm not your pet! I'm your partner! Somewhere along the way you assumed you could just lead me around by the nose. We're in this together, you evil bitch. You're *nothing* without me."

She paused. Her head came up, unfocusing

from the task in her hands. She turned slowly, smiling, incredulous. *"I'm* nothing without *you?* Did you forget that you came to me with your tail between your legs and your cock hanging out? You're the most despicable man I've ever met, Bergeron Nacht. Hard up on money and living in a hole in an alley with a corpse, and you dared to negotiate. I only employ you because you secretly love it. You *love* it, Berge. You wake up every day and *revel* in the vileness that we do. And when you're bathed in gore and filled up to the ears with self-loathing, you come panting after me to fill me up with your putrid, stinking, worthless soul. You *need* me, Berge. You need me *far* more than I need you."

He sucked in a breath and prepared to unleash hell, ready to put her right back in the place she belonged. But Nerys chose that moment to faint, her small body going limp in his arms. He instantly went into damage control mode. Each and every prisoner of Zanje's castle was his responsibility. If they died, it also fell upon him to obtain a replacement. It was in his best interest to keep them alive.

It was *not* because this one happened to be Nerys.

He shook her gently, cradling her in one arm. He used his other hand to pat her cheeks. Her lips had faded to a whitish color, and the blush in her cheeks was gone. "Nerys!" he barked.

Zanje started laughing. "Oh, so this one has a name. How interesting."

Berge ignored her and carried Nerys out into the hall. "Nerys!" Ashes scrambled out of his pocket, hooking into the fabric of his shirt with her sharp little claws and leaning toward the unconscious woman. Ashes' nose twitched. Her front paws reached, looking for something to grab ahold of, all the while Berge checked for a pulse, peeled back her eyelids, checking for signs of life.

Ashes took a leap of faith from Berge's shirt pocket and landed in Nerys's hair. She twisted under her chin, coiled up into a ball, and spun in circles. Nerys stirred and whimpered. "Berge?"

"Yeah, it's me."

"I don't feel well." She licked her lips.

"I can tell. Come on."

"I don't want to die."

"You won't."

He helped her to her feet. Her hands hooked around his shoulder and clung to his arm, fingers digging into the flesh of his arm. He expected her to realize what she was doing and pull away, but she didn't. Instead, after a few unsteady steps, she readjusted her grip even tighter and leaned into his body for support. It was a strange feeling, being needed. He thought about making a wise crack, but for some reason wasn't in the mood. A long list of flawless insults simply died on his tongue. Then Nerys halted, squeezed, took a few panicky breaths, and vomited on the floor. She remained bent, heaving, whimpering.

And then, to his surprise, she apologized. "Sorry…"

"For what?" he asked.

"For…getting it on your boot."

He looked down. There was maybe a drop of puke on his toe. "It's fine. I've had much worse than a little vomit on my boots." Her fingers held to his shirt with all the ferocity of rigor mortis.

After a few more shaky steps, her face scrunched with confusion. "My blood…"

"Hm? What about it?"

"…What's it for?"

He frowned. Blinked. Realized no one had ever asked him that before. It was their most closely guarded secret, though. If anyone found out, there could be competition. Zanje wasn't the only rogue scientist, but she was the smartest. If her competitors ever found out, they could charge less. Still, Nerys wasn't going to leave this place alive. What was there to lose? "It cures Red Death."

She stopped him for a minute. Frowned. Considered. Digested new information. "Oh."

Then she started crying. Not the messy, showy, dramatic kind, not like the prisoners from the dungeon. No, not Nerys. Her tears were the silent, tough kind. She was trying not to do it. She didn't ask for help and she bit back every sob. All the way back to her cell, she never said another word. He had to admire that; he'd seen a lot of people after they'd lost blood.

She was silent all the way to her cell. He helped her to the ground, staunching the feeling that she ought not sleep on a cold floor. Even considered putting her up in his bed until she felt well enough to return to the cells. That, he dismissed immediately, angry with himself for thinking it. He was conscious of all the eyes upon him. He didn't have time to sort out newly fledged protective instincts where the Null was concerned. For the others, he had a reputation to maintain. He lay a hand upon Ashes, instead, hoping she understood he meant for her to stay. Then, he left Nerys shivering on the floor of her cell, curled up with his precious pet.

The Rare's eyes glittered in the witchlight. He said nothing. Berge said nothing. Just before Berge turned to leave the dungeon, the Rare smiled a crooked, knowing smile.

Chapter Twelve

The brute—Berge—lowered her to the cold, damp floor of the dungeon. Simos held his breath and didn't move. Something was different. Something had changed. He handled her as if he might break her. He spared no breath for his usual vitriol. Didn't bother glaring at the prisoners or snarling insults. He ignored the lot of them. In fact, it was this strange deviation in behavior that convinced Simos that Berge had changed at all. He was too careful about hiding his thoughts and feelings. Too concerned with remaining silent. He was so worried about staying silent on what had occurred that he may as well have shouted.

Berge cared for Nerys.

He probably wasn't even aware of it yet. Berge wasn't a man accustomed to emotions. He was a walking atrocity. The list of his victims was longer than Zanje's. The act of killing was more deliberate. He was not kind. He was not good. In Simos' eyes, Bergeron Nacht was irredeemable. Berge actively wronged for the pleasure of wrongdoing. His reputation was well-known throughout the land. He had earned his share of unsavory nicknames. He wielded power stronger than any man had a right to wield. Whereas most people had a small amount of control over a small amount of heat and light, Berge was able to summon fire and shut out the light of the sun. He didn't give warnings. He didn't show mercy. He had no scruples left. Man, woman, child…no one was safe from his chaos.

Berge was a walking nightmare.

Simos observed, quietly, gleefully gloating in his cell. Berge, it turned out, was not so inhuman after all. The slow destruction of Nerys would prove to be his undoing. It was only a matter of time. Berge would fray. Berge would balk. Bergeron Nacht was not the type to accept an unfavorable condition. He would pit the value of Nerys against the value of Zanje. What he decided mattered not. That he had to decide made him vulnerable in the interim. Not only would Simos soon be free, but the stars were aligning. He might also be able to cleanse the world of Nacht's taint.

Simos' opportunity was nigh.

His hell-dark eyes met Simos through the bars. Simos stared right back, challenging hell with madness. Berge's expression rippled with a fractional second of uncertainty. It was only the barest flash, a darting of the eyeballs toward the weak and trembling girl in a cell all alone. He wanted to go back, but knew he could not. He wanted to hold her and care for her while she regained her strength, but knew it would damn them both. And just like that, it was gone. Nacht's gaze fell to the ground, looking away first. He left them there in the darkness alone. No insults. No abuse. Just an unexpected, dulled sense of confusion.

Simos listened as he made the slow, tired plod up the stairs. Cocked an ear as the door creaked. Smiled as it clicked shut gently, leaving Nerys in *his* care. Berge couldn't help her now...but Simos could.

Nerys whimpered. Simos' senses sharpened immediately. She took a slow breath. It shuddered free of her lungs, rattling her teeth. She sobbed once. "Berge," she whispered. "Please." He wondered if she knew what she was saying, though he was certain he was the only one who overheard, her voice was so faint. If she survived this...if she were freed, too, that connection could never be known. It would mean great danger for her.

"Nerys!" he called. She didn't respond. No sound could be heard but the chattering of her teeth. Alarmed, he pounced forward. His fingers curled around frigid bars, face pressed through from in-between. "Nerys! Nerys!" Still nothing. He smacked both palms against the bars so hard as to bruise. "Damn it!"

"Dead already?" Mirdoz.

"Blacked out," he replied. "Damn. Nerys! *Nerys!*" Blacking out was dangerous. The reactions from blood loss weren't severe, usually, but any condition could be fatal—no matter how mild—if left untreated. She could have passed out and swallowed her tongue. She might not be able to breathe. If her blood pressure was too low, she might go into shock and die. If she had a hope in hell of surviving, she needed to stay awake. "Nerys!"

"Nerys!" Mirdoz joined in. "Nerys!"

He wasn't expecting that. As an unspoken rule, they mostly kept to themselves. Residents lived and died. It was just a part of their reality.

"Nerys!" Mirdoz continued.

"Nerys!" That was from Megra. Most of the time Simos forgot Megra was there. She was designated 'Baggage.' She shared her cell with four others—Nellan, Seph, Illis, and Kopep. They hadn't left their cells in a long time. Simos often wondered why they hadn't been killed already. It had to be costing Zanje a fortune just to keep them fed. After Megra opened her mouth and started shouting Nerys's name, her four cellmates joined in soon after.

Other voices joined in after. All except for Marc. Berge had cut his tongue out after a particularly cutting remark.

Simos went silent, unsure of what was happening. Simos had had only few conversations with other prisoners. They weren't exactly friends, but what Mirdoz did was *almost*...alliance. For the first time since they'd been thrown into their cells, the inmates were united.

"Ashes?" Nerys peeped.

Simos blinked. *Ashes? Berge's weasel, Ashes?* He crafted a small wisp of witchfire and sent it floating into Nerys's cell. Ashes stood by Nerys's head, leaning back on her haunches with her ears perked up, senses on high alert. Her milky, blind eyes saw nothing but tried. She gazed into the void. Nerys's hand trembled toward the little weasel. Ashes looked over her shoulder, nose twitching. "Well, I'll be damned," Simos muttered.

The little creature was actually *guarding* her.

"Simos?" Nerys croaked.

"She alive?" Mirdoz.

"She's alive," Simos confirmed.

"Oh, thank God."

"Simos?" Her voice trembled. She sobbed.

"I'm here, Nerys. We're all still here."

"Oh, God! So weak. Can barely...move."

Her breathing was still labored. Not good.

"Shh," he cautioned. "You're going to be fine."
She whined, a wordless, frightened cry.

"That bastard Berge," Mirdoz hissed.

"Give her your breakfast, for fuck's sake!"
Nellan.

It was a good idea, one he'd wished he'd
thought of. Simos swiped up his bread. He
always saved the past two days worth, just in
case. He wasn't always certain what he'd need
it for, but knew for a fact he didn't need it for
right now. He stuffed today's cheese into the
soft center and reached as far as he could
through the bars between them. Then he bent
his wrist and tossed it gently.

It hit the bar of her cell and bounced back to
the center of the aisle. "Shit."

"You fuck it up?" Mirdoz hollered.

"It hit the bar," he groaned. He grabbed his
other ration of bread. "I'll see what I—" He
froze mid-sentence. Ashes had darted into the
space between and snatched up the bread and
cheese. "You little shit!" He snarled. "That's not
—" He stopped midsentence again as Ashes
disappeared behind Nerys's head, obscured by
a red wave of hair. She poked her head up
above Nerys's ear, looked about, and
disappeared again. "You're shittin' me."

"What?" Mirdoz demanded.

"The fucking weasel got it."

"God damn it!"

"No, I mean, she got it. She brought it back to Nerys."

"Oh."

"Yeah."

"Wow."

"Yeah."

"Listen, Nerys," Simos continued. "The first one is always the hardest. You're going to be—just—fine, you hear me?"

She wasn't moving. "Nerys! Nerys!"

"Nerys!"

"Nerys!"

It was going to be a long night.

Chapter Thirteen

Berge did his best after Wex and Zanje left to avoid all human contact. Pretending he was alone in the castle helped to numb his troubled thoughts. He tried not to think of Nerys because she challenged him. And he tried not to think of Zanje because he hated her. And he tried not to think of Wex because he still didn't know why he'd saved the guy in the first place, and after spending some time with him, was glad that he did. And he sure as hell tried not to think of Dair because Dair was about as appealing to him as a bag of dicks and he really just wanted to cut the guy.

So in the meantime, he lost himself in the castle with Ashes and Maxine. Hilarity ensued.

For starters, Maxine wasn't allowed in the castle. So naturally the first thing Berge did when Zanje and Wex fucked off into the sunset was let Wex's dog indoors. She was very hesitant to do so, though, and mostly stood at the doorway pretending there was some kind of invisible force field there that was stopping her from crossing into the interior. "Maxine, what's wrong?" he asked her.

Ashes seemed to think the poor dog was confused about how doors worked, so she jumped down from Berge's pocket to show her how. She dove beneath Maxine's legs, crossed into the castle, ran around behind Berge's feet, then hopped back outside and repeated it over and over again. Maxine watched her, eyebrows raised, as she spun around and around in circles, inside, outside, beneath and betwixt. When that didn't seem to educate the dog, Ashes hopped. She sat on her haunches on the outside, coiled her leg muscles, leapt as high as she could across the threshold, and then leapt back out.

Berge watched the whole thing and laughed. "Come on, Maxine. Come inside."

She stared at him with her head down, looking ashamed. She was exceptionally trained. So polite. Nothing he did seemed to work. Then he got the idea to do something that always seemed to work with Ashes. He walked a ways into the main hall and turned around. She was still there, shuffling at the doorway and watching him carefully. He tried to call her one more time, just in case, but to no avail. So he dropped to the floor and pretended to be hurt.

She came running right away, poking at him with her nose. He got up and dashed to the front door, rammed it with his shoulder and slammed it shut. He leaned back against it and looked at the dog. She stood there wagging her tail and looking rather sheepish. "Now what?" He grinned. Her tail wagged.

He'd lived in the castle for fourteen years and never had a reason to explore it. From the main tower, he got the impression that any room not in use was simply empty. All that was supposed to be in the castle was dust and witchlight. Nonetheless, he had nothing better to do until Zanje and Wex got back, and something about exploring a castle with a blind weasel and a dog just sounded cool.

He took the stairs up the main tower. He'd never been up to the top of the tower before. He didn't have a fear of heights, but every man had a limit, and his was somewhere around the level of the clouds. Zanje's main tower went up into the sky further than he could see on a day with clouds, and something about that bothered him. There was no good reason for a tower that tall.

No good reason...except for one. And it was one that he was counting on. If there ever came a day when something unspeakable happened to Zanje, Berge had no trust fund. It would be convenient to know where she kept her lion's share of the treasure.

He passed by the seventh floor where they usually frequented. He passed the eighth where she preferred to sleep. He kept climbing, up and up, until he picked a floor at random just to see what was up there and stepped off the staircase. He had already quit keeping track of which floor he was on. Counting wasn't his favorite hobby. Wherever he was, it was at least thirty or forty floors up.

The floor was furnished. That was a new view for him. There were upholstered wooden benches in the hallway outside some of the rooms, waiting areas for visitors for...what? Visiting nobles? The master's staff? Extended family? There was a runner carpet down the center of that hallway, wall sconces with candles still in them. He thought they were brass, but upon closer inspection, discovered that they were, in fact, made of gold. "Well," he said to his two furred companions. "There's enough gold on the wall sconces to keep us going for a while. There's that for plunder, if nothing else." He smiled. Maxine's tail wagged as if she understood. Ashes was too busy sniffing along the baseboards, probably hunting for mice.

He poked his head into one of the rooms. Surprisingly, it looked to have once been a library. There were shelves all along every wall, some shelves standing up in the center, obscuring his view of the rest of the room. Same as with the hallway, there were old decorative rugs, benches for waiting—or reading, he supposed—cushioned seats up against the windows, and hand lanterns.

What it didn't have were books. Not one of the shelves had even a single book. Zanje sometimes lamented the loss of a civilized age, and the loss of books of learning was her greatest sorrow. Seeing so many empty shelves at once helped him see the true scope of it. He'd mostly only heard rumor of the book burnings, for he himself had not been all that interested in reading books. Zanje, on the other hand…sometimes he forgot that she'd grown up in this place. This would have been her library. If even one of the shelves of this place had been full of books, he could see why she might have been put off by the loss of them. If all of them had once been filled with academia…

He whistled and stepped inside, walking slowly along the edge of the room. He felt like one of the old explorers stumbling upon an ancient ruin. It wasn't that far from the truth… libraries of this nature were relics of a dead age. Light streamed in from the windows, illuminating every dust mote from the fine layer of filth he stirred with every step.

The library was quite large. He passed by

several other doors that returned to the hallway. Eventually, he got bored of the library. It was intriguing, but didn't truly interest him. Before he'd even made it to the other end, he crossed the hallway and opened the door on the other side.

He didn't have a name for the room the door opened into. It was just as large as the library, but more...cluttered. There were dozens of small round tables with curved bench seats. Here and there were folding dividers, providing a measure of privacy if desired. There were dead—very dead—plants along the walls and hanging from planters and several decently sized chandeliers. "What do you think they did in here, guys?"

Maxine and Ashes didn't have any more of an answer than he did. At last, he decided the floor was boring and returned to the stairs. He did want to get all the way to the top today, and he imagined it might take some time. He climbed and climbed. It was exhausting work; he didn't know how many stories the tower rose into the sky, but it was more than he could climb without a few breaks in between. Maxine started panting at about the same time Berge did. Ashes quit way before that, jumping up onto his shoulder. "Don't know why you won't just sit in the pocket," he huffed. "Not like you can see anything, anyway."

After that he went quiet, conserving his breath for the journey, and it was a long one.

Finally, the stairs turned out and ended. There was not another step to take. He smiled to himself, chest heaving, and took the opportunity to sit upon the top stair. Maxine walked a few more steps past him and flopped to the floor against the wall. She groaned.

"Agreed," he said, glancing about. "Wow," he breathed when he saw where he'd come. The room itself was etched entirely out of marble. Every several feet started a new slab of marble, each a different color. Some were black with veins of white, some white with veins of black. There were even blue, green, beige, and silver with veins of gold. But even better than that, every slab was carved within an inch of its life, to a level of detail so fine as to defy belief. Each panel was a different kind of scene. Some were of animals, some of flowers, some of people. The animals were fighting or traveling or hunting. The people were fighting, kissing, making love, speaking, and learning.

Directly across from the stair was some kind of altar. It was a huge gold chair, polished to a beauteous shine, though no one sat upon it. Before it was a symbol that was more or less a circle with some stylized writing and design crossing the lines. In that one room, he understood her better. If this is what civilzation was meant to be like before the purge and before the Red Death started picking them off one at a time, he could easily see why she couldn't rest until she'd returned to such a state.

What he didn't see in that room, however, was the one thing he'd been looking for: money. The god-chair was pure gold, but it wasn't budging. He stood and walked over to it, looking for somewhere she might stash gold, perhaps a cubby hole or a lockbox or even a loose floor tile. "Look for shiny things," he murmured to his two companions. He ran his hands over every piece of art up there. Maxine stayed right where she was, breathing heavily and waiting for him to be ready to go.

Ashes happily helped, scurrying around the floor and weaving in and out among the carvings. She probably wasn't actually helping, but it looked that way, so he accepted it.

"Where would she hide a bunch of gold?" he wondered aloud. His friends weren't very forthcoming with their answers. "And how heavy is this room? Shouldn't this tower have toppled over by now?"

After about an hour of searching, he gave up. There clearly wasn't a hidden trove of gold up here, unless the enormous throne counted. And it didn't. It really didn't. Because he couldn't fit that in his pocket and spend it on whiskey. He rested his hand on the carved banister at the top of the stair, then looked longingly over his shoulder at the strange altar to Zanje's god. He sighed. "Nothing here, I guess. We'll try again tomorrow."

He started on his way down stairs. As he passed the first floor descending, he caught something at eye level as he continued on his way down. At first he was sure that his eyes deceived him. He walked backwards up the stairs until the floor was at the level of his chest. He was certain, then, that he hadn't been imagining it.

Footprints in the dust. He grinned.

Chapter Fourteen

Wex had never been so nervous as he was around Zanje Vangelic. He did not feel as if he was worthy to remain in her presence. She had an air about her of superiority, and whether or not it was true didn't seem to matter. He felt it to the marrow of his bones, and it instilled in him a need to submit. He was the employee, she the employer. And so, he pandered to her needs, bowing and scraping though it felt ridiculous to do. He led her to the snowcraft. She held the small wine-colored globe out before her like a black lantern. The medicine inside it sloshed from side to side, syrupy and potent.

Wex struggled not to be sick, all the while transfixed by purpose for it. It looked like blood. It had to be blood. The pieces of the puzzle shifted, turned, and clicked into place one at a time. The reasons for all of it—the secrecy, the emotional detachment, even the sanitary environment. The medicine...was blood. Of course, realizing that sparked a lot of other questions, like where they were getting it from. The castle was a large place, but he'd never seen anyone go into or out of it. Maybe it was their own blood? That would certainly explain the high price.

He focused instead on her eyes. They were a pretty, icy blue, like winter itself. It wasn't as easy as it should have been, though. She stared right back into his own eyes, her will forcing him to look away. His heart thudded steadily in his chest, telling him what he already knew. He had a job to do. She was a passenger on a mission. His purpose was to deliver her unto it and allow her to work her miracle.

It felt...good.

He went to her side of the vehicle and made to show her how the door opened. But when he started to explain it, she interrupted him by saying, "Just open it," and waited like the queen she was.

He felt foolish. Of course he should get the door for her. She was holding a precious commodity that was probably worth more than his life thrice over. "Right."

When she settled in, the dark glass bottle cradled upon her lap, he started up the craft. She neither smiled nor frowned, but stared straight ahead, already focused on their destination. For a moment, Wex wished he'd been allowed to bring along Maxine instead of Zanje. He couldn't think of a more awkward journey than the one he was about to take. But Maxine couldn't do what Zanje could. He took pride in knowing that he was a cog in that machine, aspiring to finally be the noble human Maxine saw through her adoring eyes. Yeah. That would do.

They spent the first hour in silence—uncomfortable, for him—before Wex quite forgot she was there. It was a sunny day, and for a wonder, it wasn't snowing. It seemed to him to be a good day to be alive. Before he knew what he was doing, his lips parted and song came forth. He sang a hymn his father used to sing from time to time, droning on in his deep, rich bass about the meaning of existence. It was a quietly hopeful kind of music, appropriate for the weather. It was too much to hope that winter might break, but the sun seemed to be trying to do its best. It had been written in some of the old history books that such a thing as summer existed, though Wex knew it to be a fairy tale. It was a sweet tale, though. Summer was a pleasant concept in theory.

He reached over unconsciously to pet Maxine, naturally expecting her to be sitting in the passenger seat. Instead, he accidentally groped Zanje's breast. Worse, he remained there, hand splayed out as he tried to work out the unexpected softness of silk and the yielding consistency. When he glanced sideways to make sense of it, he was met with an icy death glare, as cold and dark as a night on the frozen sea. "Sorry," he blurted, yanking his hand back from the scorching contact and the frigid stare. "Thought you were Maxine."

"I wasn't aware you and she were that close," she drawled.

"No, it's not like that," he tried to explain. "I thought that—usually she's—we drive around together and—you know what?" He sighed. "Never mind." He bit his lips shut, cursing himself for a fool. There he was, fumbling again as usual. He never could understand people properly. Too much human contact, and he always managed to mess it up somehow. He missed his dog. Dogs always made it clear exactly how they felt. They always listened, and they always had your back. He liked people—in theory—he just had a hard time understanding them.

She laughed softly. "You have a gift for singing," she said at last.

"Thank you," he mumbled. He made sure not to say anything more than that.

She waited as if expecting more. When he didn't continue, she said, "You can keep singing if you like. I don't mind."

"I'd rather not." He wasn't about to risk embarrassing himself again. He focused on her presence there and kept his mind on the road and on the mission.

She sighed, a long wistful exhalation, and stared out the window. "That's a shame."

He glanced at her askance. She was watching him from the corner of her eye, and he wasn't imagining that. It gave him just enough courage to ask, "So how did you get into this line of work?"

The corner of her mouth turned up just the barest hint, dimpling her cheek with a touch of pride. "I was born into it, actually. On my father's side."

"It's…science, right? You don't mind if I ask, do you?"

She watched him carefully for a few moments, as if trying to figure out what his motivation might be for asking. He could only guess at what she might be thinking. It almost felt like she was testing his moral fiber, deciding if he was worthy of the knowledge. The moment stretched on long enough that Wex nearly apologized for having asked.

"It's quite alright. Yes, it's science. Medicine, specifically. Most of the teachings were lost long ago. I learned directly from my father, and later I found his books."

"There are still books?" he gasped.

"There are still books," she confirmed. "But mine. Only mine. I keep them hidden and locked up and I won't let another touch them. They are all that's left of a wiser era. So much was lost in the Fires."

He whistled appreciatively. "So what did he teach you?"

She eyed him suspiciously. Trying to ascertain the direction of his thoughts, perhaps.

"I'm only curious," he promised. "I love learning new things. It's a hobby of mine."

"So I've noticed. A noble pursuit, academics. Too bad it's not appreciated anymore."

"I completely agree."

"Do you? How interesting." She nodded slowly. "Tell me, what do you know of genetics?"

"You mean, like with dogs?"

She rolled her eyes. "Yes, if you like. I suppose dogs aren't much different than men."

"You cross two animals that have desirable traits, and the offspring are selected for those traits," he explained. "You mean like that, right?"

"Yes, like that. And what do you know of the Red Death?"

"Well. As to that…" He thought about his father and nearly didn't continue. His father wasn't a fool, but he was perhaps a bit too pious. If he'd been less of a God-fearing man, he might have found Zanje in time to...no. Best not to think of that. "I don't know anything that's worthwhile. It's an illness."

"And do you believe it's the work of God?"

He grimaced. "I don't know. Maybe. My father always believed that God was a benevolent being, but then he got sick and, well...why would God do such a thing? That's what's never made sense to me."

"Earlier you asked me a question that was much like that one. This time, I'll hear your answer, Wex. Why would God do such a thing, indeed?"

"I think, if he were to do such a thing, it might be...to test us?"

She smiled, a slow curling of sinful red lips. "Close enough to the truth."

"What do you think?"

"Genetics is the science that evolves the weak into the strong. When you take two strong animals and cross them, the result is an even stronger one. The stronger offspring survives the harsher environmental condition. And the Red Death is...?"

Wex's mouth fell open with realization. "I see. You think that the Red Death is an environmental stressor that's meant to push human evolution into the next age?" She nodded with satisfaction, her vicious smile too knowing. "And you think God allowed the Red

Death to further that along?" She nodded again, her lips pulling back to reveal perfect teeth. "Ohh," he mused, nodding to himself in understanding. "But where does the magic fit in?"

She laughed. "Magic was the test. And mankind chose to use it to destroy their only hope of salvation. With science gone, mankind has no chance in hell of surviving this cataclysm. And that was my father's work."

Wex was confused. "Your father engineered the cataclysm?"

"No. My father rescued science. Through his teaching and through my own innovations I learned how to reverse the effects of the Red Death. There are virus-like particles in the red blood cells of a few. When you introduce those virus-like particles to the system of a diseased individual, the virus overtakes the cells of the sick and rewrites the genetic code. It overwrites the Red Death and makes a person healthy again."

"Wow."

She nodded. "Yes. By sacrificing only a few, we can save hundreds. It's a necessary evil to protect the future of mankind."

His heart fell. He glanced at the globe in her hand. "So we *do* sacrifice?"

Her gaze followed his. She lifted the globe. "Yes and no," she allowed. "Taking this much blood won't kill a person. The body catches up and replaces this much blood in only a few weeks."

"Oh! That's...well. That's encouraging. I thought—it was wrong of me to think that. It makes more sense now." He smiled, feeling lighter than he had in weeks.

"Does it? That's good."

"Yeah. It makes sense now. So in essence what you're doing is borrowing that much blood from someone and then giving it to someone who's sick, and it makes them better?"

"Yep, it forces evolution."

"Why *that* much blood, though?"

She watched him impassively for a moment. "What do you mean?"

"How do you know exactly how much blood you need? Why not...a teaspoon? Or a gallon?"

The fingers of one hand fanned over the curve of the globe. "A teaspoon isn't enough. The disease itself causes blood loss, so enough is needed to recoup the loss and assist in healing the afflicted. A gallon is too much to take at a time. The source individual would not survive."

"Oh, okay. I see. And then the person you take the blood from recovers from it in...what, three weeks?"

"Usually about four to six."

"Okay." He nodded. "Okay. So, then what happens if you use that person again before they've had a chance to recover?"

"Depends on how long it's been. Best case scenario, it wears them out and makes them weak. They might get temporarily sick and exhausted."

"Worst case scenario?"

"They die."

Chapter Fifteen

Berge seethed with something foul and untapped. He immediately named it Hatred, though it didn't have an aim, an outlet. Zanje was out of the castle, off on a fool's errand to save the bloodletter's whore. Dair's woman was dying slowly of Red Death, and Berge couldn't be more ecstatic. It was about time that Haddig and his brood suffered for the crooked business they operated. The more he thought about it, the more he reveled. The more he reveled, the more he reviled himself. It coalesced and recalibrated, over and over, hatred amplifying over evil, head over heels into infinity.

He lounged in Zanje's favorite ballroom, naked, hoping that when she returned, she sensed the defilement that seeped into the cushions. He hadn't washed in a while. He uncorked a bottle of her fancy wine and drank it from the bottle, taking satisfaction in knowing that she took grave offense unless wine was sipped slowly from a wide-based glass. He opened up her box of music stones and tossed them all over the balcony, smiling when one of them broke into three pieces at the bottom of the precipitous drop.

"Fuck her," he muttered to himself as he tossed the wine bottle back and drained the contents. Fuck Zanje. Fuck Dair. And Haddig. He frowned at the empty bottle and then threw it across the room in a spontaneous fit of rage. It shattered against the stone wall, green fragments of glass trembling to a halt. A spatter of wine stayed behind upon the wall. His eyes locked onto the smudge as it dripped down, down. It looked a lot like blood.

He'd seen a lot of blood in his lifetime. First, out of desperation. Gambling was a dangerous life. He'd gotten into more than his fair share of fights, and the first ones he'd only just barely survived out of sheer dumb luck. He didn't have a spark of the Craft in him and they did. The only way a man survived those kinds of odds was to get down and dirty with the worst of them. He didn't fight fair and he didn't make exceptions.

No fucking exceptions.

He opened another bottle and leaned back against the couch, feeling pleasantly fuzzy. It blocked out the insanity his mind churned out. It didn't block out the abiding hatred he had for *everything.*

He thought of Nerys. Then he swore at himself for thinking of Nerys. He thought of Zanje. Then he hated himself for thinking of Zanje. The cycle repeated itself until, at long last, he accepted what he'd known all along. Humanity was a cancer. He was naught but one ugly blotch in a tumor of human debauchery.

"Nacht!" someone hollered. The voice drifted in from a distant place in the world. It was far away and insignificant. A man shouting his name in anger. How original that was.

Berge sucked on the bottle neck. Wine surged into his mouth and rolled around his tongue. He began to understand Zanje and her desires. Complex flavor and the spice of alcohol. It tasted clean and dark at the same time. If blood were distilled, perhaps. And maybe that was her logic, too. He probably spent too much time trying to understand what happened in her terrible, beautiful mind. "I'm in love with Zanje," he said aloud. The words were a lie, and he well knew it. He only said them because he felt he must. It was the only logical explanation for his actions. Love was the only reason—the only legitimate reason—for people to do the unthinkable. Men could only embrace their darkness in their desperations born somehow from love.

"Nacht!" someone shouted again. But who

was it? And did it, in fact, even matter?

"What do you want?" he muttered. Whoever it was would never have heard him, but he just didn't care. His mind stilled anyway, though, and he listened to the disembodied voice. It roamed the corridors of the castle like a ghost, searching for him. "Oh, Death," he mused with a wry grin. "Is it that time already?" He threw one arm over the back of the couch and tilted his chin back. His mind went fuzzy and his vision twirled in a slow circle, back and forth and back forever.

"Nacht, you bloody sack of spaff, where the fuck are you? Nacht!"

"Shut up, you filthy faggot, I'm right here!" He put the wine bottle down, but it went too hard, hobbled, hobbled, and tipped over, spilling its contents upon Zanje's expensive ermine rug. *Ermine*. For the first time since she'd bought the fucking thing three years ago, it dawned on Berge what was meant by it. Ermine was weasel fur. White weasel fur. He stood of a sudden and kicked back the couch. This rug… simply would not do. "Fucking *ermine*," he growled. "I helped her pay for it, too. I'm going to gut the bitch when I see her next." He held himself firmly and aimed for the center, though his treacherous body swayed back and forth.

He was midstream when Death himself appeared in the doorway. "Are you out of your fucking mind, Nacht?"

Berge blinked and swayed. He pissed down his leg but couldn't be bothered to give a damn. "Yeah." Death looked an awful lot like Dair of the Untamed. Berge supposed he shouldn't have been surprised. "You wanna fight or something?" He stared, uncaring of whether he lived or died. He felt invincible, resigned to the knowledge that he was worthless. Nothing to lose, nothing to fear, nothing holding him back. He was certain, in that moment, that if Dair were to fight him, Berge wouldn't hesitate to crush his face into mash beneath his bare knuckles.

Dair must have sensed it, too. He took a step back into the hallway.

"What the fuck are you waiting for?" Berge demanded. "I thought you came to kill me?"

"Oh, I think you're doing just fine."

Berge grinned, a lopsided crooked grimace. "She does it," he slurred. "She kills me. I'm dying, sure as shit I am."

Dair shook his head incredulously. "You're one fucked up son of a bitch, Nacht. Look at you."

Berge stood straighter and held his arms out wide. His grin broadened. "Look at me."

"You're drunk and buck ass nekkid."

"I am."

He only shook his head again. "Well, look. I

had something I was going to ask you, but I'll ask it tomorrow. If you're still alive. But before I go, I just want you to know—"

"What? Ask me now."

"No, I'll—"

"I said, 'Ask me now.' I'm this fucked up all the time. Not a day goes by I'm not fucked up. That's me. That's Berge. All day, every day, fucked up as shit. How're you?"

He laughed humorlessly. "God, man, but you're a sorry piece of work. Fine."

Berge's eyebrows climbed his scalp. He figured he'd won this series.

"I could have killed you, just now."

"I doubt it," he drawled, barely able to keep his balance anymore.

"I could have killed you, Nacht. Hear me. Listen again. I could fucking kill you. Right now. And all I'd need to do is push you off that balcony."

Berge scowled, dropped to his ass right there on the ermine rug. "Kill me, then. I deserve it."

"You do. But I'm not going to. I'll tell you why tomorrow."

"Tell me now." Dair turned to go. "Dair! Tell me now!" Dair left him there and didn't return. "Dair, you tell me! Tell me right now! You tell me right the fuck now! Hey! I said tell me!"

His head had been cleaved in two, stomped

into the earth, and pissed on. He was sure of it. His nose was even pressed into a rug that smelled strongly of piss. And when his eyes opened and the light filtered in, he was equally certain that it was the wrath of the gods that seared his mind, not your average run of the mill morning sunshine, despite the fact that he denied the existence of any god at all. He pressed the heel of his hand to his temple and squeezed his eyes shut again. "Damn," he groaned.

"Ah, you're awake."

Berge froze. He recognized the voice. It had once haunted his quietest moments. It was a voice that stalked his peace, demanded vengeance, and relented not. Dair, the Cur of the Untamed. Haddig's faithful pup. Dair would track a man for thousands of miles to collect a debt, and he always collected in blood. "The fuck do you want?" he grumbled.

"To collect on an old debt."

"Go fuck yourself."

Dair chuckled. His shoes were polished, his suit crisp, hair combed back perfectly. Dair was a man in his prime. A villain in his element. He was completely at ease on Zanje's favorite couch. As to that, Berge smiled, knowing his balls had been all over that couch, that his unwashed body was now infiltrating Dair's perfect suit. "I have a proposition for you."

"Not interested."

"I wasn't asking," he threatened.

"I wasn't either."

"Nacht." His voice was warning. But there was a hint of something else there. Slightly more desperate. Just enough to make Berge peer at him from between his fingers. And that was when he saw it and knew once and for all that he had the upper hand.

Blood. There, at the corner of Dair's mouth. He caught it immediately after, his tongue flicking out to capture it before it gave him away. And there, the hairline fractures in the skin. Dair had caught the sickness. Dair was doomed to die a slow and horrible death. Bleeding. Spitting blood. Pissing blood. Shitting blood. Choking on it, swimming in it, yearning for it. Berge saw and Berge celebrated. Still on the floor, he leaned back against his usual chair and crossed his arms, plastering a smug smile all across his face. "You're dying."

"We're all dying," Dair replied evenly.

"We all deserve it, too," Berge agreed.

"Even you?"

"Especially me." Satisfaction permeated his bones. Berge expected to die. He didn't even mind, really. Dair, on the other hand, had an empire. Had a family. His family had long held the city of Raddolf down by the throat, iron jaws slowly closing. Dair didn't want to die.

Berge wanted Dair to die.

And most beautifully of all, *Dair* needed *Berge* if Dair *didn't* want to die. He said what he was thinking. "I could rape you for every last grimy penny and leave you to die anyway, and there isn't fuckall you could do about it."

He smiled ruefully and held his arms out wide. "And yet I am here anyway."

"Zanje could have helped you."

"Zanje doesn't owe me money."

Berge laughed. "I'm not giving you any money anyway. Your mistake is in assuming I fear you. I don't." He leaned forward and sneered. "Bleed and die, you greedy fuck."

Dair's eyes widened. He lunged across the space between them and wrapped his fingers around Berge's neck, but he didn't even flinch. The fingers crushing his windpipe made it hard to breathe. He smiled anyway, wheezing as he tried to laugh at the desperation evident in the loan shark's craggy face. Dair's gray-blue eyes burned with a wild brand of hatred, unrestrained and urgent. He was a man without choices, and he had begged with everything except words.

And then he begged with that, too. He released Berge's neck and fell upon his knees, making a slow production of clasping his hands together in prayer. It took him a minute to properly school his features into those of earnest and sincere need. Berge's cough and laugh took turns using his throat while Dair struggled to find the right words to beg for aid. In the end he went with, "Berge, please. *Please.*"

Berge grinned and waited. Dair shook his hands, beseeching. His perfectly ironed suit was subjected to a pissed-on rug, spilled wine, and Berge himself. Such a fine man to beg thusly from one such as Berge. And then, like a line of sad poetry, a single tear of blood dribbled from the corner of Dair's eye, tracking unchecked down the groove beside his hawkish nose. Berge's smile flattened out as he observed its journey.

Blood. Blood had held so much significance for him throughout his years. The perfect color. The sickening coppery smell of it. The absolute necessity of it. But against Dair's face, shed in supplication, he thought only of Nerys.

It's not for us to judge, Wex had said.

"No," he found himself saying, but it wasn't as a response to Dair's begging. "No. No, that's not right." He jumped to his feet, snatched up his pants, and left Dair there on his knees. "Don't you fucking move," he ordered.

Chapter Sixteen

Every day was the same—dark, with a chance of breakfast and dinner—but for the days Berge came down to steal one of them away. It happened maybe twice a week, and so far, none of them had been for her since that first day. She counted herself among the lucky ones. The Primes and the Majors definitely saw the worst of it, while her and Simos and the Baggage never left their iron prisons.

She therefore had days upon days of quiet, contemplative solitude. Though she was surrounded by people, to a one they most appreciated their own company. It was likely a survival mechanism. There was no reason to be attached to someone who could be dead any day. It was a dark and dismal thought. A true thought.

So she let her mind wander and explored the pathways slowly, savoring every minute. What she found in there challenged her notions of what was life, and what were men, and how might she have wanted to die, if she'd had a choice. She was a young woman without a whole lot of experience behind her, so she endeavored to ask another for a second opinion. Unfortunately, all of the second opinions in the room were extraordinarily biased. They'd been caged for God knew how long. What was life but a dark hole in the earth? What were men but beasts in a battle for dominance? And death? They didn't want to die, and even if they did, the only thing they were certain of was that it wouldn't be here in this godforsaken hole.

"Simos."

"Nerys." She couldn't see him in the darkness, but she could imagine his expressions as he spoke.

"What did you do? I mean, what did you do before you were here?"

He was quiet a moment before replying. "I was a teacher."

"What did you teach?"

"Painting."

Her heart leapt against her ribs, yearning to connect to a fellow artist. "What did you paint?"

He sighed heavily. In that unhappy breath of air was mourning. "The stars."

"I'm sorry. I shouldn't have asked."

"No," he answered gently. "It's okay."

"I grew flowers in my little greenhouse," she confessed. "I dried them and glued them to paper, then framed them to hang on walls."

"That's...lovely," he responded. "Where did you learn that?"

She shrugged. "It just seemed like a nice idea. Naiora needed life."

"Self-taught," he murmured appreciatively.

She smiled to herself.

"Why, though? Why pursue art in a world like this?"

She hugged her knees. "It just...felt...right."

"Yes...that it does."

The thought of seeing another artist's work sparked hope inside her. If Simos could paint again—if she could glue flowers again, and show him, too—there was something to look forward to, on the outside. "Would you do it again, if you were free?"

"*When* I am free, yes." He stopped fidgeting and took a breath. Let it out slowly. "We're getting out of here, Nerys." Witchlight bloomed slowly as he lifted an object. Nerys couldn't quite see it. "This...is a key. A skeleton key. I've been working on it since the day they threw me down here. It doesn't quite fit, yet, but it will."

Nerys's pulse sped up at the thought that freedom might, perhaps, be possible. But then..."I learned what they use our blood for," she admitted.

"Oh yeah? Are they painters, too?" His voice was tinged with wry amusement.

"No. It's medicine."

He went silent. She wanted desperately to know what he was thinking, to know if he thought the same as her. It was difficult to understand how people like Berge, who were so awful, were doing something so noble. "If that's true," he offered up at last, "they're not doing it out of kindness."

Nerys thought of the tormented soul inside the shell and wasn't sure. She didn't dare say it, though. Simos despised Berge. He could never believe there was kindness in him anywhere. "Why else then?"

"They're not good people, Nerys," he growled. "Put that from your mind now. There's nothing in them that can be saved, no shred of gentleness anywhere. Even if what you say is true—and I don't believe it; it sounds like a lie—then there's something in it for them. Probably a lot of money. They're definitely the type to profit from suffering. What kind of medicine is it?"

"I'm not sure. It wasn't clear, but... supposedly it's for the Red Death."

Simos laughed, but it was a hollow, humorless sound. "Now I know it's a lie." He shook his head incredulously. "You're a sweet girl, Nerys, but you can be so naive. There is no cure for the Red Death. It's a heavenly scourge upon humanity for all of our crimes as a people. We squandered our time here on earth, were given so many gifts for the betterment of mankind, and we wasted them. Every single one. We turned our backs on science in favor of a weak but exciting form of magic"—he flared a tiny wisp of blue flame to illustrate his point —"and now science has turned its back on us. God has turned His back on us. He tempted us with this magic to test our moral fiber, and we used it to destroy academia."

Nerys hadn't considered that. "I wouldn't have guessed you to be a religious man."

"And why not?" he pondered.

"No reason. I just didn't, that's all."

"Hm."

"So, you hate magic, then?"

He grinned, a flash of light in the blackness. "No. No, I don't. Quite the opposite in fact. Magic keeps me warm at night, down here where it's so cold. No one alive would ever discredit the many benefits of the Craft." He eyed her from beneath his brows. "Aren't you cold?"

"Yes, constantly."

"You must lack it, then."

"Magic? Not totally. It's just that there isn't much down here to work with."

He nodded slowly. "Then what do you think of it?"

"Hm?"

"Craft."

"It seems useful."

"Mm-hm. That it is. It's warm. It's bright. It's an inexhaustible resource. We're like catalysts. More or less."

"What's a catalyst?" she wondered.

"Ah. Yes, the butchery of science. I'd already forgotten," he said bitterly. "A catalyst is something that facilitates a reaction without being used in the process. The Craft gives us the ability to convert one form of energy to another. It costs nothing for us to use. That's one of the infallible laws of the universe. There's a constant level of energy in the world at any given time. All we do to master the Craft is direct one form of it to become another. Light to heat, heat to light, and…so on and so forth."

"Are there other types of energy?"

"Of course."

"Like?"

"Very few actually know."

"Do you know?"

"…No. What about you, Nerys? What are your thoughts on God?"

"I haven't thought about it much. Just because people believe in a god doesn't make it real."

"No, it doesn't," he agreed. "And I'll be the first to admit that the way most people see God doesn't sit right with me, either."

"How does it sit with you?"

"My God is for me," he hedged. "If you want God, you have to find Him for yourself."

She went quiet and considered his words. Meanwhile, he scratched at his makeshift key. With what, she had no idea. "Hey," she interjected a short time later. "You never talked about your philosophy of science."

"Science is dead, Nerys," he lamented.

"Right, but, what do you think of it? And how it relates to God, and magic?"

He sighed heavily and stopped scratching at his key. It was a long time before he answered, and when he did, he didn't sound happy. "The three things are one in the same. All three exist for the same purpose."

"And what purpose is that?"

He smiled. "The exploration of wonderment."

Berge stormed down the stairs, a perfect fury, at his absolute worst. "None of you say a fucking word," he said softly, menacingly. "Or I'll torch all of you. And I'll sleep like a baby while your corpses smolder in the pit." And then, just to illustrate his point, he sent blue flames licking up and down both sides of the aisle. The fire coiled its way up iron bars, and all of the prisoners ducked away.

Except Mirdoz, who pressed his face up against the bars and bared his decaying teeth. "A fucking word," Mirdoz dared. He cackled.

Berge stalked up the center of their cramped dungeon. He came to a stop in front of the Major's cell and glared into it. He only peered into the face of the one laughing, almost curious, like a cat watching a beetle crawl toward it instead of away. There was a dull roar and a gathering, sucking vacuum, and then flames exploded from the cell, parting way before Berge himself and jetting out behind to either side. Berge stood stoically, his face set in a grim expression befitting one of his caliber of wrath. Several voices from farther back in the dungeon yelped, shrieked, screamed and cried, astonished by the brutality and the surprise of it.

Nerys squinted against the invading brightness. Then, horrified, she realized what had just happened. Berge had just murdered the Major in cold—hot—blood for naught but a flippant comment. Worse, Larric was in the cell with Mirdoz and hadn't stood a chance. She gasped and bit down on the sob that threatened, lest she attract attention.

The occupants of the cell designated Baggage began shouting. The blue of Berge's attack died down yet the light remained. "He's burning!" someone shouted. "Oh my God, he's on fire!"

"Put it out, put it out!"

"Kopep, hold still!"

Meanwhile, Kopep yelled wordlessly, terrified.

"Almost, almost. Hold him still so I can put the flames out." Fabric flapped frantically. Fitful flames flickered.

Berge shot a glance in her direction. His dark eyes fell upon her. She froze. The look in his eyes was tortured and pitiful, as if he could no longer govern his own actions and lashed out in pain like a wounded animal. She stopped breathing, certain she was losing her mind. Evil didn't feel remorse. Murderous actions were unforgivable, and yet that seemed to be what he was asking with his eyes. For an apology, or perhaps not even that. She didn't know what he cried for, but cry for it he surely did, even if his scream was silent.

Beyond him, the light went out and someone exclaimed, "Oh, thank God!"

"God is dead," he threw over his shoulder. Then, without another word, he turned on his heel and stalked further down the prison. He stopped again before the cell that held the Primes. They were exhausted, all three of them. Lissa, Kalyria, Marc. "I'll be kind today," he cooed to the three within the cage. "I'll let you choose who goes."

Immediately the two women whimpered and started crying quietly. The expected pleas for mercy came next, but they didn't affect Berge. Without the light from his fire, Nerys couldn't see that far down the cold dungeon. But then she heard the metal rasp open, the clank of it being laid aside, and the crying increased in volume.

"His name is Marc," Simos said softly.

Nerys and Simos made eye contact. She couldn't see his face, but the connection was there, heart to heart. A tear slid from her own eye. For Simos. For Marc.

And for Berge.

"It doesn't fucking matter what his name is," Berge snapped back.

"Berge!" she shouted. She didn't know why she called to him and wished immediately that she had it back. Wounded animals knew not friend from foe. Of course, at this point she didn't know which she was to him, either. She didn't know what possessed her to try to stop him, only that she needed to. Marc wasn't going to make it through another bleeding. *Something* was happening between her and Berge. She might have been the only one who could change his mind. She had to try.

There was silence in the dungeon, though the weeping quietly continued. Simos was watching her carefully, neither approving nor disapproving. He lounged against his wall as was his way, the king of caged wolves, biding his time.

What did that make her?

There was the heavy thump as Berge dropped Marc to the ground—and the heavy grunt that followed when Marc hit painfully—and left him there. He sauntered over to where she sat. "Nerys."

Her voice was barely audible, but somehow she managed to say it. "Don't."

"Why not?"

"This isn't you."

He laughed bitterly. "Are you an expert?"

She bit the inside of her lip. His bitterness pained her in ways she'd never known. She didn't know where to begin to make the pain go away. It was a challenge she couldn't overcome, and that bothered her.

"Why not, Nerys? Hm? Why not?" When she didn't answer, he slammed his body up against the bars. She flinched, startled by the ferocity of his madness. *"WHY NOT?!"*

She choked on her words. Swallowed them, and failed to stop the steady stream of silent tears from betraying her weakness.

"We're all dying, Nerys," he hissed, every syllable punctuated. "You. Me. Him. He dies, another lives. Maybe that one dies for another.

Maybe that one *kills* a dozen others. Life and death. Love and hatred. It's all meaningless, don't you see? None of it fucking matters. You're going to die here, don't you understand that? Hang on for another hour, another day, another *week*. And in the end, it still won't fucking matter because you will still be just as dead as you would have been if you'd died yesterday. All the way dead. So die today, or die tomorrow, or hang onto your pathetic threads of life if you must. But he dies today and another lives because of it, and it's not for me to judge why *him* and why *him*." He pointed at Marc and at the ceiling.

"Berge," she finally managed, her voice breaking on his name. She couldn't speak. Couldn't dare to ask him to deny his nature. She didn't have the words to say that she had any faith might convince him otherwise. She only hoped that whatever showed in her face might give him pause.

He held her stare for longer than was appropriate, his chest heaving with the breath of adrenaline. Then he wrenched his gaze away from her. It imprisoned and released her at once, to have seen and to have known, to some degree, the chaos within. Her heart pounded and her thoughts panicked, and she didn't come to until she heard the sound of Marc's body sliding across the stone floor. He groaned and grunted as he was manhandled and shouldered. Then Berge carted the man upstairs slung over his back and was gone.

She looked over at Simos' patch of shadow, wondering what he must be thinking. Abruptly, he shouted helplessly, wordlessly, an expression of impotent rage. On and on his voice roared through the dungeon, fluctuating in volume but not in emotion. Simos only voiced what all of them were feeling—grim, helpless, but unwilling to be ignored. Normally, Simos kept his voice to himself, lending it to Berge for only moments at a time to remind the man who tormented them that his victims were people, not just sacks of blood. Now, however, he displayed a rare moment of opinion.

Nerys hugged her knees to her chest. She clapped her hands over her ears to try to drown out the sound, but it was ineffective. That was the point, of course, but Nerys didn't need to hear Simos scream. She remained firmly aware of the injustice of Bergeron Nacht.

And that was when she realized what it was she should have done.

Chapter Seventeen

Wex stood in awe in front of Dair's estate. It was the tallest building he'd ever seen—except for the castle of course. It was twelve stories and built with immaculate white marble. Surrounded by snow-heavy trees on all sides, it looked like a king's palace out of a fairy tale land. "Wow," he breathed softly.

He had thought that maybe Zanje would take time to admire it, too. She had indicated an appreciation for the arts. Instead, though, she slid off of her seat in the snowcraft and sank into snow up to her shins. She stepped gingerly through the snow, careful not to trip as she made her way. He decided to follow suit and trudged after her, shoving his cold hands into his pockets. She led him up to the gate of the estate, melted the lock off, and let herself in.

They were immediately stopped by some tough-looking guards. Wex thought they might have been in a few street brawls in their time.

One had the look of a man who'd had his nose broken more than once, and another had the deformed ears of a man who'd been hit in the head too many times. "Hey! Who are you and where do you think you're going?"

"I'm Zanje, on behalf of Dair. This man works for me."

"Uh-uh," the one said, holding up one very thick hand and making a severe frown. "No one goes into the manor without express permission."

"Do you know who I am?" she asked with a sardonic smile. "Maybe you should find out, first."

"Doesn't matter who you are," he shot back. "No one means no one. Go."

"I suggest you find out. Otherwise, I'll be happy to educate you."

Wex sensed an imminent confrontation and stepped forward. "Excuse me," he interjected, stepping between them. "We're committed to saving lives." He leaned in and lowered his voice. "Dair came to Zanje to ask for help for his wife. She's ill."

They exchanged looks.

"We know she has the Red Death," Wex continued. "Zanje can fix her up. She saved me."

"Yeah? And who are you?"

"My name is Wex Kincaid, but I'm just the

driver. She's the special one, not me."

They looked at her. Really looked, this time. At the glass bubble she held with its questionable contents. At the serious look upon her face. "What is that?" he asked her, indicating the globe.

"Blood," she replied shortly.

"What do you intend to do with it?"

She smiled.

"Please," Wex supplicated. "We've already accepted payment from Dair. He's your master, isn't he?" The man narrowed one eye and nodded. "He's not going to be happy if you hold us up."

"Where is he?" he asked suspiciously.

"Back at our place. He's fine, I assure you. We traveled by alternative means and for reasons that take too long to explain, I can only bring one other person with me, and she's it. Can you just let us through?"

He nodded, one slow nod, and stepped aside. "Right this way, Miss Zanje."

"Just Zanje. 'Miss' makes me sound like I'm thirteen."

The guard captain dismissed his buddies and led them inside, up a few flights of stairs, and down a hallway. He dismissed four guards outside a room, too, then opened the door and led them in. The smell hit Wex full force. He lifted his sleeve to cover his face, but Zanje didn't even flinch. The guard gave him an incredulous look. It took Wex a second to realize that he was being inadvertently rude. He dropped his hand, though the smell of rot and death threatened to make him sick.

The guard shut the door behind himself and locked it, then turned back to them. "My deepest apologies," he said in a deep bass. "Dair is protective of his Fionah. He won't accept that she's dying and there isn't a way to save her. It's made him a little crazy, so there are those that wish to kill Fionah for him just so he'll go back to work. He just spends all his time in here with her, watching her bleed out."

"Touching," Zanje said.

She turned away from him and went to the bed. The woman wrapped in sheets was a tragic piece of work. The fat of her cheeks was sunken, her eyes dark and closed. Her hair was matted with blood. The sheets and blankets were soaked red. "Oh, God…" Wex began, his heart breaking just to see it. He had never been so close to late-stage Red Death before. His father had managed his illness much better, or maybe he was just better at hiding it. This woman…she was dying, right before his eyes.

"Wex, give me my bag," Zanje commanded. He nodded and unshouldered the bag. "And that table." She pointed. He brought the table over next to her. She opened her bag and purposefully removed every item. She set out a clean, wax coated needle. Wex leered at it, wishing it wasn't there, yet glad it was. She set down a brown bottle and unwrapped some clean rags. There was a length of rubber hose he recognized. "Is there a chair?" She addressed the guard.

He nodded his head. "Yeah, I'll get it." He began his slow plod over to one side of the room.

Wex watched him until Zanje snapped her fingers. "Attention here, Wex. I need your help."

"Yes ma'am," he responded instantly. "What can I do?"

She dabbed a rag with some of the contents of the brown bottle. "This is alcohol," she told him. "Clean her up a bit while I get ready.

"Alright." He took the rag from her and leaned over the dying woman. Her chest rose and fell, breath rattling like dead leaves. Blood oozed out of her ears and wept from her eyes.

"Don't worry about touching her," Zanje told him. "You've been cured and you're immune now. You can't catch it anymore."

"Really?"

She didn't answer again.

"That's nice," he said to the lady. "It'll be good for you, too, then." He dabbed at her face, smudging the blood off of her forehead and her cheeks, taking especial care to try to make her look pretty—not because he was shallow, but because he imagined it might have been what she would have wanted if she were awake to say so. He turned down the blanket and sheet and hissed. His eyes darted back over to Zanje. The guard was back with the chair. She asked with her eyes and forewent her words. "She's... rotting," he whispered.

"I know. I smelled it when we walked in."

His jaw dropped, horrified. "Why?"

"The disease breaks open the skin. Anything and everything can get into the wounds that way. She hasn't been out of this room in too long, wrapped up in blankets with no air circulation. It's the perfect environment for bacteria and fungi to grow. She has an infection of the most heinous kind. We're going to be here for a while, Wex."

"How long is a while?"

"Does it matter?"

He looked back to the patient on the bed. At the black and white fungus that was growing on her nightgown and the seeping fluids that soaked the mattress. "No," he croaked. "No I suppose it doesn't." He went to put the sheet back up.

"No, don't do that," she cautioned. "Get rid of those sheets. Burn them. And we'll get her fresh ones when we're done, here, too."

He nodded and tugged the sheet the rest of

the way down. "How do you manage to stay so calm?" he asked her as he began trying to clean her arms. He quickly soiled his rag, turned, found a dresser to set it on, and retrieved another.

She smiled as she affixed the hose to the wax-coated needle. "It's a secret."

He nodded. "I think she's clean."

Zanje looked up. "No, wash that arm better. It needs to be perfectly clean, or she's going to have a lot more than Red Death to worry about."

This time it was the guard who asked, "What's worse than Red Death?"

"Every other fatal illness in existence," she clipped back. "I have a cure for this one. I don't have a cure for the others."

"Oh."

She handed Wex the blood-filled globe. "Do not drop this," she warned. "If you do, she dies."

He took the glass gingerly. "Blown glass?"

She shook her head. "Don't you start with me, too. Just don't break it."

"Got it."

Wex watched, fascinated, as she worked. She made sure all of her tools were in order precisely where she needed them, arranged herself carefully on the chair the guard provided. She took a fresh rag and soaked it with alcohol, cleaned the woman's arm thoroughly. Then she wrapped a loop around her arm and tied it, slid a rod into the loop, and twisted it until it fit tightly around her bicep. "You," she beckoned to the guard.

He pointed to himself and gave his name. "Aengus."

"Hold this until I tell you not to." He did. Between him and Wex, the side of this lady's bed was very crowded.

She unclipped something on the tube, and blood started crawling down the line. Wex swallowed and shut his eyes. "Wex!" she snapped. His eyes flew open. "Your idiotic fear of needles won't serve you here. If you pass out, you break the glass. She dies. Get over it, understood?"

He swallowed. The rebuke worked. He nodded. He didn't feel good, but he could stomach it. "I understand," he managed.

"You ready?" she asked the guard. He nodded. "Wex?" He nodded, too. She nodded, then bit down on the wax and pulled. She jabbed the woman's arm and unclipped the tube. Wex watched the globe in his hands as it emptied. So did Zanje and Aengus.

"That's all it is?" Aengus asked.

She glared at him. "Is that all it is, he asks," she grumbled. "Centuries of scientific advancement, medicine so elite that it's been banned, and 'that's it' is the thanks I get." She shook her head and started putting the tools she didn't need anymore into her bag. "Do something useful and track down this village's apothecary or healer person or whatever you call it here."

"What do you need?"

"Nothing I'm going to tell you," she said as she reclipped her tube. "Get me someone who knows what she's doing."

He gave her a stormy look, but it didn't even faze her. She glared right back, stare for steely stare. Wex was awed; Zanje was maybe a hundred and fifteen pounds of bone. Aengus was bigger than Wex, perhaps three times Zanje's weight and with excess muscle packed on. And under her scrutiny, Aengus withered and went off to do her bidding.

When he'd gone, she pulled the needle and pressed clean bandage to the wound. Wex was amazed. The entire process was less nausea-inducing than he had initially thought. There wasn't a gaping, messy wound; the illness that plagued the lady of the house was worse than Zanje's method of restoring her. He cheerfully helped Zanje clean up her tools. "You did well, Wex," she praised him. "Now that we're finished, do you have any questions?"

He thought about it. "No, that was brilliant. Thanks for bringing me along."

"Don't thank me yet. This isn't going to be pretty. Remind me to get more money out of Dair when we get back."

Wex looked around at the fine house. Unlike Orelia, these people could afford it. He nodded and said, "Yeah, okay." He looked at the face of the woman whose life he'd just helped save. "It's amazing," he said again. "Amazing, how people come up with these things. How does someone even get the idea of where to begin?"

"Begin what?"

"Looking for a cure. Where do you even start?"

"Well, what do you think?"

He thought about it, standing with his arms crossed and looking out the window as she buttoned the bag closed and regarded him. "Hm. Well, you'd probably have to understand how the disease works, I'd think."

"Correct. Illnesses are caused by many factors. Some are viruses, some bacteria, some fungi. Some are even a person's own immune system attacking their own body."

"You're kidding me!"

"Pathogen interactions are varied. So the first thing to do when you're looking for a cure is to figure out the cause. Discover how your pathogen enters the body and causes ailment, and target the interaction."

"Alright, I'm intrigued. How does this one work?"

"The Red Death isn't a fair example. It's a scourge sent by God."

"Still, I'm curious."

"Still, I won't tell you. This is the one thing that sets me apart from others. A woman can't give away all her secrets."

"You don't trust me?"

"No."

Chapter Eighteen

She was already awake but facing the wall when Berge shuffled down the stairs one heavy step at a time. He went to her cell first and merely stood there, an unwanted presence radiating blue light. She pretended to be asleep, curious as to how long he meant to stay there, watching her. She could smell the fragrance of fresh bread—just baked, not the cold, hard, stale stuff she usually got—and the complex aroma of beer, too. Her stomach snarled in response, but luckily Berge didn't seem to hear it. He sat down on the floor just outside, feet splaying out to either side of his seat. Then, he slid the tin cup of beer over and set the bread next to it. "Nerys," he beckoned.

She turned over in her cell, fixing her gaze upon his knee cap instead of his dangerous eyes—eyes that drew her in and rewrote her sensibilities. She didn't answer. She wasn't sure what to say, so opted instead to let him know with the flicker of eyelashes that she was awake and that she was listening.

He blew out a breath. It sounded unhappy. "You confuse me."

"Is Marc coming back?" she asked instead, ignoring his introduction to an uncomfortable conversation.

"No."

She turned back over on her side, facing the wall. "Go away, Berge." The smell of beer and fresh bread was tantalizing. Putting up a strong front had never been so difficult.

"You're mad at me," he observed.

"Don't treat me like we're friends. The things you've done…"

"Horrible things. Yeah. I know."

"Are you even sorry about it?"

He huffed a short laugh. "Not really."

"Then you confuse me, too," she replied unhappily, curling tighter and willing him to go away. "How can anyone be so cruel?"

"Nerys, I'm just as confused as to how someone can be so…you. You act so self-righteous and saintlike. Yet in doing that you're only denying your baser nature."

"I don't have a base nature," she mumbled.

"Oh, you don't? Have you never wanted to kill? Hurt? Lie? Steal?"

"No," she answered. She had, though. She'd wanted to hurt *him*.

"I don't believe you. All of us are that way, down to the core. Strip away all the pretty. Peel away the layers of pretending to care, charitable intentions you don't even mean, making sacrifices to help out strangers…at the heart of it, deep down, we're all just animals with a need to do violence. Even you."

"You're wrong. It's the opposite. People are good, and when pressed to desperation, have an instinct to lash out to survive."

He went quiet. She didn't want to talk, either.

Ashes pushed underneath her forearm and curled up in between her arm and her face. She snuggled into the creature's sinfully soft fur and let the tears come. He couldn't see them from where he sat. She took slow, measured breaths to stop the hitch of a sob, refusing to cry where he could see.

"Ashes," he barked. He clicked his tongue, summoning the weasel back. She only spun in a circle, curling tighter against Nerys's skin. Berge sighed again. "She likes you. She's never liked anyone except for me. If anything ever happens to me…" he trailed off and hesitated, for so long that Nerys was concerned that he might know something about his near future that he wasn't about to share. "If I die…Would you take care of her for me?"

She didn't answer right away, but she

scratched the creature's tiny skull with a fingertip and promised in her heart. Ashes wasn't guilty of Berge's crimes. She could care for the weasel if the man was dead.

"I have no right to ask it of you, but...she hasn't done anything wrong."

It was an echo of her own thoughts. She smiled to herself. "*When* you die," she corrected cruelly, "I'll care for Ashes."

He breathed a sigh of relief, her asperity apparently lost on him. "Thank you. Nerys."

"Berge?"

"Hm?"

"Why me?"

He hesitated. "I don't know what you mean."

"What's so special about me? What's a Null?"

He swore. "You're asking me a question I don't have an answer to. That's Zanje's smart person crap. I've tried to listen but it bores me."

"Do you know *anything* about it?"

"Yeah. Certain blood goes to certain people. Yours can go to anyone."

Her eyes widened. "Anyone?"

"Yeah."

"Even you?"

He snorted. "I'm not sick. But if I needed it, yeah."

"And Simos?"

"The Rare? Yeah, him too."

"And can he give to me?"

He laughed. "Hell I'm not sure. But I don't think so, no."

"How does that work?" she wondered.

"You're really asking the wrong person," he muttered. "That's just the way it is. I know who I need to find, and she knows who we need to use. I prefer to keep it simple."

"Oh. I see." She did, too. That explained why she was the only Null. What a responsibility to carry. It made her feel special, though, somehow. "I can save anybody," she whispered, her fingertip resting atop Ashes' fuzzy ears.

"Yeah." He went quiet, caught up in his own train of thought. After a few moments, the tin cup scraped against the stone again. "Eat your breakfast, Nerys. It will help you regain your strength."

"I don't want anything from you," she grumbled stubbornly.

"While I can appreciate your toughness, Nerys, you need to eat."

"I'm not hungry." Her stomach growled, betraying her.

Berge laughed. "Oh really? Come on. I made it fresh this morning."

She closed her eyes and gave a surreptitious sniff. The aroma of warm bread and good beer wrenched another voice from her empty belly. Sighing, defeated, she twisted over and sat up. She tugged the plate and the cup toward her, mouth watering.

Ashes uncurled and ran around her in a circle. She shuffled around sideways, chortling. She dashed toward Nerys and back again, as if trying to fight. "What does she want?" Nerys asked him.

"Something to play with. Here." He reached into his pocket and withdrew a small round wafer. He tossed it down between them. Ashes wove in and out around the bars, snagged the toy, and wove in and out back again. She wove back and forth through the bars, a weasel crafting an invisible basket. The two of them only watched and smiled.

"What is that?" she wondered, nibbling on her bread.

He grinned."One of Zanje's socks. Zanje hates Ashes, so…I sewed it together into a toy for her. She loves it."

"I see that. So you sew?"

"Only enough to repair my clothes."

"Too cheap to buy new ones?"

"You got it."

"Looks like someone has taken a shine to you," Simos muttered from across the aisle. Nerys's eyes were drawn there. Simos was just waking up from sleep, rubbing a sore neck and stretching cramped muscles.

Berge stood and bristled, preparing for a fight.

Simos grinned up at him, the picture of provocation. "What's the matter, Nacht? Something on your mind?"

"Setting you on fire comes to it," his chilly voice replied.

"She's not yours." He stood.

"Says who?"

He rolled his shoulders and flexed his fingers, limbering muscles. "I know the kind of man you are, Nacht."

Nerys shivered, suddenly colder than she was a moment before. It was also bluer in the room than it was before, a little brighter. A closer look revealed pinpricks of witchlight, spattering through the air like mist. She didn't know what he planned to do with it, but after seeing how he'd disintegrated Mirdoz and Larric, she really didn't want to find out. "Berge," she beckoned.

Berge ignored her. "And what kind of man is that?"

"A rotten one," Simos easily replied.

Nerys glanced between them. They were remarkably calm for two men that sounded so angry. Simos' grin had flattened out. His eyes promised his death.

Berge glanced at her and then back at

Simos. He grinned, the hostility draining away. "Is that what you say to the man that brings you breakfast?"

Simos's eyes narrowed. "I don't see a second cup of that beer."

"Well I only have two hands. Rather unreasonable for you to expect that I can carry enough down here for all of you."

"Did someone say beer?" one of the men further down questioned tentatively. "Oh, I haven't had a beer in ages."

"Ohh, I smell fresh bread," one of the women moaned. "It smells *so good.*"

"Yeah. In my infinite generosity, I baked for you sad sacks this morning. Two shakes." He flashed a grin at Nerys and then went back up the stairs.

Simos was quiet before snapping his gaze back to Nerys. "What the hell just happened?" he wondered aloud.

She shrugged. "He baked."

"Hm. I'll believe it when I see it."

She smiled to herself, wondering if maybe she didn't have a positive influence on him after all. A couple minutes later, he came back down the stairs with a basket loaded with bread, a string of tin cups, and an earthenware pitcher. "Say please," he demanded, standing in the center and waiting.

They were quiet, unsure of what to do. This

was quite outside the realm of possibilities until just now. It was Megra that broke first. "Can I please have some bread and beer?"

He turned toward her voice and made his way. He handed over a lump of soft bread, a little larger than a dinner roll, handed her a cup and asked that she hold it. Then he poured a little beer into it and tilted the pitcher back up. The rest of Megra's cellmates caught on quickly, asking politely and crowding around the front of the cell. In no time at all, the group of Baggage had a hearty breakfast. Berge shot a look at Simos cell and a smile at Nerys before he moved onto the Minors. In no time at all, the prisoners all had bread and beer except for Simos.

He stopped in front of Simos' cell. "Want?"

Simos' expression was carefully neutral. Nerys could only imagine that he was having trouble coming to terms with what had just happened. Berge had always been the face of evil to him. This new Berge did not make sense. When Simos refused to answer, Berge simply set his plate down on the floor outside his reach and poured a cup of beer. He leaned against the prison wall and slid down until he was seated much the same way as Simos himself. Then he drank from the pitcher and nibbled on the bread, leaning against the wall between Nerys's cell and Simos'. He watched Simos and made a show of his enjoyment, moaning with every bite.

It was so normal, like two bickering friends at the cafe, that Nerys laughed. Berge smiled. And then finally Simos broke. "Would you pass it here, please?"

Berge looked over at him, his head tipped up against the wall. "I don't know. Would I?"

"Don't toy with me, Nacht."

"I'm the one with the beer." He raised the pitcher in a salute and drank. Simos glared at him. Berge smirked and said a single word. "Dance."

"What?"

"I said dance. Dance for it."

"No," he denied, hostile once more.

"Alright. I'll give it to Ashes, then." He turned back toward the weasel. She was on her back, locked in a battle to the death against Zanje's former sock. Berge clicked his tongue. "Ashes, come here, now." She stopped kicking at it, and turned her head in his direction. "Want some breakfast?"

She kicked the sock viciously and shuffled on out of the cell. He held out Simos' bread to her. She snatched it and ran behind Nerys to eat it. Berge turned back to Simos. "Still time."

"It's pretty good, Simos!" one of the others shouted to him from down the prison.

Simos looked past Nerys, though all he

could see of the weasel was her twitchy ears. He licked his lips. The sound of his stomach rumbling filled the space. "At least give me the beer," he muttered. "Weasels don't drink." He added a belated, "Please."

Berge clicked his tongue. Ashes leapt over Nerys's leg and came back out to the center. She sniffed up over the rim of the tin cup. Simos was indignant. "You've got to be fucking kidding me." She put her face into the cup.

Simos leapt to his feet. He made sure to give Berge his healthiest glare. And then, much to Nerys's amusement, he began to dance.

Chapter Nineteen

A cold breeze ghosted over her bare shoulders. Were her blood not a raging inferno of heat, it might have forced her to put on a warm coat and a scarf. As it stood, it only made her shut her eyes in appreciation. She tilted her head to the side, leaning into it like a lover's caress. She inhaled the scent of the wind. Luckily, it was a west wind. Were it an east wind, it might have carried the scent of the pit with it.

She laced her fingers together and leaned over the rail, reflecting on her recent medical miracle and how hotly opposed to it Berge had been. Now that she was returned, it was only a matter of time before he sought her out. His pattern was as predictable as the phases of the moon. Far off in the distance, she could just barely make out the lights of Quorath. They turned the sky a russet color, like a blotch of decay in the otherwise crisp and flawless night sky. Oddly appropriate, given the fester of humanity that lived below that sky.

She felt him like an black omen before she saw him. She smiled, taking perverse pleasure in having him figured out so well. "Berge," she greeted the night.

His arms encircled her from behind, and he crushed her against his chest. His hot breath fanned against her ear. "How dare you," he breathed. His voice and his words were often at odds. It was clear by his actions that he wasn't angry.

She smiled and leaned away from his face. "What have I done now?" she drawled.

"First you run off to save the viper's wife. Then you leave me here with the viper himself." He swayed back and forth with her in his arms, his face captured in the crook of her shoulder.

"Mm, except he's a dog, not a viper."

She felt his grin against her ear. "Did you save his bitch?"

"In a sense. Did you kill him yet?"

His breath stopped. Zanje's smirk deepened. His hesitation could only mean that he hadn't been quite as evil as he believed he was. Berge's resolve was weakening. It was possible he was nearing the end of his usefulness after all. "No, I didn't kill him," he grated from between clenched teeth. "But that doesn't mean I didn't want to."

She chuckled from low in her throat. "Oh? Is

that so? Bergeron Nacht didn't kill a man he so badly wanted to kill?" She turned out of his hold. Her fingers curled around the railing, and she leaned back against it to scrutinize. "Dare I believe that you spared his life to please me?" She regarded him from beneath long lashes.

His eyes drifted half-closed. "You wish. Doing so would mean that I cared about you."

"And you don't?"

"You know how deeply I hate you, Zanj. Don't pretend anything's changed between us."

Her gaze fell to the floor of the balcony. She put on a show of mock disappointment, even going so far as to pout. "How tragic. And here I thought we were just warming up to each other. You wound me, Berge." She turned back around, leaning on her elbows and looking out across a blank field glowing dimly in the quarter moon. She knew how the position would inflame him, and it did.

He came up behind her and leaned as she leaned. They fit together like lock and key. His arms splayed out in front of them both, caging her in, a predator honing in on its prey. Meanwhile, she only relaxed, just a woman at ease upon her balcony at the end of an evening. She always ignored him, and it always pissed him off.

"You aren't going to ignore me today," he snarled, nipping at her ear. "You've made me very unhappy these past few weeks. I'm not taking no for an answer." He buried his nose in the hollow of her throat beneath her ear and began running his hands all over her.

"Do you remember when we first met?" she mused aloud.

He paused, his throat rattling with a frustrated growl. She could have laughed.

"Do you remember how you told me you thought mankind was beyond redemption, and how we ought to just let ourselves go, embrace our...what words did you use? Our basest selves?" He remained still. "I think that first day was the day I loved you the most."

He released the breath he'd been holding as a resigned sigh. "And now?"

"Ever since that day, we've hated each other just a little more each day. Where are we now?"

"I don't know, Zanj," he muttered. "Why don't you explain it to me? Use all those big science words you love so much."

"Hm," she sighed. She withdrew a cigarette and took her time about lighting it. Berge gave up on his advance and joined her at the rail. He leaned back against it and crossed his arms, watching her. She took a slow drag, held it. She savored the taste, then let it stream out from between her lips. "When they burned down the gates, my father holed himself up here in this room, but not after hiding all of his best books and me. He never told a soul what he was working on, but he taught me everything he knew. 'Someday,' he said, 'they're going to want it all back. When that day comes, we must be as we always were before. They can't help it,' he said. 'They can't see the way that we see. But a day will come when they will need us again.' I always thought he was crazy. If they were going to kill us before, why should there ever come a time when we help them?

"My father thought mankind was worth saving. But my father was just a theory that needed to be improved upon. Mankind can be made better, but the only way we're going to fix it is to purge this godforsaken plague."

"We've been over this before. Why are you bringing it up now?"

She smiled and looked away. "You're drifting," she accused. "And you're only here now to test your rot."

"My what?"

"Your rot," she insisted. "You're starting to doubt what we're working on. You're starting to have hope, and hope is a poison."

"I've never had hope," he shot back angrily. "I'm not about to start now."

She chuckled. "You haven't? The first time we went to bed, what was that?"

"Lust."

"Oh," she responded sarcastically. He

scowled. She straightened and rested her hands upon the rail. "I appreciate your work, Bergeron Nacht. You've always been a ruthless bastard. The streets fear your name. That's useful. But you remember what I told you, that day we negotiated the terms of our relationship?"

He bared his teeth and got in her face. "You said you'd kill me the moment I wasn't useful anymore. Are you threatening me? Is that what you're trying to say, Zanj? That I'm no longer useful to your cause? You going to kill me now? Do you think I care about that any more now than I did? Because I don't."

She threw her cigarette off the balcony. "It might be. Is it true? Are you going to betray me, Berge?"

He grabbed her shoulders tightly, squeezing, his face a tight portrait of rage. His pupils were blown out. She could see she'd touched a nerve, perhaps saying all of the thoughts aloud that he'd been plaguing himself with. She watched the emotions wrestle with his face, watched doubt turn to anger turn to melancholy and back again. Toying with Berge was one of her favorite pastimes. His grip was painful but not worrisome. Berge would never dare to hurt her.

He wanted her too badly. Always had, and always would. She knew him like she knew herself. He was a despicable man who flirted

with disaster.
    She was the disaster.

Chapter Twenty

"No you can't come in with me. Zanje says you're not allowed in the house." Her fat tail shuffled back and forth. She shifted on her feet, nails clicking on the stone, but never crossed the line of the threshold. Her greying muzzle fell open with a puppy smile. *Please, Wex!*

He went to shut the door. She stared up at him. He stared back. Her tail wagged faster. He looked toward the castle interior, wondering if he could get away with sneaking her in this one time. Then he remembered Zanje's comment about killing her. She wasn't the type to crack jokes. He looked back to Maxine. Her tail picked up speed again. "Look at you. You're adorable." He grinned and rubbed her head. "Tell you what. I'll leave the door open so you can see me. But you stay out here, okay? Wait here," he bade Maxine. He held his broad hand out, fingers splayed. She tried to lick it, but missed. If she only crossed the doorway, she wouldn't have, but she was a good dog and waited outside. He wondered, as he often did, if she understood his words or just his tone.

When he was sure she wouldn't follow him in, he walked further into the house a few steps. Then, he turned around to check. She stood in the doorway, tail wagging slowly back and forth. *I'll wait.* He smiled and said, "Good girl. You stay there. I'll be right back, okay?" Her tail wagged faster for just a second.

He crossed through the enormous main entry hall. It boasted a peach colored marble floor, an expensive remnant of a previous age. He appreciated the artistry, but the floors saddened him. They were a lovely piece of architecture, but up in this dark castle, they were never seen. They also hadn't been cleaned in at least a decade. Zanje didn't seem to value keeping the castle clean, probably because she only used a few of its rooms. His footsteps left a trail in the grime, but he appreciated the floor nonetheless. Perhaps, someday he would clean it just to please his own sensibilities. Someday.

He made his way through to the back hall. A set of stone stairs led down into the lower level where Zanje kept her laboratory. There was a grander staircase in the main hall that led up to the rest of the castle, the part that towered into the sky. This one, however, led deep into the eaves of the earth. First, her laboratory. Further down, who really knew? Castles usually had dungeons. Of course, with the rate at which Zanje went through wine, a cellar was a more likely option. Maybe a dungeon repurposed into a wine cellar. He whistled a song as he descended the stairs. Berge had left him a note telling him to clean up the laboratory. He and Zanje were seducing one another on the balcony, and he hadn't had a chance to tidy up whatever he'd been working on in the lab.

Not for the first time, he marveled at Zanje's witchlights swaying just below the ceiling in the hallway of the lower level. They were bright enough to keep the entire hallway illuminated, and yet she wasn't even in the room. It took extraordinary control over the Craft to be able to do such a thing, and Zanje kept the entire castle lit at all times. He filed a mental note to ask her about it sometime.

He shoved open the door to the laboratory. Blue light flooded the hallway. He squinted against the onslaught of brightness and stepped into the lab. Zanje didn't usually like people to be in her lab unless she was there, but given that it was Berge that had given him permission, he figured it was probably okay.

He took two steps into the lab and froze. His stomach lurched into his feet, his mouth went dry, and he forgot how to breathe. There in the bed he'd once woken up in, so long ago now, was a corpse. There was a needle stuck in the forearm still, and the tube hung from that. Where the tube trailed upon the floor like a vine, the man's blood had spilled upon the floor. The entire laboratory was covered in it. Blood made sticky, dried up rivers all the way to the drain in the center of the laboratory floor. Wex had once seen the laboratory as a room of learning and exploration. This time, to his eyes, it looked like little more than a slaughterhouse. He dug a fist into his own stomach, quelling nausea. His eyes wouldn't leave the bloody floor. He refused to look at the dead man.

"Left a mess for you to clean up in the lab," the note had said. A mess. Just a mess. Just a little clean up job for you to do real quick, Wex. No big deal. Wex sucked in several deep breaths, but each one tasted more like blood than the one before, until his tongue was bathed in the flavor of iron and death. His stomach heaved and pitched. Not wanting to vomit all over Zanje's laboratory floor, even if it was a disaster already, he ducked back out into the hallway and shut the door behind him.

Time for a pep talk. "Get ahold of yourself Wex. You knew something was up. She's outright mean and Berge clearly has a screw loose. What were you expecting?" Not murder. Definitely not murder. He crumpled against the wall and slid down, his thoughts whirring with what his eyes had just seen. Logic. Logic, logic, logic, he told himself. Why would two people committed to saving lives take a life instead? She said blood restored itself. She said they gave them time to recover before they bled them again.

He peered into the doorway again. At the body. The dead body.

His mind conjured up the image of Zanje coming at him with a needle. There was a needle in the arm of the dead man. Then there was the blood all over the floor, leaked straight from the dead man on the bed. Blood out. The globe in Zanje's hands. Blood out, for a reason. Needles, needles…"I don't know," he muttered. He did, though. It was shockingly clear. "This is madness. Madness." He dropped his head into his hands, taking slow deep breaths to try to calm his nerves.

Zanje lied.

His first reasonable conclusion was that he wanted out. Desperately. He considered jumping into the snowcraft with Maxine and picking a direction at random and just driving. Wherever he ended up would be just fine.

But there was no outrunning the Red Death. It was everywhere, or so he'd been led to believe. And Zanje and Berge had the only cure to it, even if they were obtaining it by grim method. Unless…he could maybe steal the cure and give it to someone else? Maybe they could take the knowledge and come up with something better?

Or maybe they'd kill him just for having it.

There had to be a better way. There just had to be a better way. Unless there wasn't. And the more he thought about it, the more it looked like there wasn't. If the cure was in the blood, then they needed the blood. There were really only so many ways to obtain blood.

In truth, though he'd done some studying, he hadn't been interested in biological science. He much preferred physics and chemistry, machines and forces and reactions that ended in a boom. Zanje *had* studied biological science. And while he didn't always like her attitude, he had to admit that she was classy, sophisticated, and remarkably intelligent. She was the most self-aware person he'd ever met. Whatever had happened in this lab, it simply had to be related to how his life had been saved. In the end, he decided that it wasn't for him to question. He liked Berge, and Zanje didn't strike him as the kind of person who would be cruel without cause.

Yeah, that was it. In fact, it made a lot more sense that way. It explained why Berge and Zanje were so secretive and short shrift about it. Their methods were controversial and costly. It might even cause them a measure of emotional pain. They were doing a dirty, detestable job in order to save the lives of others. It was a concept that his heart accepted, and the only one that the man could accept and be okay with himself. Nodding, he got shakily to his feet, mentally preparing to go face-to-face with the corpse.

Besides, when he thought about it, he realized Berge had tried to warn him a long time ago, and he'd kind of shrugged off his attempt. Decent guy, Berge.

He opened the door slowly, as if he might actually scare the dead person. He tilted his face up and away and watched the corpse out of the corner of his eye, as if only seeing him with a small portion of his eye might make the scene any less grisly. "I'm sorry about your luck," he murmured to the dead guy. It did make him feel better to talk to the dead. "Rest easy, though, friend. Your sacrifice has made it so that other people might live. You won't be forgotten. You will be missed." And then, on a whim, he kissed his fingers and pressed them to the dead man's forehead. The skin was cold and rubbery. Of all the thoughts he could have had, the one that pervaded was that he thought that was odd. It didn't even feel real. He frowned, still wrapping his brain around being in the same room as a dead body.

"I suppose by cleaning up the mess, he

wants me to remove you from the lab. And maybe to wash up the blood. Don't know if I can handle that part, but I'll at least have to try." Sighing unhappily, he grabbed the dead man's dangling arm. He yanked the needle free quickly and cast it across the floor, not wishing to dwell upon it. Then he dragged the man up and slid him over his broad shoulders. He was heavy, but settled nicely and didn't slide. Deciding he'd have to clean up the blood later, he turned slowly and made his way toward the door. It took some careful maneuvering to keep the corpse from bumping his face into the frame —though he was dead, Wex didn't wish to be disrespectful—but eventually, he made it out alright.

Maxine's tail picked up speed when she spied him. She was still standing patiently just outside the door. She barked when she saw him. Then her nose went up into the air. She sniffed, and immediately Wex felt guilty. "Don't worry, Maxine," he warned her. Her head hung low. Her tail wagged in shorter arcs, as if she wasn't sure if she was supposed to be happy to see him or upset by the corpse upon his shoulders. "I know, I know."

He made it about fifty feet before he realized he didn't know where to take the body.

"Oy, Wex!" It was Berge.

Wex turned toward the door, but there was

no one there.

"Up here!" Wex looked up. Seven stories up. There was Berge, standing on that balcony from before. He was waving one long arm over his head, and he wasn't wearing a shirt. "If you go that way"—he pointed—"about sixty yards into the trees there's a big-ass pit. You can drop him in there."

Oh. That was where. He nodded and got to work.

Chapter Twenty-One

Two months later...

Berge swirled his glass of whiskey, thinking about how Zanje swirled her wine. It wasn't the same. It was better. The ice made a lovely crystalline chime as it tapped against the glass. He smiled.

Wex looked into his glass and frowned. "So what is this?"

Berge pouted. "It's whiskey. You've never seen whiskey?"

"No, can't say I have. Beer, yeah. Whiskey?" He shook his head. Then he took a long, deep swallow of the stuff. Then he looked at his glass with unpleasant surprise and even blew out a breeze of what Berge could only assume was some of the most scalding air to have ever traveled the man's throat. "Hoo!" he exclaimed.

"Yeah?"

"Oh. That's delightful."

"Fuck yes it is." He clinked his glass against Wex's and took a drink from his own.

"So."

"So."

"You and Zanje."

"Yeah?"

"How long have you been together?"

Berge shook his head. "We aren't."

"Oh." He looked genuinely confused. "You're not?"

"Nope."

"I saw you…it just looked like…I thought you were is all."

"Nah. Zanje's…Zanje. She's like smoke on the wind. The moment you try to grab her, she dissipates."

"Ah."

"Why? You wanna have at?"

He frowned into his whiskey glass. "No, I don't think I should."

Berge was filled with a perverse glee just to think of it. "Ohh, come on! You should! You two would make a great couple!" His voice was too earnest, and Wex wasn't falling for it.

He shook his head and frowned. "No, she's…above my pay grade. A little too much for me, I think."

Wise man. Wiser man than me. He clapped Wex on the shoulder but said nothing.

"Hey, Berge…"

"Yeah."

"How old were you when you killed your first man?"

"Oh, let's see…fourteen? Yeah. That sounds about right."

"Still a kid? Didn't your parents find out?"

Berge grimaced. "Sort of, I suppose." He took a long swallow of whiskey, finding comfort in the burn.

His face scrunched up with confusion. "Sort of? How does that work?"

"Well. The first man I killed was my father. Not sure what happened to my mother."

Wex was shocked. Poor guy. "You killed your own *father?*"

"Yeah, he was a real bastard."

"Still. Your father. Wow." He threw back his whiskey. Then he stared at his glass and grinned. "Delightful," he said again. He shook his head in awe. "Mind if I have some more?"

"Help yourself. I can't remember the last time I had a drink with someone I didn't want to stab or fuck."

Wex gave him a sideways look. "I hope that's not you suggesting either of those things."

He couldn't help it; the images conjured themselves. Wex was a big, burly man with a beard and a bald head. Berge burst out laughing, and it felt…good. "You know, Wex… you're not a bad guy." He poured another whiskey.

Wex grinned and reclaimed his glass. The glass looked tiny in his hands. He just about had the glass to his lips before his smile slid away and he gave Berge the same askance look. "You saying that only has me more worried."

"Relax. I'm not going to poke you with anything remotely pointy or phallic. Drink your whiskey and shut up."

He laughed back. "You know, that day you had me take that body to the pit. You know, the first one?"

"That was months ago, but yeah?"

His tone grew more serious. "I almost quit that day. I was about to grab Maxine and run."

"You probably should have."

"No!" he denied.

Berge frowned and looked down into his glass, guilt souring his conscience.

"No, Berge, I mean it! This?" He made a sweeping arc with the hand holding the glass, amber whiskey sloshing to the rim. "All of this? It's just one tiny, ugly piece in a bright, big picture."

"I think you've lost your goddamned mind. This kind of job is alright for people like me. I was born in filth. I thrive in it. I live for it. You, though?"

"Oh, am I not rough enough to handle a little blood?"

"Wex. You're not a bad guy." He frowned at that, realizing the words that were leaving his mouth. He tasted the syllables, then nodded, coming to a decision. "You're not a bad guy. It's not that I don't think you can hack it, man, it's that you shouldn't."

"No." He shook his head. "This is…man, if I believed in God, I'd say this is God's work. We're doing good things. Have you ever heard the phrase 'the end justifies the means?'"

"No."

"It means that if the end result is more favorable than the unfavorable conditions needed to reach it, then…that's okay. So if we have to hurt a select few people to save ten times that many, then we're actually doing more good than harm."

He didn't like hearing those words from Wex. Anyone else, yeah. Not Wex. "It smells like horse in here," Berge declared, changing the subject.

"Yeah," he agreed, albeit slightly confused. "It's a stable."

Berge glanced about, noting the placement of the rafter beams and the quality of the roofing. When the wind blew, not a breeze of it cut through the walls, and nothing creaked as if it might fall over. "Yeah, I got it, buddy. It's just that there hasn't been a horse in the stables since before Zanje was even born."

"How do you know that?"

"She told me."

Wex looked around, too, thinking about what he said. Then, "Huh. That is weird."

Berge shook his head. "I fucking hate this place. How do you live out here?"

"It's not so bad. It's pretty warm out here, actually, and the castle—" he cut off abruptly.

"The castle...what?"

Wex's eyes darted sheepishly. "I shouldn't have said."

"Said what?"

"It's just...a little dusty in there for me."

Berge stared. He'd been expecting something more dire. "You're a *clean freak?*"

"I wouldn't say that," he defended. "It's just...well, it's filthy. And you've got old, beautiful marble in there just dying to shine. You know what I'd do? I'd throw all the shutters open. Just for a day. One good, long, beautiful day. Let the wind into your lives for a day and blow all that dust out. Then wax the floors of the main hall and get all the cobwebs out, throw open the curtains. I bet it cleans up real nice."

"You might be right," he admitted. "But when I said I hate this place, I meant this *place*. The whole place."

"Oh. Well, I don't."

"You just got here."

"It's been, what, six months?"

Berge froze with a mouth full of whiskey. Had Nerys really survived six months? He counted back as far as he could, but he wasn't much for keeping track of the dates. "More or less."

They sat in companionable silence for a time. Between the two of them, they finished off the whiskey. Maxine even got to try it, though she didn't seem to be much of a fan. Berge knew better than to give any to Ashes. She was a cheap date. Besides, Ashes was prowling the stalls looking for rodents. For a blind weasel, she was a proficient hunter.

Finally, when he was just drunk enough, he broached the subject. "I hate her."

"Hm?"

"I hate her. Zanje. I hate her."

"No you don't," Wex argued.

He wasn't half as drunk as Berge was. And in fact, it rather pissed him off. "I do. I hate her more than anybody. She's awful. She's evil. And I hate her."

"You're just drunk," Wex told him with a sly smile. "You'll get over it."

He picked at his fingers, spiraling deeper into a dark abyss he didn't want Wex to see. "No, I won't. But it doesn't matter."

"If you say so. Hey. Shouldn't you be thinking about sleep?"

"Why?"

Wex settled back against the hay with his hands folded behind his head. "You have to work tomorrow, don't you?"

Berge didn't want to think about it. He wished he had more whiskey.

"I mean, unless you really weren't kidding about that roll in the hay." He patted the space next to him and threw seductive eyes in Berge's direction, then grinned.

It was just enough to make him crack a smile. "I'm not into the desperate type," Berge told him with a wink. "So, sleep it is." He stood and brushed off bits of hay.

"Goodnight, Angel!" Wex called as Berge opened the stable door.

"Goodnight," he chuckled back.

Chapter Twenty-Two

She shamed herself by how pleased she was when the door opened. Her heart leapt at the first creak, and her chin lifted at the first glow of blue. "Berge!" His name leapt off her tongue too easily. She only stopped herself from jumping to her feet by rolling up onto her knees. She grasped the bars and pressed her face to them, ready for the moment he came into view.

Berge only glanced in her direction for a moment. Then he turned the other way down the aisle, saying nothing.

Her heart fell, thinking perhaps she'd wronged him somehow. She opened her mouth to say something else, but Simos interrupted. "What's gotten into you, Nerys?" he whispered fiercely.

She shrugged helplessly and sank to the floor, staring between her knees. Her earlier shame increased tenfold. "I'm not sure what you mean," she lied, keeping her voice low enough that Berge couldn't hear.

"You. And *him*. It's disgusting."

She bit her lip to keep from championing his defense. Berge neither needed her defense nor deserved it. She knew his list of crimes was long. She just wasn't wholly convinced he was beyond redemption. "I can save him," she responded. "He told me I can save anyone," she added much more softly, for herself. *And I believe him*. She doubted that he was thinking of himself when he'd told her that, though, but it hardly seemed important right now.

"What is it you see in him?" Simos persisted. "There's nothing good about him. At all."

"I know," she answered, troubled. "I'm not silly enough to justify the things he's done."

"You're a sweet girl, Nerys. You don't need that kind of trouble."

"I might die here, Simos," she confessed bitterly. "I need to believe in something, don't I? You have your God. What do I have?"

"You have to make your own religion," he told her fervently.

"And what does that even mean?" she demanded, gaining ferocity. "Who am I? Why am I here? Why are *any of us* here? If your God is all-powerful, why is *he* here?" she hissed, meaning Berge. "Does not your God preach forgiveness? Does not your God tell you that He will be the judge of our actions? Does not God tell you to put your faith in Him and love the people that struggle the most?"

Simos was quiet a moment before he finally answered, "Berge isn't struggling, though, Nerys. He has abandoned all sense of human decency. He has turned his back on God and walks a path into darkness. Don't follow him down that path."

She turned back toward Berge himself. "I'll follow him," she promised. "I'll follow him just far enough to bring him back to the light. "I guess my religion is just to make the best of everything. He's in pain, Simos. He's begging for help, you just can't hear him. Maybe I'm the only one who can. Maybe this is my purpose."

Simos was shaking his head. "You're mistaken. And I fear that this mistake may cost you your life."

A scream erupted further down the hall. "No! No, please! I can't, please! Berge! Berge!" The voice devolved into a desperate wail, and the sound of a body hitting a dull surface came next.

"On your feet," Berge grumbled. The wailing continued.

Nerys pressed her face further into the bars so that she could see further down. Just in time to see Berge cock back his hand and strike the woman across the face. She yelped and fell upon her hands. It was Lissa. In the months since Marc's death, Kalyria and Lissa had had to go upstairs more than their share to make up for the deficit. Lissa was weak, probably weaker than Kalyria. Had Berge chosen Kalyria, neither might have died. She wondered if it was an oversight or if it was deliberate, but figured it was probably best not to know. Her stomach shrank deep into her belly, filled with the leaden substance of dread.

Berge was spiraling deeper and deeper into oblivion and showed no sign of slowing down nor stopping. She watched him strike Kalyria again and again, lost to his anger and frustration. She turned away and shut her eyes against the sight, unable to cope with the view. She wanted so badly for him to see something good in humanity, had tried to be that for him in every way that she could. Kalyria wailed and whimpered, her voice muffled against her arm or the ground. Nerys dared not look.

Simos's cruel voice infiltrated her solitude. "And you still think he can be saved," he whispered for her ears alone.

She squeezed her eyes shut even further, and tears spilled down her cheeks. She heard his insult, yet she still believed in Berge. It broke her heart to do so, but she couldn't not.

"Nacht, you bastard, let her up for God's sake!" Simos shouted. He hung through the bars, his arms upraised in helplessness. "You want someone to vent your frustrations on, I'll gladly tangle with you." He curled his hand into a fist, then released his middle finger in a rude gesture.

"If I had any reason to use you, Rare, I'd treat you just as sweetly. You're a useless sack of shit and I hope you rot in there and die."

"My name is Simos, witch fucker. Come over here and show me how sweet you can be."

Berge laughed. It was a sinister sound.

Nerys opened her eyes and stared at the wall ahead. To her sight, it was just her three walls and Simos. Simos hung through the bars, taking turns glaring down the hallway and shooting a piteous expression in her direction. He felt sorry for her, and she couldn't even blame him for it. She was messed up. Her happiness all hinged on whether or not her actions could pull Berge back from the darkness. And she couldn't. It was all too clear.

"Neeerysss," Berge purred. She held her breath. "Neeerysss. I know you're back there Nerys."

Her shoulders racked with silent sobs. "Berge."

"What's wrong Nerys? You crying?" He didn't sound concerned, nor sorry.

"No," she sobbed.

"You can cry Nerys. I love it when they cry.

It's my favorite part. Cry for me Nerys. Sing me a song." His voice dripped venom. He was in such a sorry state as to be hardly recognizable. He had never spoken to her as he did now. Crazed, possessed perhaps.

She shut her eyes and scooted to the back of her cell. Simos shrank away from his bars, too, as Berge came into view. His eyes were hard and cruel. He pressed his hands to the bars of her cell and leaned toward her, grinning wolfishly. "Hello, Nerys."

She forced herself to meet his eyes, trying to channel some of Simos' courage. She could only imagine how she must look with tears streaming down her face. "Hello, Berge." Her voice shook.

"Why so glum?"

"You wouldn't understand." Especially since she didn't.

"Oh? Try me."

She shook her head.

"Tell me!" he shouted. "I'm so *sick* and *tired* of people assuming I'm an idiot," he snarled through clenched teeth.

"Maybe you shouldn't act like one," Simos shot back.

Berge slammed his hands against the bars. The iron rattled and crashed. Nerys flinched. "Well, Nerys? Are you scared of me now? You've been so *brave* up until now. Now you look as meek as a mouse. You're such a cute little mouse, too." He leered through the bars at her.

She shrank into her knees and just wished he'd go away.

The sound of feet pounding up the stairs interrupted Berge's torture. "Mother fucker!" Berge growled as he whirled. Simos' gaze followed his, eyes widening. Nerys craned her neck around. Berge dashed toward the stairs, and Nerys scrambled toward the bars of her cell. She crashed into the iron just as the woman's foot disappeared from view with Berge's hand lunging after it. Lissa howled with defeat just as Berge's fingers clamped around her ankle. He pulled, dragging her down the steps as she shrieked for help. It was sad to watch; there was no one within miles of the castle that could have heard or helped, and even if there was, no one could withstand the level of witchery in Zanje's castle. Be it Berge or Zanje or both, Nerys knew enough of the castle's workings to know that no one stood a chance against them in a fight.

She watched in mute horror as the woman's skirt was dragged up as she was dragged down. Her knees banged painfully into every step. Her nails dragged at the walls of the staircase, gritting against stone, trying to slow her descent back into the dungeon. She'd had a bare taste of freedom, a chance to escape certain death. Now, no matter what happened, she'd be dead by nightfall. Either Berge would beat her to death or the needle would do the rest.

If Lissa died to Berge's fists, Kalyria would have to bleed. She wouldn't have more than a month left, either.

"Berge!" Nerys cried. "Berge, stop! Please, don't!"

Lissa howled and howled without words, begging, desperate.

"I'm gonna fucking kill you!" Berge growled, pawing, tearing, pulling. "Come here! Get over here!"

The rest of the dungeon was eerily silent but for the two of them and Nerys.

"Berge!" She couldn't see through the haze of tears. "Stop! *Stop!*" She drummed her hands against the iron bars.

He didn't.

She had to do something. There had to be something she could do to save Lissa. There had to be a way to keep him from killing. Maybe Kalyria could go. Maybe…maybe…"Berge, I'll go!"

Berge stopped fighting.

Lissa stopped fighting back.

Simos stared.

Nerys's mouth fell open, surprised at the words that had left her mouth. Despite her own measure of shock, though, she felt the right of it. It was what she had to do. "I'll go," she said softly into the perfect silence. "Don't take Lissa."

"No," Berge told her flatly. "We never use a Null where another will do. There aren't enough of them in the world."

"I want to go," she insisted. "So take me instead."

"Not gonna happen, Nerys."

"If you take Lissa, she'll die!" she shouted.

"Yeah, probably."

Lissa whimpered quietly, doing her best not to call attention to herself.

"I won't," Nerys insisted. "If you take Lissa, you'll be out of a Prime, and your other Prime will be dead within a month. If you take me, I'll be fine and you can keep both of them."

He wavered, whether because he was shocked or because he considered it was left to question.

"Nerys, no!" Simos cautioned. It was meant to be for her ears alone, but Berge heard it.

And when Berge heard it..."Nerys," he barked. "You *want* to take her place? You'll bleed, *willingly*, in the place of a stranger? *For* a stranger?"

She nodded vigorously. "Yes!"

"What?" He cupped a hand to his ear. Lissa curled in upon herself upon the stair, eyes wide and staring, hardly daring to believe.

"*Nerys,*" Simos hissed. "Stop this. You could be bled again next week. You won't make it."

"I don't care," she hissed back. "I can do this. Lissa will definitely die. I won't. I'm stronger than that. Berge, yes, I want to go. Let me do this."

"Nerys!"

"*Nerys!*"

"*I said let me out of here! I want to go!*" she yelled.

Berge stared. She stared back. His eyes were wider than usual, dark, glittering. But there was a spark of confusion there, like he wasn't quite sure what to think. She'd confused him, at least briefly. He shook his head almost imperceptibly. His lips curved in a rueful smirk. Then he tugged Lissa along, back down the stairs and back to her cell, her legs dragging along the floor behind her. If anything, Lissa wailed even harder than when she'd been removed from it. She collapsed into it in a heap.

Nerys's heart pounded, hardly daring to believe her own courage. Her knees knocked together. She was brave, but she was also scared. She'd volunteered for the unthinkable, and it was an odd mixture of feelings. Terror, and excitement. Her heart soared with the wonderment of having done something right.

Something that made a difference. When she realized that, she stood a little straighter. Her knees stopped shaking.

Berge sauntered down the aisle and came to a stop in front of Nerys's cell. He took his time about unlocking it, his eyes never leaving hers. There was something reserved and intense lurking deep within them. He never spoke a word. The key turned. The door shivered upon its hinges. It creaked and squealed as it was slowly pulled outward. Then he proffered his hand like a gentleman at a courtly dance, though there was never a dashing smile upon his handsome face. His eyes fell upon his hand, waiting for her agreement.

She took a breath. Truth be told, she was a little thrown off by his invitation. He didn't grab her, drag her, beat her, as he had with Lissa. It seemed a little unfair. In a twisted way, she rather hoped that he would. She didn't want to be special to him. For if he treated her differently, it meant that he did harbor especial feelings of fondness for her, and she was frightened of what that might mean. She held her breath. Her eyes fell upon his hand.

She slid her fingers into it.

She tripped on her way down the stairs. Her head was spinning, and the stairs were already dark. Berge spoke to her gently, though she didn't recall any of the words, only that his presence and the calming tone of his voice gave her enough strength. She couldn't see, though she knew his witchlight lit the way, but he led her by the hand. Her vision wasn't working properly. It was grey, black, and blurry, with blinding spots of blue. She felt as if she were spinning in circles though she walked forward as straight as she could. Her stomach turned in the opposite direction from her eyes.

In a way, it made her giddy, but when she tried to giggle it only came out as the whine of someone trying desperately not to vomit. "Berge, help," was the only thing she could remember saying the entire time.

She tripped on the last step and would have pitched forward entirely, flat upon her face, but he caught her before she hit the unforgiving stone floor. He said something quietly into her ear. His hand spread flat against her ribcage, holding her up with inhuman strength and willpower. He kept talking, his voice low, so that none other would hear. She remained strong all the way up until the point where he left her there shivering and had gone away. The door to the top of the stairs shut, every creak and cry of it as familiar as her own hand.

As soon as it shut, her eyes rolled back into her head and she blacked out.

She came to and blacked out more times

than she had the ability to remember. She was hot and cold at the same time, icy shivers and blazing shivers taking turns ravaging her veins and bathing her lungs with panic. Her stomach pitched and heaved. She threw up a lot, and if she was lucky, she threw up when she was conscious enough to miss her clothing. Her mind spun dizzily. She was certain she was fading and threw in all of her remaining effort to simply not die, focusing with all her might on listening for Simos's panicked voice across from the aisle, using it like a beacon on a stormy shoreline. She tried to tell him that she was going to be okay. Tried to tell him not to worry so much. She didn't know if he heard or not, but he never stopped shouting. She wasn't coherent enough to make sense of the world around her during that ordeal, but in that time she did remember one thing.

Lissa saying "Thank you" over and over again. It made it all worth it. She'd saved three lives that night.

Chapter Twenty-Three

Berge kept his calm all the way up the stairs. He kept his calm as the door swung shut. He kept his calm all the way to the kitchen. And there, he cut himself a piece of shaking bread with the added spice of his fingertip mixed in, slathered butter over the blood smear soaking into the flour, and ate it with quaking hands. He shoved the whole slice into his mouth and mashed it down. He didn't chew for a long time, only let the butter melt across his tongue. He shut his eyes and savored the taste of blood and butter, trying to block out what had just happened.

Trying to forget how it defied everything he expected of mankind and the shitty specimens of his race.

She volunteered

She volunteered.

She fucking *volunteered*.

And then she'd held her arm out like a champion and looked him right in the eye as

Zanje stabbed her with a needle. She didn't even flinch when it went in. She'd even stubbornly tried to hold his gaze while she had the first reaction, insofar as she could with her eyes rolling off to the side. Trying to tell him without words how strong she was, how she could handle it. Like it was no big deal.

His eyes snapped back open and he chewed the bread down viciously. He took a breath around his mouthful and stared at his finger. He'd only managed to snag the very tip of his index finger, but it was bleeding profusely. He swallowed his bread and stuffed his finger into his mouth. He sucked, drawing even more blood in. It was hot and coppery, but it centered him to his purpose.

Blood was life. Blood was death. Blood was Berge. This was his calling in life...to procure blood for Zanje. It was a task he enjoyed, and also one he accepted as necessary, fueled by a greater, worldly purpose. He was even sleeping with the—insanely hot—boss. He had job satisfaction in spades. He'd signed his soul away from any other purpose a long time ago. He'd done this to himself. Back when he was gambling in every sense of the word—with money, with life, with women—he'd dug himself a hole so deep he could never get out, and Zanje had thrown him a rope. He owed her everything he was, even if everything he was

was nothing at all. She'd probably saved his life, too.

And then there was Nerys. Beautiful, innocent, *stupid* Nerys. He wanted her off his mind. He wanted her name wiped out of his thoughts. He wanted her dead. If she would only die, he could stop thinking about how she might be the only person in the entire world that deserved to be saved, and how she was poised precariously close to being the next to die. In his mind's eye he saw Zanje's cruel smile and her wicked way with the needle, and he had to stifle the urge to protect the brave yet stubborn ginger.

"I'm losing it," he said to no one. He stuffed another piece of bread in his mouth and made his way to the stairs. He knew exactly what he needed. He took the stairs two at a time. Six flights of them, without breaking a sweat, fueled by necessity and challenged philosophy. He threw the doors open, his eyes scanning the room until he found her.

She sat upon his chair as if it were her throne, her flawless legs crossed at the knee, black skirt snug around them and revealing nothing. Beside her on the table lay one of her precious books, a marker between its pages. In one hand she nursed a glass of wine. In the other she held an already lit cigarette. Upon her face she wore the blush of a buzz and a smile that could crumble empires. "Berge."

Just one word. Just his name, and he was undone. She was the center of gravity of a black hole. Everything went toward her and was destroyed. He flew in and flew back out again and somehow survived, but he kept going back to her for another taste, tempting fate, lapping at a poison that grew more potent with time. "Zanje," he breathed. He knew her pattern like she knew his. There were ways of getting past the guards at the gate. Each time he'd flown at her, she'd denied him. She appreciated certain refinements and very particular base instincts. All he had to do was choose which scenario he preferred. So he hovered in the doorway and tried to use her charms back at her. He leaned casually against the frame and shoved his hands into his pockets.

She cocked her head to the side and smirked a little more, one eyebrow climbing higher for a brief second. "Hm. I sense a lurking menace upon my doorstop."

"And I sense a heartless bitch upon my chair," he drawled back.

"Clever," she admitted. She swirled her glass once and then took a slow sip. He watched the journey of red glass to red lips, not for the first time thinking of blood; blood in a glass, blood on her lips…she was a vampire in the truest sense of the word. Except vampires were fictional and Zanje was terrifyingly real.

"Quite."

"What can I do for you Berge?"

"Remind me why I exist."

"Oh." She smiled even more, her eyes falling into her wine glass. "You've come to remember your place, I see."

"Yes," he whispered.

She crooked a finger and turned her body to the side.

Instead of pouncing, he gave a sinful smile and sauntered. She tipped her face up and waited. He stood before her and leaned over, leaning one hand upon the chair, his face inches from hers. While her eyes searched his, he used his other hand to swipe her wine glass. She pouted while he drained it. Then he tossed it without looking. It hit the stone floor and shattered with a satisfying sound. He leaned in as if to kiss her. She was suspicious at first, but when she tilted forward and her eyes shuttered closed, he made a grab for her cigarette. Then he stood, slouching as he dragged out the rest of it, filling his lungs with foul smog and savoring every moment of it, as polluted inside as he felt just looking at her.

"You little sh—"

His lips crashed into hers. She tasted of wine and ash. He shut his eyes and sucked it all in, sloughing off the taint of Nerys. There was only

Zanje. Awful, evil, sexy Zanje.

When the taste of ash wore off, he stole her cigarette again. He poked it between his lips and shut his eyes. Sucked on ash as if his life depended upon it. Zanje curled to her side and scrutinized. He felt her judging eyes all over him. "What?" he mumbled through the stub.

"You've never smoked a day in your life. Why now?"

He took the deepest breath he could manage, until his lungs burned like acid and his chest ached. He held it as he spoke, smoke wisping off his lips as he did. "I suppose being with you makes me long for death."

"Being with you makes me feel dead," she sniped back with a smile upon her face.

"Mm. Appropriate."

She frowned. "Why is that?"

"Kind of feels like you're dead," he teased.

She gave him a glare that could kill a horse. "That says more about you than me," she quipped back.

"Touche."

"I've got time if you want to go again," she offered in the same tone she used for conducting business.

His head swiveled in her direction, the cigarette hanging from his lips. His eyes flickered over the object of his obsession. She was at her most beautiful this way; her smile lopsided and satisfied, every statuesque curve of her body unmarred by sloppy mortal fabric. She looked at him as if he was worthy, the only time he ever felt as such. Being with Zanje was like being dead and alive at the same time, but it was the only time he ever felt alive at all.

She gave him a smoldering smile of seduction, toying with him, before plucking the cigarette from his mouth.

He leaned over and kissed her. "No," he said against her lips. "I've got work to do. We're down a Prime and you cleaned us out of Majors again. Don't wait up."

He rolled out of bed and went to the balcony. It was a ridiculous fantasy; he hoped she'd look, drink in the view, and file it away as something she'd want when he got back. He needn't have bothered. Zanje had more self control than the entire human race; he was merely the object by which she could find some release. So he stretched, groaned, and then dressed slowly. Only twice did he look in her direction. Once, and she was on her back finishing off the cigarette, her eyes mostly closed. Her God only knew what was on her mind. Twice, and she was looking at him. Her sultry, smoke-rimmed eyes promised heaven. The look within them didn't.

He shivered as the fabric of his shirt settled

over his skin, and he was pretty sure it wasn't from the chill.

Chapter Twenty-Four

It had been three days since she'd eaten anything. She was as nauseous as she was empty, and all of her thoughts were consumed with food. The usually tasteless bread and hard cheese sounded like a regency meal. Without the extra energy, her body chilled faster. She tucked herself as deep into the back corner as she could, hoping the walls would help her insulate. She'd never been a large person to begin with, but a lack of food and sunlight was shrinking her physique.

Across from the aisle, she heard Simos's stomach grumble. "Sorry," he muttered. "Hungry."

"We're all fucking hungry," Nellan snapped from further down. "Stop fucking talking about it. We know."

Nerys bit into the meat of her arm, just so she had something to nibble on to trick her body into believing she was doing something about the ache. She would never say so, but she agreed with Nellan. She wasn't about to believe anyone else could be suffering as greatly as she suffered for having an empty belly. Her stomach mirrored her thoughts and roared. It seemed to echo against the damp stone. She never thought to be grateful for the damp environment, but at least with the steady leaking, there was always something to drink.

"Coldhearted bastard," Simos grumbled. "Evil fucker. I don't know what his plan is, but starving us isn't going to help. At this rate, none of us is going to make it through the next bleed." He shivered, his teeth rattling together.

"Maybe that's the point," Kalyria murmured. "Maybe they're done with us now, and they're just letting us starve to death to save them the effort of killing us." There were words of agreement. There were sighs. Mostly there was silence, for there wasn't much else to say.

"I hate just sitting here," Nellan complained.

"How's that key?" Nerys asked quietly.

"Almost. But even if I tried to break us out now, we'd be too weak to run, and even then, half of us would starve to death trying to get to the next town."

"Berge and Zanje have to eat, too."

"Yeah, but then we'd have to risk running into them to look for food."

"So let's kill 'em," Nellan suggested.

"I'd sure love to put a knife in his guts," Lissa snarled.

Nerys frowned. She didn't want to kill anyone. She wasn't much of a killer. When she got free, *if* she got free, all she wanted to do was put as much distance between herself and this castle forever. But what of Berge?

The door handle cranked and clattered, signaling an entry. Nerys scooted toward the bars, peering into the gloom to try to see the man that still haunted her constantly. "Berge?" He didn't answer, but sometimes that was just his way. "We were beginning to wonder when you'd come back. We're hungry."

"Even I might be glad to see you, Nacht."

"I'll let him know he is missed," came Zanje's cool voice. "He'll be touched."

The response to that voice was immediate. Simos scrambled back into the corner and curled up tight into a ball. He held his breath and tried to remain silent, completely shut off from the woman who so casually sashayed down the stairs. The other prisoners shushed as well. Nerys could hear them scrambling as far away from her as they could get. Nerys followed suit, only because it seemed wise. Simos had his head stuffed between his knees. He wouldn't even look to Nerys herself.

Nerys dared to peek at the woman. Her face was like iron wrapped in silk, all delicate features and angelic beauty, but wrapped around a hard, cold, unyielding center. Nerys had only seen her a couple of times, but Berge didn't seem to like her, though they worked together. She stopped at the decision for left or right, head swiveling from side to side as she tried to remember which way she needed to go. After a moment's thought, she turned left—away from Nerys and Simos. She heard Simos's breath hitch with relief. She took that as her cue to go back to the bars and watch. When Zanje's heeled boots stopped in front of the cage of the Minors, the lone inhabitant—Rowan— immediately started whimpering. She chuckled, a low and cruel sound. Then the rasp of metal as key fitted lock slithered through the air. The whimpering grew in volume, feet scrabbled against the stone, trying to retreat even further into the wall.

Zanje disappeared into the cell.

"N-n-n-n-o! P-p-lease, mistress. No!" The last 'no' devolved into a pitiful whine and panicked breathing. Then there was a strangled sound and a gasp. Nerys pressed up against the bars, trying to see into the cell to no avail.

"Oh, God!" It was Illis' voice, low and horrified. "God save us."

"God has abandoned you," Zanje said coldly. "And you've only yourself to blame. But fear not, little worm. With my help, we might yet regain His favor. And if not…" There was the sound of a body dragging. "You'll at least get to meet Him soon."

There was the sharp inhalation of breath, and then screaming. Rowan was dragged out of her cell by the legs. She left a dark smear behind her where her torso dragged. "Get up!" Zanje barked. Rowan tried to do as she was told, pushing against one hand to try to rise up off the floor. The other hand she pressed to her abdomen. Dark blood gushed between her fingers. She hissed, her face contorting with pain. "Up, or I'll gut you right here for all to see."

Rowan managed, only just, to get to her feet. She steadied herself shakily against the bars. Her face was resigned. The day of Rowan's death had been coming for a long time. Nerys had noticed that it was a condition of imprisonment, after a long time, to accept one's eventual death. Rowan's sad brown eyes drifted up and down the dark corridor, saying a silent goodbye. Then she hobbled slowly to the stairs, one hand still pressed to her fresh wound. She crept up the stairway, Zanje right behind her.

After the door had closed, Simos whispered into the impenetrable darkness, "Her name is Rowan."

As one, their voices echoed his, "Her name is Rowan." *Farewell, Rowan.*

There was silence for a long time. During that time, Nerys wondered what had happened to Berge, and why he was no longer the one to visit them. Had Zanje killed him? Had he abandoned Zanje? Had he abandoned them? She had never had any reason to like the man, and yet now that he was gone, she learned that she missed him. He was a predictable evil, one that had a pattern and a personality. She knew how to tease out details of his life. She found something in him to empathize with, a common human element that she could at least identify. He was a compass by which she could navigate this dismal existence. As insane as it sounded, Berge kept her sane as long as she was here. Without him, she was a bit lost.

And there was Zanje, and Nerys knew without a doubt that she wanted nothing to do with her.

And then there was screaming. A lot of screaming.

Rowan's voice was bestial. She howled and howled. With every shriek, Nerys's heart broke a little more, her sanity fraying at the edges. The threads of her mind unraveled a little more each time, until her entire brain dissolved into madness. She couldn't shut her ears tightly enough to block out the sound. She whimpered; it made a muffled sound deep in her skull that tried its best to block out the noise, but in this it spectacularly failed. Rowan would not be ignored.

It went on for hours.

Wex was gazing out the window toward the full moon, appreciating the sky for the wonders far beyond his scope of comprehension. Maxine snuggled into his side. She didn't care to gaze into the heavens as he did, but she was content to keep him company as he did.

"It sure would be awesome to be able to travel the galaxy, wouldn't it Maxine?" he asked, running a hand slowly down the ridge of her spine. "I think someday, I might be able to build a craft that can sail into the sky. Not sure if I'd live long enough to make one that could fly that far, though. How far away do you think it is? It might take the rest of my life to try to reach it, and even then I might not." He considered it for a time, working through all the pieces and parts to the process. He wondered if aluminum would work or if he'd need to learn a new skill. He wondered how much energy it might take to travel that far, and if he'd survive the trip. He toyed with the idea of bringing company to help him share the responsibility, but dismissed the idea out of hand. He wasn't sure he could build an airborne craft big enough to hold two people and Maxine, and he just wasn't going to leave Maxine behind. "I wonder if I could sleep in the sky and rest," he mused aloud. Maxine's head tipped backwards at the sound of his voice. He patted under her chin. She kissed his hand and returned to staring off into the distance.

A thin, keening wail broke the silence. Maxine's mouth clicked shut, her head tilted, and she leaned into the sound. He did the same, turning toward the source of the sound. At first, he wasn't sure what he was hearing. He thought that it might be coyotes, or some kind of nocturnal creature, perhaps an owl he'd never known before. But when the next scream broke, the voice devolving into something animal and desperate, Wex discerned a few words in the noise. Words like 'God,' 'help,' and 'please.' His heart skipped a beat, not daring to believe.

He wasn't sure how he had been so blind all this time, but it troubled him more than he could say. His morality was dissolving, one part at a time. Taking someone's blood to save a life was fine, as long as it was okay with them. Okay, taking it against their will was fine, so long as they weren't killed. Okay, killing them was fine, so long as more lives were saved and if they weren't tortured. But torture? He couldn't justify that. It haunted him.

He took a deep breath and let it out in a heavy sigh. "Maxine."

She flipped her head back again and kissed his face.

"They're good people, baby dog," he said, scratching her chin. "They have to be. It doesn't make any sense."

Another scream, this one lasting longer, more tortured.

She's dying, he thought. He buried his face and his hands in Maxine's fur. Her tail thumped against the dirt floor. "It just doesn't make sense. They can't be—it's not right—th-th-they save people."

The next scream was so raw and primal that he clapped his hands over his ears. "They saved me!" he shouted to drown the sound out. Maxine kissed his face. "Stop! Screaming!" he cried.

She didn't, not for several hours. And he thought he'd be grateful that she had stopped screaming, only...only it meant she wasn't screaming, which could only mean she was dead. "Maxine...Maxine..." He hugged her tightly, her tail thumping along to the pounding of his heart. He didn't want to think about the woman who had surely died, so he tried instead to think of the person she might have saved instead. He wrestled within himself, trying impossibly to weigh the value of one life versus another. Who was the woman that had died, and who had she saved?

How awful, he thought, his stomach tying up into knots.

Silently, he petted his dog, futilely wishing he was back at home with his father. That was impossible, of course. His father was dead, and he was already on this path with Berge and Zanje. *Saving lives. We're saving lives.* His mind went blessedly numb for several minutes, the war having settled itself out into a neutral blankness. He found a sense of calm in that, and in the calm he saw a tragedy.

The woman that had died...she was in Zanje's lab, alone with Zanje. She was dead, and alone, a corpse in a red pool of disrespect and anguish. "Maxine, I have to go," he whispered, kissing her muzzle. "I have to clean up, okay?" She kissed him back. "I have to"—his voice broke—"I have to clean up, okay?" He kissed her again, harder, holding desperately to his one sane anchor.

He got up and made his way toward the front door. Maxine walked him over, at least as far as the door. Then, polite as ever, she stood with her toes right up to the door jamb, shuffling from one paw to the other, tail wagging. Waiting. He looked back over his shoulder. She stared up at him smiling, tongue lolling. *I'll be right here.*

Chapter Twenty-Five

Berge dragged his feet along like lead bricks, step after tired step. His eyes could barely stay open, but he was almost there. The sooner he got back to the castle, the sooner he could go back to sleep.

For the first time since he left the castle, he thought about Nerys. He hoped she was dead, that he'd never again have to waver on his path of iniquity. She challenged his perceptions too much. Made him think about what it might have been like to have a soul. She gave him hope for the future, and hope was a dangerous thing.

His eyes scanned the courtyard, looking for Wex, but it seemed the man was gone. Probably out on a run, delivering lifesaving blood to some undeserving shit with a lot of money. Wex was too good a man…a man who believed in goodness. He and Nerys would have been good friends.

The first thing he noticed was the smell. It wafted through the main hall. He followed his nose, though he knew where it originated. He heard the clatter and clink of Zanje tinkering about in her lab long before he reached the door. Just as he rounded the doorframe to peek his nose into the cesspool of human decay, she murmured, "Oh, Berge. Good. You're here."

"You made quite a mess."

"I was thinking of you."

Behind him, his new Major, an ugly, stinking man who was barely alive as it was, caught the view. His eyes went big, then rolled back. He fainted, collapsing like a sack of bricks in the hallway. Berge left him there and stepped into the lab.

He eyed the disaster painted all over the chair. Torn flesh, ragged, not like it should have been if she had used a straight-edged tool. There was blood all over the bed, splattered up and down the walls and even the ceiling, smeared across the floor. Zanje's usually pristine white lab coat was more red than white. There was blood on her face, a speck of it just below her eye like a beauty mark. She smiled at him sweetly over her shoulder, though even Berge could see her eyes were crazed. It seemed that Zanje had finally crossed the line of her sanity.

And he'd never wanted her more in his life.

And that, in turn, pissed him off. Because on the heels of that spike of desire was the sharp awareness of just what exactly, she had done. "Her name is Rowan."

"What?"

He shook himself, realizing then what he had done. The Rare in the prison cells far below tried his damndest to make sure Berge never forgot their names, trying to humanize them in their tormentor's eyes. As if Berge had a conscience, and could feel remorse for the things he had done. It was an underhanded trick, a clever survival skill, and one that he'd done well staying above for as long as the Rare had been a resident. "That was our last Minor," he snarled.

"So get another one," she snapped, turning back to her counter. "That's your job. To procure."

"I'm not in any shape to go back out. I haven't slept. I haven't eaten." He started undoing the straps holding the corpse in. "And you didn't clean up, either."

"It's not for me to get my hands dirty."

"No? Have you looked in a mirror lately?"

She paused. Picked at her lab coat. Said nothing.

He swore under his breath. Tried to remove the corpse—Rowan—from her restraints. Her torso was disconnected from her lower half, though, the two halves sliding away from each other as he tried to lift her. "Motherfuck!" he exclaimed, shocked and disgusted. He dropped her without meaning to, the poor woman's remains splattering to the floor. Berge did something then that he hadn't done since he was a child. He fell to his knees and lost the contents of his stomach. "What the fuck is wrong with you?" he demanded.

"I don't know what you mean," she replied calmly, not even bothering to turn and look at him.

"There's more value in these people than even you seem willing to believe!" he shouted, gesturing wildly at the broken person. "You can't fucking *buy* these, Zanj! It takes weeks, sometimes months, to track them down and bring them in. They require food and care as long as they're here. The least you could do is not butcher them when you bleed them. They drain resources every time they need to be replaced, and my time is better served here!"

"Is it now?" she shot back too softly.

His eyes widened at her tone. "The fuck is that supposed to mean?"

"Are you any use to me here at all? All you do is pant after me, lurking in corridors, skulking about like a madman whining about his lot. I wish you were still out gambling. At least then you weren't annoying me with your nattering. And when you're not humping me you're drooling after your precious Null in the dungeon. How many times have you fucked her already, Berge? How many times more?"

"Whoa! Are you jealous?"

"Absolutely not. I'm disappointed in you. Feelings for a prisoner? Feelings for an apple-cheeked, naive little trollop who talks about the greater good and hope and sunshine. Has Bergeron Nacht left his night corridor for a splash of the sun?"

"I don't belong in the sun," he muttered, not sure where she was going with this.

"No, you don't. You belong in hell, with me. And the hellbound hellhound loves his meat." She turned and indicated the mess upon the bed, eyes wild and impassioned. "There it is, Berge, your nightly meal. A gore fest fit for the king of hell. Does it now repulse you?" She took a step toward him. "Does your own darkness evade you now when it is needed most? Have you abandoned yourself, then? Are we no longer one soul?"

"Were we ever?" he shot back. "You always kept me at arm's length, and yet on a short leash. I only ever went where you pointed. You've always led. I was never even your equal in this. *You* told me that! You remind me of it constantly! Whatever work it is we do upon this earth, it's been by your command."

"Yes. My command. Always my command. And I command you now, as I have ever. That's your mess. That's your lot. So throw the bitch in the pit and get me another one."

"Must you be so careless?"

"Careless, says he," she laughed. "That's rich. It almost sounds like you wish we could save them."

His mouth snapped shut. "Even a dog needs a nap once in a while."

"What do you think we're doing here? Saving lives?"

"Sometimes. I know it's never been for the sake of those we save, though."

"Yeah. What's it for, Berge?"

"Money. The world revolves around it. It's always been about money."

"The world's going to hell. What do I need money for?"

He stared at her, bewildered. "Why else would we do what we do if not for money?"

She laughed. It was a hollow, empty, horrifying sound. "Oh, Berge. Bergeron Nacht, my lovely, nightbound stranger. We do this because it's *fun*. A hint of hope in a black landscape like a streak of yellow. The daybreak before the longest night. It's a glimmer of humanity just before mankind is destroyed. As we've always discussed, just the way we discussed it. Mankind isn't worth saving. We're ending it right here."

"Why bother with the cure, then? What purpose could that have possibly served?"

The wicked gleam in her eye chilled him straight through the marrow. "Who says I cured them?"

He crossed the space between them and shoved her, hard. She smacked into the counter with a grunt. Glass containers rattled on the bench, and a flask fell upon the floor and shattered. Another toppled, rolled, weaving back and forth, until it, too, dropped off the edge and shattered, crystal music upon a stone floor. He jabbed his thumbs beneath her delicate chin and wrenched it upward. Such a small face, for one so vile. Such a pretty face. "What the fuck are you talking about Zanje?" he demanded in a voice no less menacing and soft as her own.

"What do you think I do to the blood between selecting from a donor and transfusing it into a patient?" she mused aloud. "You see that cabinet?" she pointed with her eyes. "I've been breeding a virus. A better virus. One that cannot be cured by any technology that even I possess. And I've been adding a healthy dose to every transfusion that I've ever done. With a healthy host to incubate, the work that I've done will only be amplified. Hundredfold for my earlier trials. Thousandfold at least for every one in the past five years. And now, with that strain in the cabinet, who knows? A million? A trillion, perhaps? And how many people have we saved, Berge? How many healthy, functioning individuals have we brought back from the brink of death?"

"You're insane," he breathed. It was too much, even for her. Too heinous. *No one* was that evil. "That means me, too. That means you."

"Yes, it means all of us," she whispered back fervently. "Just as it should be. So go," she mocked with a tilt of her chin. "Replace the Minor, by all means. And if you don't, I'll just use the Null instead. And if she dies, so be it. We lose a few customers until we catch up."

Her skin was hot beneath his hand. His skin burned right along with her. He realized then that it wasn't because of the magic she had that he shared. They'd been burning in hellfire for nearly two decades.

She pushed against his hand, daring to come ever closer to his gaping, incredulous face. "This is the part where you fuck me," she dared, "because it's all you know how to do when you can't even think of anything beyond how much you hate yourself. This is where you pretend that everything might be okay because you convince yourself you might love me, isn't it Berge?" She reached between them and grabbed at his groin, and to his shame, she was right. She was always right. "And it's the funniest part of all, because you could die tomorrow and I wouldn't care at all. Because we're all dying, Berge. We've been dying since the day we were ever born. So come on, my handsome devil. Dance with me. Dance, because nothing ever mattered. Nothing matters now. And come the end, nothing will ever matter because there's never been a point to any of this. In the end we all die."

Chapter Twenty-Six

She exited the laboratory dressed like a butcher, robed in white but painted in red. He kept his eyes trained upon her face because he knew no other way to handle it. Running off screaming into the wilderness wasn't a viable option. Because in her hand, she held aloft one of her dark globes, filled with blood—life—for someone out there in need. She smiled at him, and it was only slightly marred by the gore smeared on her cheeks. "Wex," she cooed.

"Zanje," he replied smoothly, proud of how his voice didn't shake.

"Remember Becket?" He nodded. "This is for that child of Orelia's in Becket. Would you be so kind as to deliver it for me?"

"Sure, not a problem, Zanje." He held his hands out and accepted the proffered container.

"Be careful. It's very fragile. Berge broke one, the night he came for you."

There were nuances hiding in there. Where

Wex was going wasn't a mere 6 miles away. If he dropped this one...if he broke it...someone was going to die as a result. He was reminded starkly of course that someone already had. "I understand." He splayed his hand around the bottom of it, balancing it carefully, before he took off his coat. He nestled the globe into his coat and wrapped it gently. "Not to worry, Zanje. I'll be careful."

He almost forgot she was covered in blood. Almost.

He never drove faster in his entire life. He poured his heart and soul into the engine that propelled his snow craft. He charged into the heart of a blizzard and ignored the snow and ice that pummeled the windshield. It was reckless, but it hardly mattered. Zanje had bought his life with one of her globes. If she was going to throw it away on a snowstorm, that was her right.

And anyway, if living meant killing others, he wasn't sure he wanted to be alive.

Torn between saving lives and taking them, he let go of his control over the situation and shot up a prayer to his father. Perhaps his God would decide. He kept both hands on the wheel, though, just in case. Maxine didn't seem to mind whether he petted her or not.

"You know, I don't know if I know what to

think anymore," he confessed. "I mean, at first I was okay with this. She saved my life. She's brilliant—not bad looking either—but I...I just don't know. How much of what she does is good? How much is bad? And I don't think I'm really equipped to make this kind of decision on my own. I don't see everything that goes on in there, but what I have seen...isn't good, Maxine. So I don't know. What do you think?"

She didn't answer.

The wind was squalling when he arrived in Becket, the wind chill so cold that it bit right through his clothes. He wouldn't be sad to see the last of Becket.

He remembered right where Orelia's shop was and went straight there. "Good evening, Orelia!" he called. He still had the globe wrapped in his coat.

"Good heavens, Wex, but you look cold!"

"Yeah, it's not nice out there, that's for sure."

"What's that there in your coat?"

"It's from Zanje. It's a gift." The moment the words left his mouth, he knew that it was what needed to be done. He couldn't rightly charge Orelia for what he was about to do. She needed this shop. The granddaughter needed a future.

"Oh a gift, is it? Does it come with hooks for my craw?"

"What? No. I talked to Zanje, and she understood your situation. She said she isn't going to charge for this one." Maybe he could pay for it? Or maybe Berge would help? Either way, it was something he could figure out later. It didn't have to be now. He plastered his best grin upon his face.

Orelia's face scrunched up, suspicious. "What exactly did you say to her, boy? And what did she say back?"

He blinked, hoping he was a good liar. He'd never tried it before. "I explained to her that your shop was the only way that your granddaughter would have a life once she was cured, and that you were really upset at the thought of losing it. I told her she probably had enough money to do this for free just this once." He threw in a kicker, just in case. "I have to work a little extra is all to make up the difference, but that's okay."

"You're helping to pay for this? Why?"

"Well, we're not trying to turn a profit off of this or anything."

"HA!"

"We're not! If what we do saves even one person from the dying, well...that's enough of a reward for us." He smiled brightly. *Believe me,* he willed. *Just believe.*

"Hm. Doesn't sound like the same Zanje that I knew. What happened? She getting her beans snapped?"

"What?"

"She getting her box packed? Her muffin stuffed? Her ditch filled in? Her fish fed?" He stared, confused. "Is she fucking someone?"

"Oh." He laughed, finally making sense of her analogies. Then he remembered Berge. "Yeah, actually."

"Oh." She blinked then, just as confused as he had been only a moment before. "Well. Let's have it then." She reached across the counter to accept the package.

"Eh, I'd rather carry it back for you, if you don't mind. It's very fragile, and I don't want it to pass through too many hands until it gets where it's going."

"Fair enough, boy. Come on back." She waved him back, lifted the wooden barrier between the front of the shop and the back. "Come on, come on."

He followed her back, down a narrow hallway and into a small room. There was a child there in the bed, and the sheets were soaked with blood. Her eyes weren't red yet, though. He breathed a sigh of relief. "Well, there she is. Nyra. My granddaughter. Parents both died of Blood Plague. Brothers and sisters died of Blood Plague. All her aunts and uncles, her cousins, everyone. Every person she's ever known, dead. Blood Plague. Everyone but me. I'm all she has left."

"Wow. This here," he unveiled the globe,

and the rich, dark blood shimmering within it. "This is blood. I don't confess to know exactly how it works, but something in it recovers Red D—I mean, Blood Plague. All you have to do is give it to her."

"Yeah, Zanje's got a protocol. She explains it to you when you ask for her help so she doesn't waste her time if you don't like it. So I've got these needles and such." She moved to go toward them, and Wex backed away.

"Sorry, Orelia...I don't do so well seeing needles."

"Eh? Didn't you get one?"

He laughed nervously. "Yeah, but I was unconscious."

"Right. Sorry. I'm old. Set that down, then, and I'll take care of it from here. In fact, you can go on home, now, if you like. It's colder than Zanje's black heart out there, and you'd probably be glad to head back."

"That would be wonderful. It was nice meeting you, Orelia. I'm glad to have helped." He set the globe down where she'd indicated and went to shake her hand.

Instead, she grabbed ahold of his arm and pulled him into her body. She was surprisingly strong for such a doddering old woman, with a grip like iron. She kissed his cheek. "You're a good boy, Wex. Thank you, for your help."

"It was nothing," he murmured,

embarrassed. He patted her back, then broke the hug. She wiped tears from her eyes and turned quickly so he wouldn't see.

She was a proud old woman. She probably didn't mean to let him see her cry, so he made his exit.

He barely made it home with his eyes open, spent the last hour of the journey nodding off. The engine of the craft sputtered off and shuddered back on as he drifted in and out of sleep. Maxine rolled over on her back on the seat, butting his hand with her head when he started to doze. "Thanks, baby dog."

When he got back to Zanje's castle, he made the slow plod back to the stable. He had one hand on the handle when the front door to the castle snapped open. He didn't have time to turn and see it before it snapped shut again. Whoever had exited was too hard to see in the new moon night. He strained his ears, trying to determine the identity of whoever it was. Were it Zanje, he didn't want to see her right now. So soon after lying about her good intentions, he was afraid that she might be able to read it in his behavior or his face. And if it were Berge, he had a few questions he needed answers to.

"I see you, Wex." Berge. He didn't sound happy. His voice was tired, almost worn out.

Wex abandoned his quest for sleep and

went toward Berge. When he was close enough, he could see the man seated upon the front stair, stretched out on one elbow, lighting up a cigarette. "I didn't know you smoked," he commented.

"I don't." He took a long slow drag. Held it. Breathed it out slowly, as if savoring.

"Oh. Okay then."

"I know. I'm a fucking hypocrite. You don't even know the half of it."

"You're not a bad fellow."

He laughed, but it was just air hissing through his teeth. "You don't know me at all then."

"Sure I do."

"Right. Okay. Let's talk about me, then, for a second. Okay?"

Wex was a bit taken aback by his tone, but he nodded once. Then, realizing Berge couldn't see him…"Sure."

"I was in love once. I thought I was, anyway. And I ruined it. Completely. Because I found the money she had saved up, and I stole it. And then I bet it all away and lost. So she left me, and since she didn't have any money left, I didn't even miss her."

"That doesn't sound…like love."

"Oh, so you noticed? Good. Well, it doesn't stop there. I stopped believing in a god when I was ten."

"Why? What happened to you?"

"Nothing, really. I just looked outside and saw that the world was shit, and I thought, 'you know, you'd think God could have tried a little harder.' And once I thought it, it just stuck. There's nothing on this godforsaken planet worth saving."

"You don't think so?"

"Well it doesn't fucking matter now, Wex. It doesn't fucking matter now."

"What do you mean?"

"Because Zanje fucking Vangelic just killed us all."

"I'm confused."

"You're confused? *You're* confused? I'll tell you who's fucking confused. *I'm* confused. Because when she told me that, I should have been more than happy to hear it. It's been our goal all along."

"What? That's not right."

"It's right. Oh, it's *definitely* right. Zanje and I were attracted to each other because of our mutual hatred for everyone alive. The one thing we always agreed on was that the world would be a better place without us. Without any of us. So in our early years, we dreamed about subjugating the human race, sending each and every one of us back to hell where we belonged so that her God—because *I* figured when it was all over, we'd just be ashes, and that was fine with me, but her God—could start over fresh and do it right this time. And over time, I forgot that was the plan. Or maybe I never thought she would actually do it. Fuck, I don't even know. Because all I ever cared about was the money."

"You aren't—"

"Nope. The money, Wex. Just the money. Always the money. I just told you, I'd never cared about anything else. So now for me, it's money and Zanje. Money and Zanje. Always always *always* money and *her*. And for fourteen years now, that's been the way of it. So she tells me today that she's killed us all, and come to find out, I'm not okay with it anymore." He stopped. Threw the cigarette as far away as he could, then stared straight at Wex. "Well? Why am I not okay with it anymore?"

"I don't know, Berge," he answered, feeling numb. "I always thought you were better than that. I guess I just don't know why I thought that."

"I don't either, buddy. I've never given you any reason to believe the best out of me."

"No," Wex murmured. "I suppose you haven't. Except for that one time you carried me six miles so that I wouldn't die."

Silently, he stared. Then he scrubbed a hand through his messed up curls. "Heh. You're right. What the fuck was I thinking?" He stood. "Goodnight, Wex. Pleasant dreams. If I'm dead in the morning—you know what. Never mind. Today, tomorrow, none of it fucking matters anyway." He opened the front door, stepped inside, and slammed it shut.

Chapter Twenty-Seven

He left her bed, shaking like an addict in withdrawal, unsatisfied and empty, hungry in every way. It was a new sensation, a far cry from the poisonous fulfillment he was used to. Her hold over him was finally broken, but all it had done was open him up to the sickness that dwelled inside them both. He didn't kiss her goodbye and didn't say anything, only rolled out of bed, yanked his pants back on, and made his way to the kitchen. He felt dirty, inside and out, sick and getting sicker. Her eyes crawled up his spine as he left, but he didn't care.

There wasn't anything in the kitchen he needed nor wanted. It was only a destination that wasn't near people, and when he was especially bored he had an animal tendency to go to where there was food and browse. He opened the cupboards just to look into them. There wasn't much to be found there, just some sacks of dried beans and grain. He tugged down one of them and stared at it. Hefted it. By the feel of it, probably beans. He held it out in front of him and let it drop. It hit, bent, and tipped over, spilling the contents on the floor.

Yep. Beans. It was mildly satisfying, but it wasn't enough.

He had one bottle of whiskey left. He hadn't had the time to go and acquire more, and he'd been saving this one for a special occasion, insofar as he had those. Tonight didn't qualify as a special occasion, but whiskey seemed like a good idea anyway. He bit the cork and spat it away. It didn't matter where it fell. He wasn't sure how much whiskey it would take to get him drunk, but he knew exactly how much he was going to drink.

The first shot of whiskey wormed its way into his gut. It went down like a bad decision, rendering him instantly nauseous. So he took another drink and sat down on the kitchen floor, leaning back against the cupboards. He sucked down the rest of the bottle without thinking twice. Every mouthful made him cough, burned his throat, and hit his stomach like a fester. He accepted it. Courted it, even. He'd never felt more wretched. At least with too much whiskey in an empty, churning stomach, he had an illness with a diagnosis and reason for it.

Being drunk changed his outlook on the

beans. They lay where he left them, scattered about the floor around the lopsided burlap bag. He smiled and took especial interest in them, moving each seed around on the stone. He counted them and recounted them for something to do, then arranged them in different patterns, ultimately using them to illustrate lewd pictures. He sat back, admiring, pleased with himself. Between the whiskey and his unsurpassed artistry, he felt marginally better; at least he knew just how fucked he was.

Sighing, resigned, he left the beans and the empty bottle exactly where they were and stood. He wobbled and swayed, but saved himself before he fell over and ruined his bean design. With one last glance at what he'd done to tomorrow's dinner, he turned and left the kitchen.

Somehow, impossibly, he made it down the stairs and down into the dungeon. And somehow, impossibly, he managed to do it without making too much noise. When he made it to the bottom of the stairs with exaggerated care, only tripping over the very last one and careening into the wall hands first, there was no sound that greeted him but snoring and the strangely peaceful sound of people breathing.

He grinned again, entertained. Even laughed a little at how he'd sneaked up on his own prisoners. He staggered his way to Nerys's cell. Stood there, steadied against the bars of her cell, and watched her sleep. His mind was pleasantly blank. All he did was focus on her shoulders as they rose and fell in her slumber, swelling and receding like waves. He stood that way for a long time, seeking peace where he knew he could find it, otherwise uncertain of why he'd come here. He didn't love her. He didn't want her. And yet, she calmed him somehow. He couldn't let her die.

Silently, resolutely, he removed the leather thong from around his neck and dangled Zanje's digit before his eyes. It was a crooked, macabre thing, but such a small trinket to house so much power. He'd always wondered what she meant by choosing *that particular finger*. Was it her twisted way of wedding herself to him, or was it her smug declaration that she would never be wed? He'd told himself the former, but had become increasingly resigned to the latter. To him, it was a symbol, a well of power that filled him up. With corrupted power, with hellfire, with her.

To Nerys, it need only be a weapon. The lock danced out of his blurry vision, trying to avoid its key, but eventually he won out. He was fortunate she didn't wake. He didn't have the words or the eloquence to say the things that needed to be said.

It wasn't until he'd left the dungeon and the key to Zanje's fire behind that he realized just how cold he really was. He didn't even know where he ended up until he awoke wrapped around Maxine, a very confused Wex seated across the stall. Berge squinted through an apocalypic hangover and scrubbed a hand through his hair. Then he said words he'd never uttered in his life. "I need your help."

Chapter Twenty-Eight

Simos muttered to himself as he scratched at his key. Nerys couldn't hear what he was saying at first, but as he worked it got louder and louder. "Rowan. Marc. Mirdoz. Larric. Sapa. Halina. Tragen…"

All the names of the dead. He recited them, over and over again. Nerys didn't want to know their names. It saddened her. But Simos remembered them as a gesture of respect, so after the first few turns around the cycle of names, she tuned in and counted. Thirty-seven names. But those thirty-seven had only died since Simos came to the dungeon. How many before that? In between the names, he apologized for not having the power to save them.

Rowan's noisy death had done them all in. The dungeon had been a loud place since then, and that was saying something, since Rowan had been the loudest one before.

"Rowan...Marc... I'm sorry. I'm so sorry. I wasn't strong enough." Scratch, scratch, scratch. "Mirdoz, Larric, Sapa..." Scratch. "I'm sorry, so, so sorry." His voice cracked and rasped. He recited them over and over again, until his voice was hoarse and the words were barely recognizable.

She hugged her knees tightly to her chest, thinking about Rowan, and Zanje. She shivered, though it had nothing to do with the cold today. She needed to be free. If Zanje ever got her hands upon her...she wasn't opposed to dying, but she didn't want to suffer as Rowan had.

But what of those suffering of Red Death?

She fretted and tugged on the cord around her neck, wondering why Berge had left it for her. It had to have been Berge's, but it seemed a strange gift to leave her. Why make a necklace out of bone? And what did giving such a macabre gift to a person mean? In a way, it reminded her of her flowers. Jewelry was a kind of art. Bone was a remnant of life. Creating art from the leftovers of death seemed to suit his character.

There was a scrabbling of metal on metal, then a click and a metallic squeal. "Yesss." Then the door to Simos' cage creaked, a tortured squeal that was so loud it made Nerys flinch. "I can't believe it. It worked!"

"What worked?"

"I made a key! And it unlocked the door!"

All the voices started talking at once, begging him to let them out.

"Me next, Simos!"

"Quick, before they hear!"

Simos shushed, hissing through the cacophony. "Shh, everyone! I'll let you out, but you have to stay quiet. If they find us, we're all dead. Were I better fed, I might be a match for them, but as it stands…"

Nerys didn't move. Simos made his way through the dungeon, forcing his makeshift little key into the locking mechanisms of each and every cell. He came to Nerys last. Why he'd chosen her last was a mystery. Was it coincidence? Or was he concerned that if they were discovered, she had the best chance of survival? Or had he merely left her for last because he felt she deserved her freedom the least?

"Come now, Nerys," Simos beckoned as he tugged open the door.

She couldn't see, but she sensed his hand reaching toward her. She reached, fingers groping in the void, looking for the way out. Her fingers poked into hard flesh, and then his hand entwined with hers and helped her to her feet. "Simos…"

"There's a girl," he said gently. He hugged her, holding her tightly and guiding her head to his broad chest. "I wish that I had been able to hug you before now. I think you might have needed it more than any of us," he told her quietly. "We have to go. Quickly now, come on." He released her, made a grab for her hand again.

Numbly, she followed, taking her first free step out of her cage in God only knew how long. She sucked in a deep breath. The free air was sour and damp, remarkably similar to the air of the imprisoned, but it did taste sweeter somehow. She let herself be led down the aisle and to the stairs. Then Simos released her hand and looked to all of them. "I'll go up first," he said softly. "Make sure the coast is clear. I'll whistle from the top if it's safe. We look for the kitchen first, eat as much as we can. Then we get out of here and run as fast as we can. We make for Lorent."

"Quorath is closer," Kalyria suggested. Of all of them, she was the current weakest besides Nerys herself. She wasn't going to make it very far.

Simos lay a hand upon her shoulder. "I know, Kalyria. But Quorath lies in the shadow of this place. We don't know who is a friend or who is our enemy. We make for Lorent."

"I won't make it to Lorent." Her voice shook.

He pulled her close and kissed her forehead. "Then best of luck. Go with God." He released her and looked toward the top of the stairs. "Alright. At my whistle." He crept up the stairs one step at a time as they all looked on, a knot of fearful faces at the base. The creak of the door opening, which before signaled the beginning of a trial, now sounded like the death knell. Surely Zanje and Berge could hear that, no matter where they were? Nerys felt as if Quorath could hear it from where they stood. Simos poked his head through the crack, panning slowly across the hallway above. He looked toward them. They looked toward him. Then he took a step outside. And another. He tiptoed out of there until he was completely obscured from view.

The rest of them took turns glancing between each other and the last place they had seen him. Most of them held their breaths. Nerys instead looked back toward her cage, feeling strangely nostalgic and a little numb. How many months had she lived in that cage? It almost seemed comfortable by comparison, whereas now, the moment she stepped outside this dungeon, she may as well be in the great beyond.

While she was looking back toward her cage, she saw a familar but very unexpected face. Ashes loped toward Nerys's cell, probably on her way to find her. It was strange to see her far from Berge, and in fact, Nerys's gaze shot up, glancing down the aisle in both directions, and up to the top of the stairs, thinking the man himself might be closer than any of them thought. It would be just like him to be lurking in the shadows, letting them believe they had the upper hand and were about to escape for real. It was the kind of sadism he ascribed to, giving them a breath of freedom before locking them up forever. Simos would be killed, his key confiscated. The rest of them would be prisoners once more.

But Berge was nowhere to be seen. And Ashes had stopped in front of Nerys's cell, her nose in the air, trying to find her. "Ashes," she whispered into the darkness, trying to get the weasel's attention.

The whistle came from above. The prisoners started tromping up the stairs, one at a time. They moved slowly so as not to make too much noise. The door creaked in between each one.

"Ashes." She made the clicking sounds Berge used on her. Ashes' head swiveled atop her neck, looking in her direction. Her nose dipped and rose, dipped and rose, looking for her scent. She clicked again, louder to her ears without the sounds of feet upon the stair, and Ashes started towards her at a slow jog.

"Well, well, if it isn't Berge's precious little pet rat." Nerys turned around. Kopep stood there, grinning evilly. He was a sour, bitter little man Nerys hadn't liked much. He took a step toward Ashes.

Nerys took one look at his face and panicked, certain he meant Ashes harm. "What are you doing?"

He grinned, black teeth gleaming wetly in the light from the rays of freedom at the top of the stairs. "Berge loves that fucking rodent. I'm going to leave him a parting gift." He bent over and crouch-walked toward the weasel. Ashes paused, then made a sidestep and continued onward. Toward Nerys.

"No, don't. She didn't do anything wrong." Her hand curled around the necklace Berge gave her, wishing he were here. Panic lanced through her.

"Come on, ye little fucker," he clipped in a sing-song voice. "Come on and let me twist yer little feckin' head off." He reached. Ashes didn't move.

"No, please!"

"Shut yer fool lips, ye cunt," he snarled. He swiped at Ashes.

"No!" Nerys darted forward, meaning to rescue Ashes. Kopep stood and backhanded her in one move, and she flew across the aisle and landed hard on her backside. She yelped in pain as Kopep crouched back down. "I said no!" she cried angrily, flinging a hand toward him. The heat from within her surged outward and with it went a blaze of brilliant purple-blue. It engulfed Kopep. He screamed and fell backwards, immediately rolling all across the floor to put it out. Ashes scattered, dashing back towards Nerys's cell. Nerys fought against the pain in her spine and dashed after her, ignoring the burning man, teeth chattering from the cold.

Ashes was in the corner, trying to find her way through it, butting her head into the stone wall, backing up, and ramming it again. She darted from side to side, looking for a new section of wall. "Ashes." She clicked her tongue again. "Come here, baby, come on." She crept close to Ashes and held her hand out. Ashes paused and hunkered down, shaking all over. Nerys's eyes fell on her hand. She turned it over and stared at her palm, wondering where she'd suddenly gained the power she'd always lacked. Ashes craned her neck out and nudged Nerys's fingers. Tiny, cold paws pressed into Nerys's skin. A second later, she leapt over Nerys's wrist and climbed her skin.

This time, Nerys didn't mind the way her claws dug into her skin, even if it wounded her. Ashes found refuge beneath her hair, behind her neck, just as she had done when they first met. Berge had asked her to care for Ashes if anything happened to him, and she hadn't seen him in a long time. "It's okay, Ashes," she murmured, rubbing her arms for warmth. "I'm here."

She listened, straining her ears against the oppressive silence. There was a hollow, roaring quiet from the end of the hallway she'd not yet seen. It was eerily quiet without the other prisoners; no breathing, no whimpering, no weeping. Not even Simos scratching at his skeleton key. In the end, the silence was too much for her. She chose instead to sing. It was a lilting jig her mother used to sing when she was gardening. Ashes trembled against her neck, little pulses of fear, as Nerys's voice sifted through the darkness. She would wait. For him.

Because she could save anyone, and everyone else was already free.

Chapter Twenty-Nine

She stalked the halls like a prowling, spitting cat. If she'd have had a tail, it would have been lashing back and forth. A visit to Quorath gave her two different orders for Primes, and both from very prominent clients from distant locales. It was a choice opportunity to spread her reach and rob the world of more of its money. The only problem was that Berge was nowhere to be found. She could probably go down to the dungeon on her own, but she didn't relish the idea of getting her hands dirty today. "Berge!" she shouted. Her voice echoed through the hallways and up into the eaves of the airy castle.

Her two clients waited in the main hall. One of them paced and paced, impatient for results. The other sat quietly, eyes focused on some distant point outside the tall window.

"Berge!" Her heels click-clicked as she climbed her six flights of stairs, thinking perhaps he might be awaiting her in her favorite ballroom. Her fingers slid along the rails as she climbed, trailing behind her like skeletal wings. "Berge!"

She swept around the banister and slammed into the door to the ballroom, shoving it open with all her might. Both Wex and Berge were there. They looked up at her when she entered. A slow, lazy smirk spread out upon Berge's lips, as if he laughed at some kind of private joke. Wex, for his part, wisely focused on something else. "What are you doing?" she demanded.

"It's evening. We're having dinner."

Her eyes popped incredulously. "Did you not hear me calling for you?"

"Sure I did," he replied. He hunched over his plate, one hand resting casually upon his knee. "I just didn't care."

"What?" she snapped.

He straightened and fixed her with a chilly glare. "I said I didn't fucking care."

"We have clients downstairs."

"So?"

"So we have work to do. Leave your plate and go downstairs."

"No."

"Excuse me?"

"Something wrong with your hearing today, Zanj? I said no."

She looked between them. Wex, his eyes

fixated on the plate before him. Berge, immovable and calm, waiting for her next move. "If you're not—"

He sighed, exasperated. "Oh, shut it, Zanj. I'm eating. You want me to help you? Then sit down on your couch, look pretty, and suck down that fancy piss wine of yours. When I'm all done with my beans, I'll be glad to help."

"Right now, Berge," she snapped, pointing toward the open doorway with one finger.

He smiled with half his mouth, scooped into his beans, saluted her with the spoon, and delivered them to his open maw. Then he chewed them slowly, grinning the whole time, daring her to stop him.

Her blood flared to life, searing through her entire body. Fire gathered up, in her eyes, in her hands, all the way to the elbow. "You dare? You're asking for a fight, Bergeron Nacht."

"Kill me then," he mumbled, his mouth full of half masticated bean mash. "You won't hear me complain. But I've had enough of your bullshit and I'm not going to die with my lips pressed to your ass." His eyes dropped to his plate, more intent on the food than on her fury. "Even if it is a really nice ass," he added, trying not to laugh.

She stomped her foot, bursting a wave of kinetic energy, shattering every window in the ballroom. The boom was loud enough to make eardrums bleed. The glass fell like crystal upon the stone floor.

That got their attention. Berge threw down his fork angrily. "Damn it all, Zanj! You really are a cunt, you know that? Noth—"

She blew the couch over, and he and Wex both splayed out upon the ballroom floor. Wex rolled over to a sitting position, but Berge snapped right back up onto his feet, his face a picture of a perfect storm, brows drawn forward, black eyes burning. Her blood sang with pure ire, ready to torch him. Were she interested in being blood soaked today, she might have. But today—only today—she needed him. She used her power to pick up all of the shards of glass, swirling it toward the center of the room, sending it into orbit around the two men.

Wex watched the glass circling, a concerned expression marring his otherwise calm demeanor. "Berge..." he cautioned.

"Yeah, I know." Berge stood, the man at the center of the eye of the storm. "You want to dance? Alright, sweetheart. Let's dance. Kill me."

She turned the swirling mass of glass fragments, jettisoning them toward the fragile hunk of flesh at their epicenter. Berge held his arms out, waiting for it, daring. He knew she wasn't about to kill him. The glass shot to within inches of his vulnerable skin before arcing out and away, cycling back up toward the top, a storm of blades that never touched the man. She wanted to kill him. Oh, did she ever!

Berge laughed. "It seems I'm not the only one who has gone soft," he purred. "Do you love me after all? Huh? Do you, you evil bitch?"

The glass froze, suspended in air like a cloud of broken crystal. She glared at him, imagining him shredded and bleeding out on her floor. Imagined him on fire, burning. Imagined him laid out beneath her, terrified. Imagined him on his knees, begging for his life. She smirked, just thinking about it, deriving pleasure from hypotheticals that might never come to pass. "I *hate* you," she told him earnestly. She let the glass fall. It crashed to the floor all in a rush.

Then, without another word, she sauntered over to her couch and curled up upon it. She picked at her skirt, arranging it around her knees. Smoothed her hair—no reason not to look her best at dinner—then withdrew a cigarette and lit it. "Well? Eat your beans then, Berge."

"Thank you," he sniped. He righted the couch, then fell upon it, the force of it rocking the couch back onto two feet and back again. He stabbed into his food, eyes boring into hers, defiant and hateful.

She would kill him. She would kill him soon. But not today. *Maybe* not today.

"Wex," he beckoned over one shoulder. "Come finish your steak."

Wex stood, every muscle taut with caution. His eyes darted between the glittering glass and her face, watching her every move. She smiled, a predator toying with her prey. He slowly came around the couch, one hand in contact with the cushions the whole time.

Zanje inhaled the toxic vapor of her cigarette. Held it, as she held Wex's suspicious gaze. And then, as he came around from behind the couch. She blew out a stream of smoke and blasted him backward. He yelped as he went flying, fifty feet across the ballroom. His legs hit the window sill, and then he toppled over it, yelling as he dropped seven stories to the ground below. The sound of a body hitting the ground—and the sudden silence as his yell was cut short—punctuated the dinner conversation.

Berge had paused with a bite of steak halfway between his plate and his mouth. He peered over his shoulder, confirmed that Wex was indeed gone, then turned back toward her.

She looked at him from beneath hooded eyelids, smiling and self-satisfied. Testing. She wanted him to react, to prove he had the heart that he denied existed. She wanted him to rage, to tangle with her. To fight.

Instead, he finished putting the bite of steak into his mouth. Chewed it slowly, eyes never leaving hers. He reached over and grabbed a hold of Wex's plate, then passed it over to her. "Wouldn't want to let it go to waste," he told her with a shrug.

Very good, Berge. She claimed Wex's fork as well, speared an already cut bite of steak. "Our order is for two Primes," she informed him. "They brought vials, so I was able to test this time." She popped the steak into her mouth and bit down. It was very tender, perfectly seasoned, and as rare as she liked. "This is good," she complimented.

He stared at her. "Zanj, we only have one Prime left. The others are already dead."

She shrugged. "It doesn't matter to me."

"Even if we were to take everything the Prime has left, Zanj, it's not going to be enough to fill two orders."

She leaned back on an elbow and sucked on her cigarette. "So get the Null."

"So we kill them both?" His temper flared.

"If we have to."

She watched him furiously stab at his food, tracing the path of his thoughts. He was always worried about that precious Null. He was too fond of her. *Your move, Berge.*

"No."

"I'm not asking."

"No. You'll kill them both, and we won't have anything left."

"Your logic won't work here. I already told you yesterday that the type compatibility and our ability to fill orders meant nothing to the plan I'm pursuing. So we kill them both. I see no problem with this."

"Zanj—"

"What's the matter, Berge?" she baited.

He gave her a look of displeasure.

She smiled a knowing smile and waited. He took too long, so she finished her cigarette and then did away with the rest of Wex's steak.

"I won't bleed the Null," he informed her quietly.

So. He'd drawn the line. "You will bleed the Null," she ordered.

"I won't."

"You will, or I'll bleed you instead."

He dropped his fork. It clattered to the floor, but he ignored it. "I don't see what that could possibly accomplish." His arms crossed over his chest, and he slouched back against his cushions, skeptical.

"Oh, I think you do."

"No, I don't. Enlighten me, oh powerful being."

"It's that rat you keep."

"Weasel. And her name is Ashes. What are

you getting at?"

"We've talked about that stupid rat more times than I care to remember, and every time you bring her up, it's for the same reason. Oh, Ashes! She has this uncanny ability to sniff out Specials! Oh, Ashes! She doesn't give a damn about anyone who isn't special! She can't see a fucking thing, Berge. But more importantly, she can't even smell anyone who isn't somehow the recovered permutation of the genome for the Red Death. So what does that mean, Berge?"

"It means you're a self-righteous hag who's jealous of a weasel." He shrugged.

"No, it means your blood is also a cure for the Red Death. And I know you've typed your own blood, Berge. I know I have. And you know what I learned when I did it?"

His mouth parted slightly.

"You're a Prime. So we don't have to bleed your Null." She shrugged and rubbed her cigarette out upon the steak. "I can bleed you instead. But if you make me resort to that, I'm going to bleed you for everything you're worth to fill both orders. Then you'll be free of me, my clients will be happy, and you won't have to bear witness to what happens to your whore in the basement." She smiled and met him stare for stare.

"You wouldn't dare."

"Wouldn't I?" The taste of blood was like

honey in her mouth.

Chapter Thirty

He kissed her sweetly at the brow and then he promised he'd take care of everything. He bade her meet him in the lab in an hour, after she'd had a chance to listen to a few of her shitty songs, smoke the rest of her cigarettes, and drink a case of wine. And then he left her in her ballroom with the strings whining and the piano shrinking his eardrums. The door he shut softly, so as not to disturb. When it latched its way closed, leaving Berge alone in the hallway of the seventh floor of a heavensward tower, he resisted the urge to drive his fist into the heavy painted oak. Instead, he mouthed the words 'damn it,' and ran a hand through curls that were long past overdue to be shortened.

He pounded his way down to the main level, mind abuzz with panic for desecrated plans. Wex was dead. That changed everything.

Wex was dead.

"Shit," he hissed. The word echoed lightly off

the empty stairwells. "Shit, shit, shit."

When his feet hit the main level, he took off at a jog. Two men peered over their shoulders at him as he passed by, prematurely expecting results. Smoke curled up from the cigar of one. Berge smiled instead of shaking his head—more smoke?—and tossed up a hand in greeting. "Not to worry, gentlemen! We'll take care of everything. Make yourselves at home!" As soon as he rounded the corner, he bowed his head and scowled. He hated Zanje. Hated her to the core of her rotten being. Hated her so much that he considered stopping off in the kitchen, hovering just outside the door for a moment, wavering on the idea of grabbing a knife. It was odd, though, thinking of carrying weapon after so long not needing one.

In the end, he passed up the kitchen and headed down the stairs into the dark underbelly of earth, toward the lab. And toward the dungeon. Without Wex, though, there was no way he was going to be able to get Nerys out of here. She wouldn't survive out there alone. When the door to the dungeon came into view, he came to a full stop, gazing at the door. Such a simple door to hide such a horrible secret. Cold iron, wrought, black. He didn't want to open it, not ever again. His feet carried him toward it anyway. He had to. There was no other way. This was his lot in life. This was what he had signed himself up for. Step by unwilling step, he dragged himself toward it, a puppet on strings controlled by the devil above.

He shivered. It had been a long time since he'd been cold. What he wouldn't give for a better coat. Every moment felt like he was freezing to death.

But as he walked past the door to the lab, defiance gripped his ankles and held him still. "No," he whispered. It was for himself, for the sole purpose of needing to say it. He wasn't going to play her games anymore. Would no longer dance her wicked dance. Nerys was down there, waiting to die for her grand cause. She was foolish, but she would go willingly. Berge wasn't going to feed her to Zanje. It simply wasn't fair. Nerys would go thinking she had done a good thing, and she would die for it. Zanje would take her life and desecrate it, and…and…he just wasn't going to do it.

His face turned toward the lab, the clinical representation of all of their atrocities. It was styled as a place of healing. A place of advancement. It was the place where Zanje put all of her extraordinary brilliance to work for the ultimate goal of proliferating evil. It was about as far from advancement as one could get. She was devolving the human race, bringing them as close to origin as was possible. She would use the pinnacle of their achievements to wipe them out.

He was drawn to the cool blue lights of her witchlight like a moth to flame. Overhead, the blue lights swayed back and forth like a sailboat caught in a swell. And then his eyes fell upon the bed and a fury like none other overcame him. He descended upon it, angerblind. He pushed it with all of his might, sending it flying across the lab and careening into a counter. The cupboards and shelves upon it jarred, jolted, and the glassware there dropped to the countertop. Some of them cracked. One or two of them rolled off and shattered upon the ground.

It wasn't enough.

He swept the rest of the glass off the counter. They broke upon the floor, and he did it one better and stomped upon them with his boots, reveling in the way the glass sounded crushed beneath his heel. It sounded like gravel and looked like spilled sugar. That pleased him, brought him a level of satisfaction he'd never known. But it did nothing to assuage his wrath. So he turned and kicked over the shelf that held all of her empty blown glass globes. She paid a fortune for those and had them shipped all the way from beyond Anthia. Each one of them cost more than a horse. He shattered all of them in one go. They hit the floor with an even more delicate sound than the glassware had, as fragile as a wraithfly's wing. "Should have bought steel!" he sneered before kicking the shelf. One of the steel shelves dislodged from its frame and clattered across the floor, shoved up against its fellows.

He opened every overhead cupboard and ejected all of the contents. Bottles of iodine, of alcohol, of ether. That last was probably dangerous; the fumes could make him faint, but he didn't care anymore. *Kill me,* he thought. *It no longer matters if I live or die, but then it never did before, either.* In defiance, he breathed deeply, greedily wafting all of the chemicals drenching the floor as they hurried their way into the drain in the center of the room.

All that was left was the cabinet that held her greatest crime. This he approached, wild-eyed, light-headed and giddy and fueled with righteous purpose. He unlatched and jerked open the little door, tearing it askew upon the fragile hinge. The dishes in there rattled but remained, resilient to his tampering. He dug one out and stared at it, musing at the simplicity of science. Such a dangerous, horrible thing… yet contained upon a dish that looked as if it held nothing but tinted water. He dashed the water out of the dish and held it up, looking at what was contained therein. It looked like nothing more than a dirty lens. He rubbed at it with one finger, disturbing whatever she'd attached there. *This is science*, he thought. *A dirty dish in a cabinet that could destroy the world.*

He understood then why magic had brought about the end of the scientific age. Science did seem like a dark magic. It did seem like the devil's work. For if something so destructive could be contained in something that was nearly invisible to the human eye—and could be engineered by a single, fucked up human being in a cold lab beneath a castle—it made perfect sense to eliminate the ability to do such a thing. At least magic was a predictable evil. Magic was a destructive force that could be seen and could be countered.

This...there was no defense against this. Whatever she'd done, she'd made sure it was irreversible. Something overtook him then he could not control, a blind rage so potent that he forgot all of his most basic teachings in an instant. He took the glass dish and slammed it down beneath the flat of his hand. The glass crumpled into jagged pieces that sliced his hand near to ribbons.

He held it there, restored to himself, realizing his mistake. Zanje had told him to cover all of his wounds. Zanje had told him to never get it into his eyes or his mouth, that all of his most vulnerable orifices could catch him the disease even if he was resistant to it, because you just never know. If even a little of it got into his body, it would become a lot of it in no time. And then, too, he remembered her words about incubation periods. Latency. How a disease could sleep in a body for months, sometimes years, before completely overtaking a person's function.

He stared at his hand. At the blood that feathered out from his palm with every frantic beat of his heart. *That's it then. In one moment, one careless mistake, I've done it. I just killed myself.* He kept staring, numb to what he had just done. The lab lay in shambles all around him, but all he cared about was this one thing. He gazed upon the triumph of science. One tiny wound...and the end of the mighty Berge. His lips curved into a wry smile. "You win after all," he murmured.

"Berge?"

It wasn't the voice he'd expected, not least of all because she should have been locked into a cell in the dungeon below. He whirled, shoving his injured hand into his pocket. She'd be worried about it—she was too kind—and he didn't want her to touch it. "Nerys!"

She was a sight for sore eyes. The jacket she'd worn when he captured her had been discarded. The top she wore was sleeveless and thin. It had once hugged her body snugly, acting as the first layer of defense against the winter. Now it hung in dirty tatters away from her skin. She'd lost weight, and she hadn't had much in the first place. And she was still the most beautiful woman he'd ever seen. But he didn't want her that way. She wasn't the kind of woman he wanted to ravage, but the kind that needed his protection. He wanted to wrap a coat around her frail, shivering shoulders and lead her away from this place, kiss the top of her head and warn her to never return, and then say goodbye to her forever. *Get away from me, Nerys.*

"Are you alright?"

He stared, for a while saying nothing. Why was it that every time she laid eyes upon him, her first thought was for his well being? "I'm fine." What else was there to say? "Are you okay?"

She shrugged.

Chapter Thirty-One

She wasn't sure what she was hearing when she heard the first crash. Her chin tilted upward toward the ceiling, toward the source of the sound. She squeezed Ashes between her arms, trying to shield her from the noise and the vibrations. "Shh."

There was another, even louder crash, and on top of it all, she heard him yelling. He didn't use any words, just yelled, over and over again. It sounded as if he might be in a fight. Her instincts warred within her for what to do about it. Her first thought was to charge in and help, but she'd never been a warrior. She wasn't particularly strong or brave. She should probably just stay right where she was and wait. If he won, he'd come for her. If they won, she should wait until they went away.

But then she remembered that he'd given her his only defense. Her fingers curled around the bone on a string around her neck. It abhorred her to have such a thing, but it had already saved one life, though it left her body cold. She kissed Ashes' neck and shut her eyes, trying to figure out what she should do. Her heart pounded. She tried to gather up the courage to dash up the stairs and rescue him. She wasn't sure if she could do it, or if she should. What if she ended up getting in the way and distracting him, and costing him the fight?

The crashing stopped. She waited for another broken glass, another ceiling-crumbling slam into the floor, but nothing came this time. Whatever was happening upstairs, it was over. She guided Ashes to the back of her neck. The weasel's claws tangled in her hair, but she snuggled up comfortably, chuckled, and stilled, perfectly content to be there.

Nerys crept up the stairs quietly, unconvinced that it was safe. But she made the entire journey without being stopped by anyone. It yet remained silent.

The door to the lab was open. Pale blue starlight spilled into the otherwise dim hallway. She poked her head in and peeked. The first thing she saw was the hated bed with all of its leather buckles against the wall of the lab. It was overturned, and left a wake of destruction behind it. Several deep grooves were cut into the stone where the bed had scuffed up the floor. Her eyes followed the grooves, came to rest upon the wet drain. It wasn't red, though. It only looked like water and something darker, brown and maybe yellow. The air was thick with chemical smells, including the one he'd used so long ago to knock her out. The shelves were broken. The glass was broken. Everything was broken, and he stood stock still in the midst of it all.

Berge stood before a counter with his back turned to her. It almost looked as if he was working on something where he stood, but from what he'd said to her during her time there, she didn't think he knew anything about the concepts and theories behind what he was actually doing here. "Berge?"

"Nerys!" His breath left him in a rush. He looked surprised to see her there. She figured that was fair, considering that she was usually trapped below.

"Are you alright?" Her eyes swept over his body, searching for wounds. He looked fine. A little upset, perhaps, but unharmed.

He stared, blinking. Then his gaze fell upon the mess before returning back to her. He looked to be confused. "I'm fine." He paused. "Are you okay?"

She shrugged, suddenly worried about telling him what had happened. "I'm not sure I should tell you this, but…the others…"

"I see."

"I…" *I stayed.*

"Why didn't you go with them?" he asked.

She looked around the broken lab, mourning its loss. All that glass…"Because I believe in this."

He shook his head. He kept shaking it, slowly back and forth. "I don't understand you," he admitted.

"I know," she answered. She offered him a shaky smile. "We're all different people, but that's what makes us so interesting. But I've already saved a few lives and if I have the chance to do it again, I'll endure."

"You're going to die."

"I know. But…we all die eventually, you know."

His eyes flashed. "We have to get you out of here," he said suddenly.

"I already told you, I'm staying."

He raised his voice. "No, Nerys, you're not."

"You can't make me leave," she said, drawing herself up to her full height. It wasn't much, though, and she didn't cut an imposing figure.

"Actually, I can." He crossed over the battlefield of broken glass, reaching for her.

Her muscles tensed, preparing for a fight. Then Ashes dove out from beneath her hair and took a leap between them. She caught his shirt, climbed up his arm, hesitated on his shoulder for a minute, and then dove into his pocket. "Ashes!" he exclaimed, a relaxed smile overcoming his face. "Where've you been, eh?"

"Um...that bone you gave me?"

He relaxed. "Yeah, what about it?"

She couldn't look him in the eye. Couldn't say what she'd done. Even if it was necessary, she was ashamed. "Thanks."

His expression darkened. "What happened?"

"One of the prisoners...one of the Baggage...he was going to hurt Ashes."

Berge stared at her. "What did you do?"

"I... think I... well." She smiled nervously. "I think I set him on fire?"

Something unexpected happened next. He scooped her up in his arms and hugged her fiercely. He rattled her a couple of times, as if he'd just learned how much he enjoyed hugs and reinitiated. Then, his voice thick with emotion, he muttered, "Thank you."

She hugged him back. "It's okay, Berge."

He broke the hug as abruptly as he'd started it, then hurried across to the other side of the lab. His eyes fell upon a hard leather case. He unbuckled the catches and opened it. Inside were a handful of wicked looking cutting tools. Nerys made a face, wondering what he intended to do with them and wishing she hadn't wondered. He retrieved the smaller of the knives, with tiny little serrations like Ashes' teeth. He tucked it into his belt and put the kit back together. "Look, Nerys…there's something I need to tell you. It's going to make you upset, but there isn't a lot of time, so I just need you to just listen, okay?"

"Okay."

"I just learned this myself. Zanje isolated the…the whatever it is that causes Red Death. I don't know what you call it, but it's invisible to our eyes, and she had it in these fucking little dishes." He made a half circle with his thumb and forefinger to emulate and indicated the broken glass all over the floor. "She made it worse." Nerys nodded, horrified, but she stayed silent as he asked. "And all the times she's used your blood—and the blood of whoever was in the prison with you—to save people, she's been adding a version of this that sleeps. It sits in your bloodstream for months, maybe years, before it's going to wake up and start killing again. And it's going to be worse than anything you or I could imagine." He paused. "Because Zanje Vangelic is brilliant. She's one of a kind. She would have done this so flawlessly as to make sure we can't do anything to stop it.

"So every single life we saved…we only turned them into time-release sacks of death and then sent them back into the world thinking they were healed."

She gasped, one hand covering her mouth.

The thought of it was too terrible to comprehend.

"Yeah." He waited for it to sink in before continuing. "You've seen what we've done. You know how it's done. At the top of this tower, however many floors up it is…and then down one floor…that's where Zanje keeps her money, and it is a lot of it, Nerys. More money than any person needs in a lifetime. When it's safe, go up there and get it, and then you go set up something like this. Except you do it right. Find people like you. Find people willing to help. Take only enough from them to save a life, and then give them time to recover. Save people. Really save them. Do what it is you thought you were doing all along, but this time, you do it right."

"Okay."

"I don't know how I'm going to get you out of here, but we'll manage somehow."

"You're coming with me?"

He hesitated, looking between the disaster he'd wrought, the empty door beyond her, and at her face. "Yeah. I'm coming with you."

She hugged him again. "I'm glad."

"I can't for the life of me figure out why, but I'm glad, too."

"I knew I could save you," she mumbled into his chest.

His arms fell around her gingerly, as if afraid

he might break her. "I didn't even want to be saved," he said.

Chapter Thirty-Two

Seeing the two of them embrace angered her more than she thought possible. It wasn't because there was affection. It wasn't even that she thought they might have a chance at making it. Nerys was doomed to die regardless, and Berge was never going to be anything better than what he was. He was too far gone to be fixed, a wooden beam, termite-gnawed and soft with rot.

No, what pissed her off was that Berge was *her* pet, *her* creature. His entire purpose was to amuse her. He was her plaything. And this…this *girl*…this weak, naive, artless *wench* had helped him slip her collar. It wasn't that Zanje truly wanted him, it was that he'd broken her hold over him. He was free, and she hated that. He was a magnificent tool of destruction, and he was mangled and useless now.

She stood in the doorway with her arms crossed tightly across her chest, blocking their one exit out of the laboratory. She wasn't a large person, but in a battle such as this one, all that mattered was that escape was impossible. While they hugged it out, she cast a furious survey across the destruction of her lab, racking up a list of their sins before she decided how best to tear them apart. The beds, the glass, the counters and shelves…those could be replaced. That cabinet, however, and the pestilence she'd been cultivating with such great care…that was invaluable. They would pay for that. She could harvest the strain again from those she'd infected, but to do so would set her back months. Breeding a cell line that was hardy enough to survive in a dish was a challenge and she wasn't eager to do it again.

There was enough alcohol and ether in this lab to torch them with barely a spark, but to do so might cause an explosion that would injure her, too. Or cause unsightly scarring.

Berge noticed her first. He slowly uncurled the girl's arms from around his shoulders and pushed her behind him. Zanje smiled, wryly amused that he thought to protect such a pitiful child against her own raw power. "Oh come on, now, Berge. Do you really think you're going to win against me?"

"Hey baby," he teased. "Give us a kiss."

Her eyes narrowed a fraction, lips curving into a wry smile. "You made a bit of a mess."

He smirked, but the smile never touched his eyes. They were alight with something foreign that she didn't like, not empty and soulless like she remembered. "I was thinking of you."

"How nice." Her eyes fell upon the girl, peeking around from behind Berge. She had to suppress the urge to torch her. Fire would have been the most spectacular way to kill her. But there was plenty of debris in the room to bludgeon or shred her in all sorts of interesting ways. Unfortunately, all of it was on the floor and had little potential energy to convert. She could pull energy from elsewhere in the castle, but it would take too much time. It didn't leave much at her disposal except for the light. Too much warning, but...that only meant things were about to get messy.

The witchlights above went out.

The lights went out, which only meant that Zanje had reclaimed them for her next attack. Berge grabbed Nerys by the arm and flung her as far as he could. He heard her cry out and trip on something broken, but whatever it was was a kinder fate than she'd have otherwise experienced. He didn't have any idea what Zanje was up to, but he knew of what she was capable. She'd foregone fire, probably because of the chemicals he'd spilled. She could attack with anything at any moment—broken glass, potentially dipped in horrible death—but she couldn't see in the dark.

Berge was a scrapper in his younger years, though. He knew when there was an opportunity to subdue the greater fighter. Zanje had Craft and he didn't. Returned to his default state, all he had available to him was the need to survive. He tackled her around the middle and dropped them both to the ground before she could use Craft. He tried to pin her wrists, but she was stronger than she looked. She struggled and broke free again and again, all sharp bones and writhing muscle. They turned and twisted on the only bare spot of floor there was, fighting for who'd get to use their arms.

She kneed him in the groin. He fell over to his back and groaned, clutching himself to protect his sensitive parts from further insult. He sucked in unbreathable air and went lightheaded and dizzy all at once. She laughed and straddled him, sharp knees digging into his ribs and hips pinning his trapped hands. Her hands closed over his throat and squeezed. His heart pounded furiously in his ribs, frantically struggling against the need to breathe, the need to strike, and the need to escape all in one.

Her hands were ripped away from his neck. Zanje grunted and was flung sideways. "Berge!" Nerys cried out. Her hands pawed at his chest, finding him in the dark.

He had enough presence of mind to push her aside and roll over atop her just long enough to tell her to stay still. "Find a wall and stay there," he told her. He didn't have time to deal with her.

Her hands fell away. "Okay."

Zanje groaned. Whatever her plan had been, she abandoned it, instead using the reclaimed energy to make witchlight again. She wasn't going to fight in the dark.

His pulse quickened. She had to know it put her at a disadvantage. She wasn't a fighter. She was a mage. She'd given up her ability to use Craft in favor of a melee fight. Then his eyes fell to the serrated knife in her hand. His hand went to his waistband, but the knife he'd grabbed was gone. Her smile was ghastly in the blue light. She knew she'd won.

She lunged. He maneuvered out of the way by inches, grabbed her by the wrist. She twisted in close to his body and elbowed him in the gut with her other arm, stepped on his foot, and delivered an uppercut to the jaw.

He let go, letting her think she'd won. He'd been in more fights than she had. He stumbled, playing injured. She'd chipped a tooth, but his body had suffered more damage in an average fight. Most of his earlier years had seen him beaten within an inch of his life about once every season. He'd learned how to take a punch.

She was sharp, though. She didn't waste time toying with him now. She'd get all of her digs in when the two of them lay dead. She sneered, wearing a small smile only for herself. Then she tightened her grip on the knife and jabbed.

His hand shot out and stopped her arm cold. With the other he came down upon it hard. Her fingers jolted open and she hissed in pain. The knife fell and clattered away. He lunged for her instead of it, wrestling her down. He didn't have any other plan other than holding her still. It was all he needed, though. "Nerys, get out of here!" he shouted over his shoulder.

"What about you?"

"I'll be fine!"

"But you don't have your—"

"Just go!"

Zanje slid her knees between his legs and laughed. "Yes, Nerys. Go and leave my pet with me. We'll be just fine." She tilted her chin down and looked at him through her lashes. "Hardly the first time we've been in this position. Isn't that right, Berge? It won't be the last."

He didn't hear Nerys's footsteps, but he could feel the fire rising beneath Zanje's skin. He didn't have much longer to stall, and he was out of tactics to restrain her. He had but one idea left. "One more kiss, eh?" She laughed as their lips met.

Then, suddenly, her lips went cold. She gasped and arched beneath him, her entire body going rigid. The heat of her skin dipped dramatically. Berge scrambled off her, shaking his hands for warmth, utterly bewildered as her terrified face glazed over. "What the—" He retrieved the knife and held it before him, his only defense against…whatever was happening.

Zanje's skin turned blue as she choked for air and reached quaking fingers toward him. Then, her eyes turned white and frozen, and she curled into a tight ball to die. She fell silent and still. And then, to his horror, ice crystals blossomed upon her skin. He blinked, staring and confused. Then he did the same with his eyes on the witchlight, wondering why they still sparkled overhead. There were more of them now, and they seemed brighter.

Then the rest of his wits returned, and he turned to his charge. Nerys's face was set in a grim line. The color had returned to her cheeks. She no longer shivered. She was standing, straight and tall, passing judgment upon Berge's lifetime tormentor. She turned to Berge, her expression softening. "I know, now, why you've suffered," she said softly. "And now you, too, are free." She coiled her fingers around his and led him from the destruction.

Chapter Thirty-Three

They heard shouting before they reached the main hall. Some of it was the sound of batttle, angry men intent on killing another man. There was the sound of breaking things, the sound of chaos, of destruction, of the end of all things. He pushed her aside and then bent towards her, speaking in a voice that only she could hear, so as not to attract attention from the men in the room. "It's your friends," he told her.

"They aren't my friends," she rejected vehemently.

He gripped ahold of her shoulders and steadied her, willing her to see reason. "They are, Nerys. You're definitely going to need them after this. All of them are like you."

"But they don't want to help," she argued.

He shook her. *"Make them* want to. That's your gift."

She looked away, uncertain.

"Now look…" He knew she wasn't going to

like what he said next, and tried to soften it as best he could. "They're not going to leave here until they've killed me."

Her eyes flashed. "They aren't going to kill you."

"Yes, they are."

"No, I won't let them." She grabbed at the necklace she wore, missing once before she found it. "You gave me the power to save you. I won't let them hurt you."

"Nerys," he barked. "Listen to yourself. You don't know what you're saying. Now listen to me. I've earned my death. I've hurt every one of these people. I've racked up a list of horrible deeds that beg for my death. I gave you the power to save more than just me. The things that you know are greater than you. Greater than me. I need you to live, and if you try to save me against them you won't make it. Do you hear me? You won't make it, and you *must*." He shook her again.

"You don't have to fight them. Let's just sneak around! There has to be another way out of here."

"No, I already told you. They aren't going to rest until I'm dead. And don't tell me that Simos hasn't given you a lot of shit for protecting me."

She looked away, and he knew that he'd won.

"So here's what we're going to do. I'm going

to go out there and pick a fight. They're going to win. Then you need to be strong." He tipped her chin up and looked into her eyes. "You hear me Nerys? You have to be strong. And I know that you are. You're a master at holding back your tears. Don't you cry for me, okay? Don't you fucking cry for me, Nerys. I haven't earned it, and I don't want your tears. Promise me." Tears welled in her eyes. He brushed them away. "Promise me."

"You're really going to do this? You can't really mean to walk willingly to your death?"

"You taught me how," he said gently, giving her a smile. "Dying for a reason? I'm not afraid of this."

She bit her lip, swallowed. Swallowed again. Nodded, though she clearly didn't want to. "I promise. No tears."

"Good girl. When it's all over, let them find you. Tell them you got held up because of me. Tell them how I betrayed you. Make up something awful but believable. Make it sound like I changed the way you think about me, and you're upset about how I tricked you. You can cry then, okay?" She nodded. "Make them believe, and make them trust you. And then you and them will change the world."

She didn't't want to. Every cell in her body rebelled, but she nodded anyway, and then she did the unthinkable. She wrapped her arms around his neck and kissed him.

It was the only time someone had ever kissed him and meant something by it. It was a precious gift. He wouldn't squander it, so he kissed her back, pouring all of the withered soul he had left into it, to give her something good in return. It was all he had to give her for what she had done. When she'd taken the rest of his kindness with her and withdrew, he dug his fingers into his pocket. There, he scooped up the sleepy little weasel. He lifted Ashes to his lips and kissed her. Her paws raised and tried to hold him back, not wishing to be disturbed. He chuckled and forced through it anyway. "Goodbye, Ashes," he whispered. He handed the creature over to Nerys with a smile on his face. She cradled her arms against her belly, and Ashes snuggled there, happy to be asleep again. "Goodbye, Nerys," he said.

Without waiting to see if she obeyed his command not to cry, he turned the corner, his damaged hand against the wall. It was an odd sensation, being a hero. It brought him strength. It made him feel invincible. He knew he was going to die, and yet…he was calmer than he could ever remember being. Prouder than he could ever remember being. For a wonder, he finally had something to die for, and it didn't seem stupid at all. He wasn't worthless, because there was value in this death. She would live because of it.

What a strange concept.

"My name is Bergeron Nacht," he whispered. It was for himself. A prayer of the godless, that someone might remember his name when this was all over. He withdrew Zanje's jagged cutting tool and held it before him. He didn't know how to use it. Weapons had seemed so useless before when he had a limitless potential for bone-melting fire. He knew how to stab and slash, but he had no real strategy for how to win a knife fight. But if he was going to make this convincing, he needed to put up a fight. Maybe he could at least take down Simos. *That* cheeky fucker the world could do without. He didn't even have a useful blood type. The idea of killing Simos pleased him. He might have been redeemed, but he wasn't altogether changed, and Simos pissed him off.

"Simos!" he shouted into the main hall. The word shot up to the eaves, echoing in the large hollow space. He resolved himself to fight, squaring his stance. His center remained calm, though his blood pulsed with pure adrenaline, unsullied by the heat of the magic he'd once borrowed. It was an appropriate way to die. He would die himself, nothing within him but what he was born with. A little bone and a few quarts of blood, shivering from the cold. No magic, and no religion. He briefly considered infecting Simos with his affliction, but that would only make more complications for Nerys's future, and that he would not abide.

There were nearly a dozen of them, men and women alike, painted in blood and gore and wearing the grim determination of warriors bent on justifiable murder. Berge's eye fell upon the unfortunate objects of their bloodlust—the two clients Zanje had picked up from Quorath. He didn't have time to consider what words might have been said between the two parties for their lives to become forfeit, but he wasn't sad about it. They could have been another Dair, or Haddig.

He smirked as the recognition lit the faces of the prisoners. They knew him. Oh, they knew him well.

"Nacht." Simos stood furthest back from him. He wasn't covered in blood. It bothered Berge, for that only lent more to the impression he'd developed of the man being a self-righteous fuck. He reminded Berge too much of Zanje, too good for the common man, omniscient and wise. There he was, the rebel king, watching on in abject silence while his fellows tore two men apart, ruining fine furniture with tainted blood. Simos didn't smile back. He waited, hands clasped behind his back as if he'd only been witnessing an art lesson at work.

"I'm going to kill you," Berge promised.

"Are you now?"

He nodded.

"Where's the help?"

"I don't need any help to kill you."

His eyes fell upon the knife. Unfortunately, Simos wasn't an idiot. He didn't know why Berge might have been separated from once powerful magic, but he could probably see by the improper way he was gripping the handle that Berge was in a desperate way. "I probably don't need any help to kill you, either. But, unlike you, I have help."

Berge calmed, taking a deep breath and waiting for the imminent inevitable. Then he advanced, one graceful feline step at a time, weaving around divans and candle pedestals, stepping over the ragged body of one of the clients. His foot pressed down upon his discarded cigar. The prisoners parted, making a way for Berge to reach Simos. Cautiously, Berge walked between them, casting furtive glances. Their eyes were cold and merciless. He'd wronged them, cost them their dignity and almost their lives. They'd lost much, and meant to collect on those debts.

Simos maintained his composure and his stance, waiting. When Berge stepped within striking distance, just beginning to form the thought of attacking, the bastard spoke. "Kill him."

Like crows to the carcass they descended upon him. They fought in the inelegant way of beasts, buoyed by the protection of the pack and unafraid to die. They grabbed at ankles, hooked arms around his middle and his neck, and his arms. He was strong. He thrashed, snarling and shouting and swearing, throwing every foul insult and slur that he had ever learned. He tried to slash with the knife, but with the arms of two or three people holding his knife hand still, he found that extraordinarily difficult. Someone's fingers wrapped around his own, peeling his fingertips away one at a time until the knife clattered to the floor.

He laughed, a quiet, desolate sound that none of them heard over their need to have him killed. He felt he'd done well. All around him was a storm of wild eyes and dirty hair. He shut his eyes and let death come for him, using his precious last few moments to remember the only memories he had worth savoring. Ashes nudging him with a tiny cold nose, the pantomime of a weasel kiss. The first time Zanje smiled at him, before he knew her heart as well as his own, back when he could pretend she might have cared. The way it had felt when he approached Wex with a plan to evacuate Nerys, a part of something great, a part of a true team for the first time. And finally, the soft yet desperate feeling of a true, heartfelt kiss.

The blade of the knife he'd killed Zanje with caught him just below the ribs in his middle. It was fire and agony and all the pain such a thing needed to be to prove it was fatal. That one wound would have been enough, but they weren't done yet. He felt every bite of their rage. His heart raced, though whether he was excited or scared—or whether it was just a stupid, biological response that Zanje might have had an answer for—he just didn't know.

In the end, Berge…we all die.

The world turned dark before the dying was over. He found peace in the blackness. Sleepy, almost, and warmer than he would have thought. At the end of all things, as life slipped away, he found exactly what he knew was waiting for him all along.

Absolutely nothing.

Chapter Thirty-Four

She watched him die. It seemed as if it should be a requirement, given their brief yet complex history. There was no one alive who might remember him fondly. From the sounds of it, he might have burned every bridge he'd ever built, and some that weren't even his. From the sounds of it, that had been exactly what he had wanted all along. And yet, the last several hours of his existence, he'd used the last of what life had given him to save her life and give her as much as he could to save humanity from a condition he'd help create. No, Bergeron Nacht was not a good man, but there was some part of him that had wanted to be, and that was beautiful enough for her to remember.

So she watched. She watched the expression of Simos as Berge approached, and though she wanted to believe that he was as cruel as his captors had been, she knew that it wasn't as simple as that. Simos, too, was a good man with glimmers of darkness breaking through. He believed Berge to be one deserving of death. In his eyes, bringing about his death was doing them all a favor. She disagreed, but she respected it nonetheless.

In a way, all of them were the same, neither good nor bad. Neither heavenly nor hellbound. Each and every being that possessed a human heart possessed good intentions, and also had the capacity to do great harm. Even Nerys herself had killed as a way of doing good. She regretted nothing. She'd done what she thought was right and necessary. Hadn't they all?

She held back her tears as he was dragged to the floor, limbs flailing, knife flashing, cruel bestial expressions upon the faces of those that brought about his end. She'd made a promise, after all, one she'd sealed with a kiss. Her fingers flew to the buzz upon her lips, the last vestige of contact with the man who would soon be dead. She remained, breathing only barely and despairing to have done so. Every breath she took was a sound to interrupt the scene she needed to witness, and she needed to hear and see every macabre detail of what transpired in the main hall of Zanje's castle. The echoing howls of wrath. The grunts of a struggle, the tearing of fabric. And, was that even the sound of soft laughter?

When it was over, there was more blood on

the floor. Blood on the couch and blood in their hair. Blood, blood, everywhere. How strange it seemed to her that so much of her time lately had been in some way related to blood. It was the reason she was there in the first place. It was as necessary to her life as to the lives of all other living creatures. It was also her strongest power and her greatest gift…the blood of Nerys Raphaen. And, too, blood was the bane of mankind, left unchecked. Their species was plagued with an illness that affected the blood. Even caused blood to leak out from the human body.

How much blood must now be soaked into the earth?

How much blood had been shed for this?

She didn't know.

As the hall quieted, bloodlust ebbing, returning her fellow beleaguered prisoners to some semblance of civilized self, she stepped around the corner. Simos espied her first. He'd remained stoic throughout the whole ordeal, bearing witness as she had to what had happened only inches from his own feet. "Nerys!" he exclaimed. He pushed people out of the way and ran to her. She didn't want to believe that he was actually concerned for her, but his voice was honest and scared. He'd disagreed with her all along, but that didn't mean he wished her harm.

She gave him a shaky smile—not feigned—and allowed herself to be hugged. She wondered if Simos knew what Berge smelled like, and if he could smell the lingering scent of his skin upon her. If he did, he didn't give any indication. "Simos," she mumbled. "I..."

"Are you hurt?" He pulled her back to arm's length, looking her over head to toe.

"No, I'm not hurt."

"What happened? I was scared something might have happened to you. Is Kopep with you?"

"Kopep is dead. Berge..." Here it was. The most atrocious lie she would ever tell. She didn't want to. Every word left her lips like a curse word, suffused her body with endless shame. "Berge attacked me." She released a shaky breath and looked away. She hoped it was convincing enough. "Kopep tried to save me so I could escape. I...saw him go down just before I got away. I hid...then I heard you all fighting, and I...had hoped...he was...he was..." She couldn't say 'dead.'

Simos was shaking his head, his mouth set into a firm frown. "I warned you, Nerys. I told you he was tricky."

She cried, then. She hated herself for saying the things she had said. But Berge had said she could cry now. "I know, Simos," she said brokenly. "I know you did. I just never expected it to end this way."

He hugged her again. "Nerys, Nerys, Nerys…it's going to be okay. We're free now. First we have to do away with Zanje." He pulled her back, his gaze drifting to the floors above.

"She's dead," Nerys informed him.

"What? How do you know? What happened?"

She wiped her eyes, trembling but trying her best to calm. "I don't know what happened. I saw her body in the lab before I came out here. I guess Berge must have killed her." She'd also caught a glimpse of Zanje's missing finger, and the last piece of the puzzle had clicked into place.

He nodded toward the group. "Someone go check and make sure?"

"I'll go," Nellan offered. He took off down the hallway.

"Can we get out of here?" Nerys asked. "I haven't seen the sun in God knows how long…"

"You won't, either," Simos said grimly. "Sun has already set. There's nothing out there now but a smear of purple on the horizon."

She smiled. "A little purple is better than a lot of black."

"You're right." He turned back to the lot of them and straightened. Trying to be the leader.

His expression neutralized. "Alright, everyone. Let's go home."

There was a collective sigh of relief and smiles all around. Their trials were over. They were wounded, tired, emotionally exhausted.

All except for Nerys. As Simos led her away, his hand entwined with hers, smiling in her direction as if he meant to wife her when this was all over, Nerys felt out of place. She peeked over her shoulder to where Berge lay. His body was broken, haphazardly dropped in with two men she could only assume were common criminals. It seemed an unfair end. She couldn't stare long, though, lest anyone believe her less good than she was meant.

She tore her eyes away before she wanted to and didn't have a chance to satisfy her need to see whether or not his chest still rose and fell. She walked away from him, but she didn't think she could ever let him go.

Chapter Thirty-Five

Wex hit the ground hard, all of his breath ejected from his lungs. The impact jarred his entire body from toes to spine to head. It shook his brain so hard that it might have scrambled. He squeezed his eyes shut as the world spun violently around its axis. *I'm dead,* he thought. *I'm dead dead dead.*

But then Maxine tackled him in the snow, thinking he meant to play. Her paws hit his chest and rebounded off as she spun away into the powder. And the only thing to do when a sixty pound dog jumped upon his chest was to tighten up his abdomen muscles and groan, the wind knocked out of him again. He rolled over onto his side, holding his belly, and watched grumpily as Maxine danced away in wagging tail circles, happier than ever to see him.

Truth be told, he was rather shocked he was still alive. He sat up, then looked up. And up, and up. At the bottom of the balcony seven stories above, replaying what had just happened. Yes, Zanje had attacked him. Yes, he had flown out the window. Yes, he had dropped seven stories to the earth below. And he *wasn't* dead. He patted himself all over, checking for sore spots and broken bones, but came up with nothing. "Huh," he said aloud. Either he was really lucky, or someone up above was looking out for him.

Maxine tackled him again.

He got to his feet shakily, taking slow, deep breaths to calm his nerves. This hadn't been part of the plan. Berge hadn't believed Zanje would try to kill him. If anything, he'd said, she might have tried to kill Berge himself, or Nerys. Wex hadn't done anything wrong. He'd done nothing to incur her wrath. Even seemed to have a soft spot for him. But whatever had possessed her to lash out at him, for the time being he was a ghost and dead to all. It was... freeing.

But it put Berge in a bad spot. He didn't have a way to spirit Nerys away. Wex wasn't sure how to help, but none of the scenarios he came up with in his mind involved him suddenly appearing and shouting "I'm alive, surprise!" Instead, he packed supplies into the snowcraft and made sure Maxine didn't need to use the bathroom. The next hour or two was bound to be quite interesting. Berge would have to improvise his plan. Wex had no idea what to expect.

Some time later, just when he was about to doze off, he heard shouting from within. It sent him running to the front door. Before he'd gotten there, it went strangely silent. Wex's pulse quickened, concerned for whoever might be hurt or dying, no matter who it was. It hadn't been Zanje, and she was the only person alive whom he wished harm. But when his hand wrapped around the handle and was ready to pull, the door suddenly flew open and about a dozen people poured out, wild-eyed and happy. "Whoa!" he shouted, too surprised to say aught else.

All of them fell in behind the two out front, a man and a woman. The man wore an expression almost of anger. He looked as if he'd seen some hard times. His face was unused to smiling, though there lurked an intelligence deep within his eyes that Wex suspected hid fascinating accounts of what the man had seen. He was ready to fight, that much was obvious. Wex held both hands up as a gesture of non-hostility. He wasn't about to pick a fight. Fortunately, it looked like the small mob didn't seem as if they wanted to fight either, though it looked like they'd just been through one. To a one, they were all somehow painted with blood.

All except for the man in the front.

He studied them while he tried to appear harmless. They must have been the other prisoners from the dungeon, which meant that they must have somehow escaped. He wondered if Berge had released them, but since he wasn't with them, he feared otherwise. The more likely scenario was that Berge had been overpowered, and the man with the readiness to murder meant to take Nerys with him. Wex couldn't allow that. Berge had been adamant that she leave with the two of them.

The woman beside the clean man was obviously Nerys. Berge had talked at great length about her in a way that had Wex quite convinced the man had been in love with her. He'd denied it, of course, but she was special to him regardless. "Nerys." He smiled, genuinely pleased to see her.

The man out front appeared confused. "Who are you?"

"Her brother," he lied, pretending indignance. "Wex. Who are you?"

He looked askance at Nerys. She was entirely impassive. Her eyes were swollen from crying and she didn't look as if she wanted to talk. "A friend," he said.

"Good," he replied gruffly. He held out one arm to Nerys. He was completely improvising. Berge wouldn't have told her who he was since he'd 'died,' so she had no reason to trust him. All he could do was hope. Dropping Berge's name was out of the question. The prisoners would react badly to it. "Come on, Nerys. Let's go home."

She looked at his proffered hand. Looked at his face. There was no spark of recognition, nor hope, nor much of anything. For the most part, she looked dead inside, like her whole world had just been destroyed. There wasn't anything left for her. Nonetheless, he waited, a smile frozen to his face, hoping she somehow gathered from the aether that this was what Berge meant for them.

Berge's pet weasel appeared from seemingly nowhere, making an impossible leap between Nerys and his outstretched arm. Her tiny claws hooked into his arm hair and his skin. He laughed and yelped at the same time. Ashes shuffled between one of his shoulders and the other, pausing for a moment on each and looking back toward the crowd. Wex was confused. He'd handled the critter before, and Ashes sometimes played with Maxine in the snow—the weasel loved Hide and Seek, and Maxine loved stuffing her face into the powder —but other than that...

But when he looked back at the crowd, he understood that Ashes was wiser than anyone gave her credit for. Life had come back to Nerys face. She was locked in a battle of wills against the man who held her hand in a clawlike grip. She was shaking her head and he was whispering in a voice low enough that Wex couldn't hear.

At last, she snatched her hand free. Then, she hugged him. And then, she came up to Wex. She smiled, though a tear had escaped her eye. Then she rose up on tiptoe and kissed his cheek. "Hello, Wex. Sorry, I've had a rough day."

"That's okay, Nerys," he said to her as sweetly as he could manage. "You can tell me all about it on the way home."

"Nerys!" the man shouted after her.

"Simos," she said back.

"If you need anything...I'm from Elisse, in the south."

Her mouth fell open. Wex understood. Elisse was far, far to the south, where there was no snow, or so it was said. Wex suddenly had a hundred questions, but he knew better than to ask him. "How on earth did you get so far north?" she asked him.

He smiled and winked. "I'll tell you the next time we meet," he promised. "Stay true to your God, Nerys. I'm glad we met."

She sobered. Then smiled. "I'm glad to know you, Simos." She waved. Then she curled an arm around his and turned them away.

"You okay?" he asked softly.

"I will be," she replied.

He nodded, patted her hand, and led her to the snowcraft. Her eyes widened, but she didn't ask. Wex got the impression that she simply wasn't in the mood to talk. He didn't usually prefer to talk, either, so he left her to her self-imposed solitude. He opened up her side and gestured for her to get in. "Oh, uh, by the way. I hope you don't mind dogs."

She came face to face with Maxine's happy face. Maxine was already at her maximum level of happiness, ready to hit the trail. She only spared a moment's glance for Nerys. Her tail thumped once.

"I like dogs," she said.

"Oh good…because you're going to need to share a seat with her. I'm afraid there isn't much room."

Maxine made a face, her lip caught in her teeth.

Wex climbed up to his seat on the opposite side. Nerys slid to the edge, all the way up against the closed door. She wasn't very large, but she still didn't quite fit until Maxine flopped down atop her, using her like a glorified cushion. Wex held his breath, worried she might be annoyed. Instead, Nerys burst out laughing. Maxine looked over her shoulder at him. *I think we're going to be fine,* she seemed to say.

Nerys's eyes were all that was visible over Maxine's happy face, but they were shining with laughter.

He nodded as he started up the snowcraft. They were quiet for some time. Nerys was withdrawn, petting Maxine and Ashes simultaneously though her expression told him she was elsewhere.

"So. What's next?" he wondered aloud. "I just need a direction to drive is all."

"Anywhere. It doesn't matter."

He didn't have any strong connections to anyone, but Orelia stood out in his mind. "How do you feel about north?"

She cringed. "Into the frozen lands?"

He nodded. "When I was driving for Zanje, she sent me up to Becket twice. There's a lady there owns an apothecary. Her granddaughter had the Death. If you're not against it, I'd like to see how they're doing now."

"It's as good a place as any."

"What about you?"

She sighed. "I'm supposed to save everybody."

He huffed. "Yeah? And how are you going to do that?"

"My blood is special." She toyed with a pendant around her neck. "And I have this."

"What's 'this'?"

"Zanje's finger."

"Really?" He peered across the cab at the object in her hands. "Why would you have such a twisted thing?"

"It lets me use her Craft."

"*Zanje's* Craft?" She nodded. He whistled with appreciation.

She stared down at her open hand and the gnarled bone resting upon her palm. "Berge gave it to me," she said softly. "And then I killed her with it."

Wex only had one thought. A question. He already knew the answer, but until it was confirmed he couldn't accept it. "He's dead, isn't he?" he asked at last.

She looked up, shocked for one moment. Then she relaxed, returning to the pets. "Yes."

He nodded again and looked out the window, resting one elbow on the door. "Damn."

"How did you know him?"

Wex smiled into his hand, remembering. "He saved my life." She didn't say anything. He kept on driving. He assumed she had only returned to her thoughts, having made an obligatory venture into conversation, but when he glanced back her way he found out just how wrong he was. She stared at him, eyes as far open as they would go, almost fearful. "What? Was it something I said?"

"He...saved your life?"

"Mm-hm," he confirmed. "It was how we met. I was dying. Red Death. Nasty sickness... He carried me to Zanje's all the way from Lorent. It's about, oh, six miles to the west over there." He pointed, but she wasn't interested. She was staring out the windshield, wide-eyed. "Are you okay?"

"I don't understand."

"Which part?"

"Any of this. He was always so adamant about how...*bad*...he was. But he wasn't. Not really. Was he? Tell me."

"Berge? Nah, he was all talk. Well. Not *all* talk," he backpedaled. "He wasn't all good, and he wasn't all bad. None of us are. But yeah. He saved my life. Looked out for my soul after, too. We were pretty good friends." He nodded again, then retreated into his own thoughts, remembering. "Even gave my father a proper cremation when I was sick, and fed my dog when I was out of town." He glanced sidelong at Nerys and caught her smiling ear to ear, her eyes closed and face turned up into the sunlight. "Best friend I ever had really. Decent guy, Berge."

About the Author

S.K. Balk lives in the frozen wastelands of Northern Michigan with her husband, roommate, two dogs, and an adorably distracting cat. She works in the blood banking industry as a coordinator and in the laboratory, and writes in her spare time.

Other than writing, she has far too many hobbies to occupy her time, including hunting, fishing, sewing, reading, playing video games, orchestrating Dungeons & Dragons campaigns, and doing whatever she can to save the world.

Lightning Source UK Ltd.
Milton Keynes UK
UKHW040607270519
343383UK00001B/8/P